SABRINA LUND

CONSEQUENCE of POWER

Isabella's Season

Goose House Publishing

Copyright © 2024 Sabrina Lund
All rights reserved

This is a work of fiction. Names (including titles), characters, places, businesses, groups, political parties and incidents are either the product of the author's imagination or used fictitiously. Any resemblance to actual persons, living or dead, events, or locales is entirely coincidental.

The historical events and public figures mentioned in this book are used in a fictional context. The author does not intend to portray any real person, living or dead, in a manner that reflects their true character, actions, or beliefs. Where historical events or public figures are referenced, the narrative is a fictionalised account, and any interpretations or representations are those of the author's imagination and should not be taken as factual. No organisations, entities, or buildings mentioned in this work have endorsed, sponsored, or are in any way affiliated with the author or this publication.

No part of this book is intended to offend or defame any individual or group, whether alive or deceased. The author and publisher disclaim any liability for any harm or damage resulting from the interpretation or use of the contents of this book.

No part of this book may be reproduced, stored in a retrieval system, or transmitted in any form or by any means, electronic, mechanical, photocopying, recording, or otherwise, without the prior written permission of the author and publisher.

ISBN-13: 978-1-0687879-2-8
ISBN-13 (eBook): 978-1-0687879-3-5

Cover design by: Michael Psaila
Published by: Goose House Publishing
Printed in the United Kingdom and Other Countries

Second Edition: November 2024
This book is licensed for your personal enjoyment only. It may not be resold, reproduced, or distributed in any form without the prior written permission of the author and publisher.

For permission requests, please contact the author at:
contact@goosehousepublishing.com
www.goosehousepublishing.com

Copyright © 2024 Sabrina Lund
All rights reserved

CONTENTS

	Acknowledgements	i
	Prologue - Genesis	1
1	The Garden of Eden	3
2	Entrance	11
3	Famille Rose	28
4	Strawberry Hill	40
5	Misapprehensions	46
6	Revelry	51
7	Into the Flames	59
8	A Rare Day at the Mantua-maker's	66
9	Temptation	73
10	The Queen Trap	82
11	Scandalised	86
12	Club de Vin	89
13	Dark Velvet	98
14	Gardens of Enchantment	101
15	Entourage	109
16	A Winter's Tale	117
17	The King Doth Keep His Revels Here To-night	122
18	Fair is Foul, and Foul is Fair	138
19	The Winter of Discontent	145

20	Nostalgia	158
21	Revelation	168
22	All is Fair in Love and War	184
23	Impressions	195
24	On Trial	199
25	Pandora's Box	208
26	Enfeebled	218
27	The Gardener's Cottage	221
28	The Precipice	231
29	Spring's Breath	236
30	If Walls Could Talk	240
31	Post-haste	243
32	The Divine Office	252
33	Sowing the Seeds	261
34	Casting the First Stone	270
35	Bone of My Bones, Flesh of My Flesh	276
36	Gather Ye Rosebuds While Ye May	281
37	Do Not Go Gentle into that Good Night	284
38	Make a Heaven of Hell	290
	About the Author	294

ACKNOWLEDGEMENTS

Thank you to my family, who have supported me in all my endeavours. Most especially, I would like to thank my mother, who first inspired my love of literature.

I would also like to thank Michael, whose wild and creative mind continuously challenges me and who encouraged me to take the leap and begin. He has been there, inspiring me every step of the way. In this, and in so many other things, we are only at the beginning of our journey...

PROLOGUE – GENESIS

Across the river, I observe the figures under the cover of darkness, each within their gondolas, progressing as though on a silent pilgrimage, closer and closer. Upon each arrival, they assume their milk-white robes with enveloping hoods that darken their faces further than the night, and drink deeply of a rich liquid.

At the toll of the bell, they float ghostly and slowly across the lawn, past statues and ruins, to congregate at the door of the abbey. A hush settles after the resonance of the final knell.

It is by my command that they have come, passing through my garden to arrive at my house. They stand at the door and knock – once, twice, echoing through the inner chamber.

From my imagination, I have created this. From seeds I nurtured, planned, designed this paradise and it is more exhilarating to see it in its physicality than I ever dreamed. They know not what lies before them, but I, the architect, am omniscient and possess all knowledge, for I repeat: I created this. Though they count among themselves heads, leaders, excelling humans and even princely dignities, they are yet to eat from the Tree of Knowledge. Patience… patience… All in good time, and only when I deem it so.

The door is released, and slowly, creaking in the silence of the night, it reveals the hallowed Chapter House, where fifty souls gather in the glow of lanterns, whispering the instructed chants that gradually rise to a crescendo. It is here that they shall cast off their known titles, and I will bestow upon them new appellations befitting their dispositions as they take up their holy orders.

I see their sincerity and commitment. We can admit none who falter in their faith or adherence to the rules. Each one has been examined, though I know their inclinations before they know themselves. Were it known, many would desire, nay, give up all, to be admitted to my house and taste of paradise. Yet many, if tested on the day of reckoning, would not pass.

I close my eyes, and yet, mine eyes, celestial and terrestrial, are everywhere, for it is the fruit of my imagination. Indeed, I can make a "Heav'n of Hell, a Hell of Heav'n." I see it in my fertile mind: the music, the chants, the ghostly robed figures glowing white in the residual light, in stark contrast to the blackness of the surroundings.

It is precisely as I had planned. I am the creator of all this. With a sonorous voice that cuts through the chants, I announce my name, my title. At this moment, I have the epiphany: in this, my theatre, I am God.

CHAPTER 1 – THE GARDEN OF EDEN

The wildflowers had been out for a full two months, and Isabella floated through the hazy field, plucking them as she went. Cornflowers, their vivid blue heads bobbing amidst the delicate natural grasses, the scarlet petals of the poppies, the corn marigolds, and cowslips nearest, received a brush from her loose chestnut hair as she bent to gather them, singing softly:

"I know a bank where the wild thyme blows,
Where oxlips and the nodding violet grows,
Quite over-canopied with luscious woodbine,
With sweet musk-roses and with eglantine:
There sleeps Titania sometime of the night,
Lull'd in these flowers with dances and delight;
And there the snake throws her enamell'd skin,
Weed wide enough to wrap a fairy in:'"

The air was thick with the heat of summer. The crickets sizzled to their own song, surrounding her entirely. As she reached to pick a cornflower, her hand hovered for a moment, and she paused. A straw-coloured cricket clung to a long dry blade of grass. Ever so slowly, she crouched to study it more closely. Its angular back legs stuck up in triangles. This was the tiny minstrel that – in a blink, it flicked off the grass, and disappeared. A short-lived flash of joy.

Isabella smiled from the thrill and picked a last oxeye daisy. Then, gathering her light blue, lutestring silk gown, she ran with ease across the meadow to the cooler sanctuary of her garden and the shades of the apple orchard. She passed the nigella and the oxlips, adding both to her floral arrangement. The scent of violets played on the verdant air as, to her delight, it engulfed her senses.

Beyond the orchard sat her mother, Lady Thornbury, with her widowed friend, the Dowager Countess Ingram, nestled amongst the rambling roses, which climbed over an arbour.

Theirs was not the magnificent, sweeping arcadian landscape of their long-established neighbour. Rather, theirs was a comparatively modest, yet elegant, home. To their eyes, it was all the more beautiful for its imperfections.

The Thornbury family had settled to the west of Henley twenty years prior, in 1742. The joy over the passing years, with the bonds of true friendships within their local community, including the Reverend Fernsby, a virtual second father to Isabella, persuaded them that there was no reason to disturb their contentment by transplanting themselves to a grander situation, in keeping with their growing fortune.

'Do consider, Sophia,' said Lady Ingram in familiar tones as she sipped the refreshing, aromatic tea. 'You will not always be there for Isabella, and do you not wish upon her the same felicity and affection that you have had with Sir Nicholas all these years?'

'Of course I do, and she can find it near home, no doubt. I am not anxious to part with her, and you know I have never been ambitious,' Lady Thornbury considered, reaching for the cream. 'I only wish for her happiness and,' she laughed, 'to keep the enchantment. Are we not blessed with such bliss?'

'What enchantment, mother?' breezed in Isabella, as she kissed each of the ladies, before planting herself at the table and helping herself to sweet elderflower cordial. A bumblebee, its fluff soft, hovered around them, before touching the white lace cloth of the table, then finding a blush, Damask rose near to Isabella.

'You should be out, my girl,' was Lady Ingram's avuncular reply. 'I have said it enough times now, and your persistent delay compels me to believe that you find the prospect of spinsterhood truly appealing.'

She paused for dramatic effect, as though addressing Parliament, before fortifying her contention. 'Mark my words,' she proceeded, 'that would be a grievous mistake. A lady of your maturity should pay due concern to your future consequence, rather than paying homage to charming widows.' She seized the wildflowers resting upon Isabella's lap.

'I am so content here,' sighed Isabella, leaning back in her chair, with the elderflower almost at her lips. 'Though I must confess, I might one day desire a companion.' She drank the sweet liquid before placing the glass back upon the table and sighing once more. 'Very well, then. Enlighten me. What does your plan entail?' she enquired, revealing some tentative interest for the first time.

The dowager seized the opportunity. 'Entail! Why that is precisely the point,' Lady Ingram declared roused, whilst establishing full custody of the stalks by thrusting them within her heavily embroidered reticule. Launching and pressing her spindly, bejewelled hand upon Isabella's, she burst forth with intensity, 'You are in a unique position, as a young lady, that your father's fortune is not entailed and will be in time – not too soon of course – entirely bestowed upon you. That is, besides your dowry. What has it grown to Sophia? Thirty-thousand pounds?' she asked, briefly turning to Lady Thornbury, before resolutely directing her attention back to Isabella. 'You are sure to make a brilliant match, my dear, certainly a title'.

Gaining momentum, she continued, 'Your father's dealings with the East India Company are all well and good, but it is his recent knighthood upon which we must capitalise. To be perfectly clear, it should aid in opening the doors of society to you.' With finality, she released her breath and her grasp of Isabella, and permitted herself to sit back in her chair.

'I suppose it could have grown so much, though I scarcely pay attention to these matters,' came Lady Thornbury's languid reply.

'Yes, it has indeed.' Lady Ingram continued her next soliloquy, for it was specifically this detail in Sir Nicholas Thornbury's last correspondence that was so fixed firmly in her mind. How could she forget? 'And so, I shall personally present you, and employ what little influence is still at my disposal. Pray, think nothing of this service, for you have been so kind as to take me in and, having shed my late husband's estate to his third cousin, you are most fortunate that I have nothing else to divert my attention.'

By now, the sun had made progress and had begun to dazzle Lady Thornbury, forcing her to shade her weary eyes. It was rather an intense discourse for so sweltering a day. As she regained her sight, her attention was drawn to the glorious vision of the Reverend Fernsby making his way across the garden, waving a book.

'Yes, yes, I hear you ladies. To what do you owe this recurring pleasure?' called the clergyman light-heartedly, acknowledging the receipt of his habitual greeting. 'Indeed, Mr Thornbury himself guided me here. I found him once again at my door and am persuaded that his ostensible motive for visiting was to seek doctrinal advice. He at least provides my conscience with a weekly absolution to my otherwise neglect of creedal duties. However,' the reverend continued, endeavouring to keep pace with Mr Thornbury, who had run ahead of him, 'I feel it my duty to report that he devoured a particularly fine sirloin of beef that I had been planning for our Sunday dinner.'

Mr Thornbury bounded forth, exerting his presence among the ladies, his paws upon their skirts, as befitting a King Charles Spaniel and Isabella lovingly fondled his silken ears. Whilst Sir Nicholas Thornbury was in foreign parts, the family and intimate circle had accepted the little canine's regency, and in turn, he provided as much humour as he did comfort and guardianship in the gentleman's absence.

Upon his arrival, the reverend bowed gently, before gazing across the table at the various delectables... sugar plums, golden French macarons with a delicate shell surrounding the ganache. There were ices made from pineapple, no less, and homegrown strawberries served with the obligatory fresh, rich cream. The cool elderflower now had dewy droplets adorning its glass, formed from the condensation brought on by the heat.

'Well, I declare! Is that a new leaf?' exclaimed the pastor. Whilst his head was inclined towards Lady Thornbury, his eyes were darting across the table and eventually settled upon the last remaining sugar plum.

'Alas, Reverend, we have not received any consignments from Sir Nicholas of late. However, we are endeavouring to refine a novel blend of Young Hyson, should you care to indulge,' replied Lady Thornbury, already pouring him a dish of lukewarm tea.

The reverend did indeed care to indulge, and found himself with a plate so overflowing that, to the delight of Mr Thornbury, a macaron, which perchance had been nudged by the pastor, rolled onto the grass.

Lady Ingram was not one to waste an opportunity and was desirous of drawing the conversation back to her favoured subject. Observing that the reverend was both well settled and, at that moment, particularly bright-eyed, she sought his endorsement of her scheme.

'We have been formulating a plan to bring Isabella out during the next London season,' she proclaimed.

Not to be hurried during the ceremony before him, Reverend Fernsby took a moment to sample the amber liquid with satisfaction, breathing in the various notes through his fine-tuned Augustan nose. He then placed his china cup and saucer down upon the lace with grace and considered, 'Well, if Sir Nicholas and Lady Thornbury have no objections, it may be a fine thing.'

'I have none, Reverend, except to ensure my daughter's contentment,' returned Lady Thornbury. 'I am certain my husband is of the same mind. You are as well acquainted with Isabella's character and situation as any among us, and as you have most fortuitously joined us at this moment, we would appreciate your counsel and elucidation regarding the wisdom of this plan.'

He could sense the atmosphere shift to one of expectation, closing in upon him as his guidance was sought. Slowly, but within reason, he rose steadily and placed his palm lightly upon Isabella's head, if only to grant himself time to recollect last Sunday's sermon:

CONSEQUENCE OF POWER

"Come to me all you who are weary and burdened and I will give you rest. Take my yoke upon you..." he thought. No, no, no, that would not do.

As he ruminated, more recent and relevant texts flooded his mind. He did not fully agree with any one in particular, but rather tended to concoct his own blend to his acquired taste. He regarded the young lady, whose eyes, sparkling like the azure of forget-me-nots, conveyed only the smallest of suggestions as to her potential in this world. She needs some invigoration, some vivacity, beyond that which her older, comfortable companions can bestow.

In her natural state, it seemed unnecessary to disrupt her tranquillity with insight that we do not live in "the best of all possible worlds." But did he have the right to deny her something greater than her experience to date and determine whether the venture was worth the risk?

At length, after clearing his throat, he settled upon the following brief speech, 'Isabella, my child, I can advise you, but to truly appreciate, you must experience for yourself.'

Then, turning to her mother, after this most succinct sermon, he said, 'That reminds me, Lady Thornbury, I return your husband's book, with thanks.' He placed a copy of Rousseau on the table out of Isabella's reach.

Lady Ingram, having contained herself until this moment, exclaimed, 'Right, that is settled. In January, we shall take a house in town for the season.'

The reverend, satisfied with his address, resumed his seat. With the alleviation of Lady Ingram's furrowed brow, the company relaxed, which permitted him to divert conversation to the particularly fine blooms surrounding them.

'I see your roses have recovered from the invading gallants,' he observed.

'You mean the deer? Yes, Jean-Claude has retreated to Lord Cheltenham's hedgerows for now, but no doubt will be back,' replied Lady Thornbury, prompting them all to laugh.

CHAPTER 2 – ENTRANCE

Lord and Lady Bute's Salon, Isabella Thornbury

Flanked by my tender mother and tenacious friend, we entered Lord and Lady Bute's Hall, a formidable gateway to society. I could not help but raise my eyes heavenward, given the height and magnificence of the entrance, with its ceiling fresco of soft blues and billowing clouds. As we crossed, our steps reverberated on the cool and polished stone.

My mother's eyes moved to mine with some ambivalence. Now the moment was upon us, I must confess, this was mutually felt. My hair, pinned, half piled high, copiously powdered and pomaded, though approved by Lady Ingram, felt mildly ridiculous, as though I wore a costume.

As we moved towards the doors on the far side, a prodigious full-length portrait emerged. A chiselled, delicate face, and what could be mistaken for a white periwig, were all that suggested a man. His majestic robe was opulence, as I had never before seen; chains of gold hung over voluminous burgundy velvet folds – not trimmed, rather layered with thick ermine.

He leaned against a plinth, his hand regally, languidly draped; one finger infinitesimally pointed more than the others. The intensity of his eyes ensnared mine, and they remained locked as I traversed the chamber. The delicate brushstrokes of the Rococo style portrayed the luxuriant intricacies and luminosity. It was perchance, this radiance, or might it have been his demeanour, that conveyed the redoubtable power of His Majesty.

'Isabella, pay attention,' whispered Lady Ingram. 'You are on the brink of making your entrance.'

Guarding the salon's gilded doors were two statues, not of alabaster, but seemingly affiliated to the portrait. This time, it was closely fitted coats of velvet burgundy, and the gold was an abundance of braiding. As we approached, with synchronicity, they opened the panelled doors to the warming lights of a large and ornate withdrawing room, adorned with further gilding.

Candles flickered and glowed in the brilliance of the chandeliers and illuminated wall lamps as a stately hearth blazed. However, an overwhelming heat also emanated from the many attendees, and the voices were a cacophony to my unpractised ear.

A few curious eyes were drawn to us, the new arrivals. I had rather they were not, for what if I should falter, or worse, fall? I became conscious of my stays for the first time, and my gown, with panniers to widen it – also a first – pristine as snow, was not exactly the mode of the majority, who appeared to favour the robe à la française.

'Right, my dear, take note of those whom I shall point out,' said Lady Ingram, poised for action. Her gaze searched the room. 'Ah, now, there is Sir Francis Dashwood, recently appointed Chancellor of the

Exchequer. Indeed, I expect political and literary figures to be present.'

Glancing, I beheld a jovial character with a slightly rounded, animated face, evidently entertaining his amused companion.

Lady Ingram continued, 'You should not anticipate dancing this evening. Nevertheless, this event presents an opportunity to make new acquaintances and you may begin to establish yourself.'

Voices continued to filter through the room. 'I say, have you heard? He has yet another in place. Certainly strategic, I grant you,' came the gossiping tones.

'Capital, capital!' exclaimed a dominant voice. 'Though not all possess the fortitude to retain their calm at the table.'

Another gentleman beside me appeared more sombre as he commented to his companion, with a slow cadence, elongating each strained phrase, 'Well, well... seven years and what has it amounted to? Fighting over someone else's land, and now cider tax – that will not be popular, I assure you.' Pausing for a moment, he then continued, 'I only hope Lord Bute will make it worthwhile... all the bloodshed... but can it ever be?' His countenance revealed the internal struggle he had fought to contain. His focus was in the depths of his Madeira, as though his wine would provide him with an answer, rather than his companion, whose emotions were equally stretched and spoke next.

'Unfathomable... spread to five continents, even West Africa and the East Indies... Dare I say, the whole world is at war, and I pray to God this is at a scale we shall never see again. You and I are few who have witnessed the...' His cracked voice broke off, unable to endure.

This was a truly jarring contrast, as their words continued to resonate within me, even beneath the pleasantries of the other attendees. It was evident that I was out of my depth. I fervently hoped that no one would seek my opinion on matters beyond the likes of the Bard. I surveyed the scene before me. The elegance and immense volume of people were more than I had ever… Stay, it could not be, surely… and yet, it was the same face as in the portrait. I turned to Lady Ingram, gasping, and exclaimed, 'I had no notion royalty would be present.'

Lady Ingram was visibly startled upon hearing this most unexpected remark. At first taken aback, she grasped the fabric of my gown involuntarily, as her eyes darted about the room in astonishment. However, upon tracing my gaze, her features were promptly restored.

'Bless you, my dear,' the dowager countess said, reflecting that we had been afforded no time for courtly training. 'Thankfully, that is not His Majesty. That is your host, the Earl of Bute, newly appointed prime minister. He is a companion of Dashwood's, although of a different variety: ambitious! Who else could achieve such a meteoric rise from king's tutor, or Prince George, as he then was, to prime minister within a few short years?' She arched her brows in a significant manner. Mother and I were left to reflect on these sentiments, as the dowager bustled away to gather some acquaintances, her voluminous silk gown rustling as she went.

Taking time to compare ourselves now, it was evident that we were not à la mode. I had been squeezed, powdered, and pomaded into something not resembling myself, and a great unease began creeping over me. I held my hands clenched, cold, and damp, with an awkwardness and a stirring of trepidation within my stomach.

The gentlemen were varied; some were quite acceptable, though all richly dressed in closely fitted coats. Many were in lustrous silks, largely black, midnight blue or darker tones of deep reds and greens, offset by white cravats of the most intricate silk cascades, which must have taken hours to perfect. To my perception, the more elaborate the style, all the more preposterous. Those who had achieve these, however, were clearly the most pleased and must have deemed themselves the height of fashion. To my disappointment, none seemed to be to my taste. I began to wonder whether I had much rather have remained at home in the country. I certainly fancied my prospects better there, with gentlemen of easy, approachable manners and looser coats, though far fewer and perhaps not well-born enough for Lady Ingram.

'Lady Margaret Hamilton-Fox and Mrs Stoughton, may I present Lady Thornbury and her daughter, Miss Thornbury,' sounded Lady Ingram's voice triumphantly, shaking me out of my contemplations. Two ladies before us, of the greatest elegance, curtsied, as did my mother and I.

'So, you are new to town, my dear. Oh, how delightful and exciting! I remember my first season, more years ago than I care to reveal, but oh, how I trembled on my first entrance,' came Mrs Stoughton's melodious tones, as she addressed me.

As I would come to understand, she was truly one of the best of ladies. Her warmth and compassion shone forth, and she extended this to many, and most especially to the bewildered young of her friends. I am immeasurably grateful to this wonder of the ton, who would be a guiding light in the months to come.

Lady Margaret, more reserved, and as I would also later discover, highly distinguished, as a lady-in-waiting to the Dowager Princess of Wales, was also accommodating.

'Now tell me, do you harbour any literary or artistic passions?' fished Mrs Stoughton with a wink and emphasis on the last word, searching for a kindred spirit with similar tastes.

'She does indeed. Isabella found *The Whole Duty of a Woman* most inspiring,' interjected Lady Ingram enthusiastically. 'Most appropriate.'

'Oh, no, my dear, most inappropriate, for how will she know her own mind?' enthused Mrs Stoughton.

The dowager frowned, clearly not relishing the turn in the conversation. 'I would prefer her not to –'

'Nothing is more exhilarating for the soul than adventure, romance, and a highwayman. Oh, the *Female Quixote* is for you!' sang Mrs Stoughton.

Even my mother appeared invigorated by the prospect, perhaps reminiscing about her own romance with Father, for their regard for each other was unwavering despite their distance. Indeed, over the past few years, when they had been apart, there had naturally been moments when she succumbed to her emotions upon coming across a tender reminder.

Most unusual for Lady Ingram not to assert herself, I sensed she was less than thrilled and had become unreasonably agitated. She brandished her fan, first rapidly fluttering it, then snapping it shut with displeasure in an attempt to bring this direction of the discourse to a close. However, Mrs Stoughton had not quite concluded her didactic speech – there was more.

'I see you, Lady Ingram. I shall behave, but you cannot object to Handel. I am planning my own musical evening featuring *Rinaldo*. Oh, how my Mr S adored those tender, beguiling arias. I cannot help but weep upon hearing *Lascia ch'io pianga* reminiscing… Indeed, who cannot?' she appealed to us all. 'What a loss we all suffered when he passed,' she sighed wistfully, almost overcome, which had the momentary effect of pacifying Lady Ingram.

Unsure whether she meant Handel, Mr S, or both, I too remained silent, but secretly longed for a rare taste of the delightful arias. The few times I had heard any, had moved me to sorrow, having no counterpart of my own. Yet, here we were, attempting to remedy this, in a manner which was beginning to feel most disingenuous.

Mrs Stoughton then deftly turned the subject to another of her passions, 'None among us entertains any delusions; you, Miss Thornbury, are here to make a match. You are indeed fortunate that Lady Ingram has taken you in hand; there is so much choice in London.' She flourished her fan, as though presenting the scene before them: room upon room of eligible gentlemen.

'I found my Mr S in a salon very similar to this, and we had many fond years together,' she sighed wistfully. 'I recommend you choose to marry for love. Love, mind you, over mere desire. There are plenty of unscrupulous adventurers and opportunists, of which you must be vigilant, even in these withdrawing rooms. Until then, I shall recommend to you some exciting romances.' Her eyes sparkled spiritedly, perhaps with a touch of playful mischief.

'Yes, you must join us at our next ladies' literary club meeting,' said Lady Margaret, in a comparatively sober tone, which was admittedly not difficult. 'We discuss a variety of topics of the day, social issues, science, the arts, philosophy and poetry.'

Despite the turn in the discourse, Lady Ingram had not quite recovered from Mrs Stoughton's onslaught, and sensing this the kindly lady turned to the dowager beaming, 'There is no need to be so alarmed, Lady

Ingram. We ladies shall have your fine charge under each of our wings.'

Mrs Stoughton's countenance transformed suddenly to an expression of pure bliss as she trilled, 'I hear the harp beginning in the music room.' Sure enough, the gentle phrases drifted through. Turning swiftly, she called, 'Come, ladies, oh, such fond memories of my youth and Mr S,' as she sallied forth, leading the way.

After the musical exhibition, which, as Mrs Stoughton observed, was greatly admired by all those with refined sensibilities, Lady Ingram set about her work once more.

'You see that distinguished gentleman in the red coat in the corner?' she began again. 'That is the Earl of Sandwich, engaged with the songstress, who entertained us so. He is no doubt refining on some of her particulars. Such a great patron of the arts, as is his friend Sir Francis Dashwood. The earl and his wife are devoted, although she does not appear to be present this evening. Such a pity, she would have enjoyed the discourse.'

She continued to cast her eyes about the room. 'Mr Henry Fitzwilliam, over there, is highly eligible. Observe,' she gestured lightly, 'in that direction, the Duke of Harringshire and the Duke of Winterbourne conversing, though one can aim too high. Let me see...'

As I gazed across the salon, the Duke of Winterbourne's intense eyes caught mine and he acknowledged me with a lift of his dark brows. His expression was of mild intrigue, yet his demeanour exuded supreme confidence, befitting his rank.

Incapable of returning the recognition, I instinctively averted my eyes to the marble floor in modesty, and vocally exhaled a breath. An involuntary flush spread across my countenance as I tensed. Partially lifting my eyes, I saw the duke share what seemed to be a departing remark to his interlocutor, before reinforcing his interest in me.

The widow, sensing my shifting temperament, heard me whisper, 'What am I to do?'

Directing her gaze towards the approaching Duke of Winterbourne, my companion had scarcely enough time to communicate, 'Simply follow his example,' before he arrived bowing.

I studied his lips in motion and though I could not conceive his words, the rich, enigmatic tones seemed to engulf me. I felt a rush and heard a single monotone note singing in my ears, vaguely aware of Lady Ingram responding in my stead, as the conversation continued to elude my comprehension. He was the first that evening to turn my head. I now understood the intoxicating paralysis in my body and the sense of the words, "my spirits, as in a dream, are all bound up." The next moment, he gently bowed, and was gone.

Truly overwhelmed now, dew surfaced my palms and with the gown even more constrictive than before, my mind moved towards an unbearable pressure on my waist. Obliged by necessity, I softly uttered to my friend, 'I feel faint.'

'I understand, my dear. Come sit here behind this screen,' Lady Ingram replied, as she sympathetically ushered me to a divan. Ever prepared, and conscious of the moment, she searched within her embroidery for the hartshorn and caressed the air with the potent concoction that wafted towards me.

The fumes instantly took effect, causing the most extreme shock that sent me rising up. The acrid intensity of the vapours created tingling sensations, coursing through my entire being, and every fibre resonated. Fully awakened from my entrancement and my senses heightened, I took rapid breaths in an attempt to recover and grasp hold of my faculties.

After some moments had passed, Lady Ingram left my side to seek some refreshments, in the hope they would aid my recovery. I was thankful for her kindness, but took the opportunity of her absence to recompose myself further, closing my eyes. Had I understood the evening's significance, I would have required more time to recover.

Shortly after, I became aware of a movement beside me, and I went to accept the refreshment. However, having caught a glimpse of her shoes, I raised my eyes and beheld a pair of shapely calves in silk white stockings, then white breaches, and a smart, black frock coat accented with modest gold braiding. Though not of the dowager, the youthful visage was strangely familiar. In my stupefied state, my mind raced as I searched for where I had seen this gentleman before.

'It would appear, Miss Thornbury, that this scene does not suit your disposition,' came his bright gentlemanly voice. 'However, you are quite captivating in your new attire, even beyond what I had anticipated. Although, there is no need for such adornments, as your natural state is charming.'

I swallowed and managed a soft whisper, 'My apologies... Sir, I do not believe we have been introduced.'

His face broke into a kindly smile, radiating warmth, and his eyes conveyed a soul which had true compassion. His demeanour suggested quiet self-assurance and contentment within, distinct in these qualities from the other gentlemen I had observed that evening.

Further, his garments more naturally befitted their owner, who nevertheless bore a graceful strength. However, his loose, light brown hair, not powdered or pomaded I noticed, betrayed his carefree disposition, as he passed his hand through it, in a gesture which felt familiar. Taking a knee to bring himself down to my level on the divan, he chuckled, 'Introduced! Do you not recollect, Isabella? I suppose you should not, for it has been many years, and my trials in foreign parts have no doubt changed me.'

'Gussie?'

His jaw moved in astonishment and delight. 'It has been an age since I heard that name from your lips.'

As our discourse proceeded, his warmth of spirit soothed me, which, coupled with a smile that extended to his eyes, was the refreshment that I so needed and he restored my senses through his ease. To experience the full effects of its properties, this restorative would require the passage of time to mature, like a fine wine.

'I assume you have given up tree climbing, at least whilst in town?' he beamed. 'Instead, I suppose Lady Ingram will have plans for you to climb other varieties. Most appropriate! Is that not her expression?'

I rolled my eyes and laughed heartily, then, leaning towards him, confirmed his recollection, 'Yes, she is indeed implacable, but she will be happy to know that I already have such an old companion here to help guide me.'

Lady Ingram, sweeping around the screen, interrupted our discourse, having procured some Champagne wine. As she handed me a coupe, she exclaimed in surprise, 'Oh, Augustus, you are in town? Are you currently on leave from your service?'

My companion raised himself from his position beside me and bowed respectfully. 'Good evening, Lady Ingram. I trust you and Lord Ingram are both in good health?'

I winced in anguish at this remark, matching the relict's customary lined appearance.

'Alas, Lord Ingram is no more, and neither is my fortune,' was her prompt reply. Only momentarily distracted, she swiftly corrected her course. 'Isabella, you cannot be squandering such an evening as this on old companions. You are evidently quite recovered. Of all the fine gentlemen in this salon, you choose to amuse yourself with Gussie, and we all know where that will lead. Lord Cheltenham is immovable and not one to be trifled with.'

'Indeed, my father has always anticipated my inclinations, even before I myself am conscious of them,' Augustus mused, passing his hand once more through his light, now tousled hair.

With that, Lady Ingram led me away to rejoin my mother and the literary ladies in the next room for the final course.

As we passed between the rooms with the aim of reuniting with our party, it became apparent that an intense energy was building in one of the salons, and captivating the attention of those present. By the time we had rejoined the ladies, the frisson had peaked to a pivotal moment. Mrs Stoughton could resist no longer and led the ladies, now also curious, towards the excitement.

The scene before us was of a Faro table in play, with four gentlemen seated around it. There was Dashwood, who seemed amused as ever, though, having conceded, he was now without cards. The second was Mr Henry Fitzwilliam, who appeared somewhat deflated and evidently had also lost his stake. He was now more intrigued by his wineglass, the contents of which had been spilled. Surrounding the gambling table were the majority of the ladies and gentlemen of the evening, murmurating like starlings, and coming to roost at a source of immense interest, twittering to each other in excitement.

Their beady eyes were honing in on the two gentlemen still engaged in contest. I recognised the Earl of Cheltenham, calm and self-possessed. The other, with whom I was unacquainted, was deliberating, his cards close to his chest, though fanned out, resembling a peacock on full display.

Positioned a few ranks behind Dashwood, I strained to see over the frenzy, as Winterbourne advanced to my side in tandem.

'Are you familiar with the game of Faro, Miss Thornbury?' He addressed me with a daring openness.

'I am not, Your Grace.' This time I was equal to replying.

'I have encountered Cheltenham many times, and he plays the man, not the cards. He currently has the upper hand,' he commented in rich tones, close to my ear. 'The other is Mr Fairfax, who has lost a great deal this evening. Knowing him, he will be anxious to recover it.'

I gazed across the table at the one person in the room not observing the two gentlemen at play, but rather speculating on myself and Winterbourne, applying her own strategy of follow the shoe, before surveying the rest of the ranks. At that moment, my attention turned from the widow and back to the game, as Mr Fairfax announced, 'Alright Cheltenham, I raise you my estate in Surrey, for all that you have taken this evening.'

The air changed instantly, and there was a collective whirring as the audience shifted and vocalised their sentiments.

'You are not in earnest, Fairfax,' rumbled Cheltenham.

'Do you doubt me?' retorted Fairfax.

'Your estate in Surrey?'

'I have five others; I would hazard the sixth.' Fairfax paused, ruminating further, before leaping to his feet and thrusting his finger emphatically towards the corner of the room. 'Sandwich, when last we played at White's, did I not wager a stable of horses?'

Audience members whispered to their neighbours, some in a flutter, others nodded and still others, with less perceptible movements, murmured to companions.

'Indeed,' came the Earl of Sandwich's swift reply.

'And when I lost, did I not have them sent to you the following day?'

'Indeed,' rejoined Sandwich, once more.

Then, turning to Mr Fitzwilliam, Fairfax exclaimed, 'And last August, when we played Hazard at Dashwood's, did I not pay?'

'Certainly, without question,' confirmed Mr Fitzwilliam. Then, addressing the room, he stated, 'You may rest assured that this gentleman's promise of payment is entirely certain.'

'There,' declared Mr Fairfax, satisfied and seating himself once more, 'will you not accept the word of a gentleman, Lord Cheltenham?'

Lord Cheltenham was one of the few individuals in the room who had utter control of his features and remained unmoved, both in his emotions and comportment. That was, except for one hand, which rested upon the table, where one finger slowly tapped… once… twice… six times the digit struck dully upon the green baize covering the wood. The tension in the room was palpable, as though trussed and ready for calving. At length, and with deliberation, Cheltenham assented.

Silence descended upon the audience as the cards were dealt. As the game came to a climax, the outcome, though perceptible to the participants, was not evident on their faces nor immediately apparent to the audience.

CONSEQUENCE OF POWER

My eyes flitted between the two, but I could not discover the emotion upon their faces. That was until, at his own volition, Mr Fairfax finally revealed a slight smirk, as though only he understood the true nature of his hand, before conceding the game with a bow to Lord Cheltenham.

Lord Cheltenham's countenance remained composed and smooth as a marble façade. However, an animated portly gentleman could contain himself no longer and, springing to his feet, he exclaimed, 'Is this not the true embodiment of gentlemanly behaviour and sportsmanship? A true model to us all.' He indicated Mr Fairfax, highlighting his dignity and grace, even in the face of such an immense loss. 'Gentlemen, you have not only thrilled us all tonight, but furnished us with ample to sustain and enliven our chatter for some time to come.'

At this, the volume of the room rose, and the music commenced once more. Enthusiastic utterances of sentiments were heard amongst the notes of the Hornpipe from Handel's *Water Music Suite No. 2 in D Major*, lively and triumphant. This was in direct harmony with people who now gathered in flocks, engaged in eager discussion, as I did with Winterbourne and other new acquaintances of the evening.

This was maintained until, given the late hour of the night, the ambiance of the room changed and the parties started to disperse to the gentle melody of *Sarabande in D Minor*, signalling further that the event was drawing to a close. By this time, even Winterbourne had left my side.

Amongst the now few noticeably fatigued guests remaining, I could not immediately discern where my mother and Lady Ingram were; they might have been seeking me in one of the adjoining rooms.

The players had long since left the table, and I reflected upon the site of the arena. The overwhelming intensity of the evening had been of a level I had never experienced.

As I meditated upon this and my new acquaintances, one of whom I must confess I was particularly drawn to, I noticed a small leather-bound pocketbook on the table where Dashwood had been seated. As I picked it up, intending to return it, my mother appeared, ready to lead me to the awaiting carriage.

Upon showing her the book and sharing my speculation as to its owner, she noted that Lord and Lady Bute had already departed to another residence, having business to attend to the next day, and she had not seen Dashwood since the game.

'It may be too delicate to entrust to a servant; not all are as reliable as our Heloise,' she considered, though visibly weary from the evening. With no doubt the prospect of sleep in her mind, she suggested, 'Do keep hold of it for now, my dear, and if you remind me tomorrow, we shall consult Dashwood. No, no, my dear, do not think of giving it to me. You know how prone I am to forgetfulness.' On this note, we departed, satisfied, from a most memorable evening.

The icy night air brushed our cheeks as we left the stifling scene of the event and took our seats in the waiting coach. Once ensconced and wrapped in rugs, we settled. We were rocked towards home. The horses' hooves clattered rhythmically.

Each of us too weary to speak. The initial effects of the Champagne and other appellations, having fulfilled their pleasurable function, now gave way to fatigue. We drooped, as the feathers in Lady Ingram's hair now did. Indeed, I could scarcely collect my thoughts.

My companion and lady's maid, Heloise, and my mother's maid, Mary, had been waiting in the servant's hall, in case we should have required their assistance during the evening.

I recollect that I passed the book to Heloise, murmuring, 'May I entrust this to your safekeeping for now?'

That is all that I can relate, for I then drifted, sleep luring me into its arms. Only the occasional jolt of the coach had means to rouse me, and even then, only to cause me queasiness that subsided to headiness and, eventually, a slumber.

CHAPTER 3 – FAMILLE ROSE

The golden light of the morning streamed through the windows onto Isabella. Her eyes fluttered slightly and slowly, the mists giving way as the brightness pierced through. The last remaining scintilla of her reverie lingered in their final moments as she ardently extended her hand to retrieve them... but they were dispelled all too soon.

On returning home the prior evening, Heloise had assisted Isabella in removing her garments, which had so constricted her. Her lady's maid had combed the powder from her hair, so that she began to feel and resemble her natural self with each stroke of the brush.

Now, the early beams slowly spread across Isabella, running over her face, and the long lengths and gentle waves of her silken chestnut hair, which shone with a rich lustre, even at some points, an iridescence of various nutty browns.

As the sun spread its rays, Isabella too extended her form to ease away the drowsy vestiges of sleep, now that the dream had truly left her, perhaps forgotten forever in that other world. Satisfied and still languid, she breathed deeply and fulsomely, as though she were lying upon the soft sward of the meadows surrounding home, for Helios' warmth that morning had transported her in those moments to that which was dear to her.

The clatter of coach wheels and hooves on hard stone cobbles of the street outside brought her back to the present, and as another passed by, it roused her further, prompting her to open her eyes. She saw the hearth which had been lit by Heloise, casting a soft amber and yellow glow, crackling and imparting a comforting ambiance with its familiar sounds.

However, as Isabella discovered, it had scarcely dispelled the chill from the air. Reaching her bare arm out from beneath the bedclothes, she soon drew it back into the warmth of the cocoon. There she rested, reflecting gratefully upon the indulgence of time, comforts and absence of social obligations, for hours observed in the city were far later than those of the country.

It was only the savoury aroma of bacon, mingled with the warm, subtle sweetness of freshly baked loaves, that at last tempted Isabella out of the folds. After a few brief moments, she had slipped on a simple morning gown and rolled her chestnut tresses into a loose chignon, before following the scent to the bright morning room.

Warm sunlight bathed the scene before her, blessing it with a delicate aura of tranquillity. Most delightful of all was the sight of her mother performing her morning ceremony, pouring hot tea, whose gentle steam rose momentarily over the brim of the Famille Rose, with its dusty pink buds and gold accents. Its translucent enamel gave great luminosity, and it was a treasured reminder of her father, who had coddled this gift all the way home on his last visit.

'My dear, come sit beside Pudding,' came her mother's soothing tones. 'Did you sleep quite well after yesterday's thrills? Pudding was somewhat out of sorts and could not settle. He finds himself not quite at ease with the clamour of the city.'

Pudding, for that was Mr Thornbury's endearment, though he acknowledged both, greeted Isabella with a lick of her palm as she took her place at the table. Then, having fulfilled his duty, he gave a blithesome thwack, thwack of his fluffy tail and turned to his own breakfast delights. This was with a slight tinge of regret that the pastor was not present, for he would have been assured of additional trifles.

Isabella involuntarily shuddered, as this room too had just begun to warm from the fire. Her mother, anticipating her need, drew the mahogany draught screen with its silk chinoiserie towards her. Then, she provided a soothing ratafia in a Stourbridge glass, saying, 'Here, my dear, take this restorative; it will aid your recovery from last night's exertions and warm your very core.'

The warmth of the fire, meeting with the sweet liquor, with its jewelled pigment, soon achieved the desired effect. The distinctive cherry and nut notes left an enduring aroma, ending with a pleasant, bitter aftertaste.

The three delighted themselves in the serene morning peace, and as a gentle quiet descended, they lingered leisurely over their repast. When all were satisfied, Lady Thornbury leaned back in her chair and confided to Isabella, 'We received an extraordinary delivery this morning, forwarded from Henley. Have you not observed?'

There, in the corner of the room, were two large chests of cedar wood, with indentations and wear, revealing the battering they had endured during their treacherous journey across land and tossed by waves at sea.

Originating from Bombay this time, as indicated by the multitude of still-decipherable labels, they had traversed westwards across the Indian Ocean, then sailed the thousands of miles around the Cape of Good Hope, up the west coast of Africa, through the unpredictable Bay of Biscay, and eventually to Southampton. From thence, they were conveyed, jolting and shuddering along the rutted terrain towards Henley, before being redirected to London.

As Isabella and her mother opened the first chest, they discovered a bundled of letters wrapped in string, nestled amongst the protective straw. These were treasure enough for the ladies, and Pudding, sensing their elation, joined in the general excitement. Upon opening the letters, they devoured them one by one.

Bombay, 30th June 1762

My Dearest Sophia, Isabella, and Mr Thornbury,

I trust this letter finds you all in good health and spirits. I am sure you have enjoyed your morning stroll around our grounds. Often do I envision you all doing so, and I long to join you one day, once my business here is concluded. I picture you reading this letter in our morning room, gazing out of the windows across the glorious meadows.

Perchance, you will find yourselves by the fire, for by the time this missive reaches you, I have no doubt the leaves will have turned or fallen entirely, with winter's crisp frost etching delicate designs on the panes. I must confess, in this stifling humidity, for indeed it is the season of monsoon, I long for the refreshing chill of our English winters.

The letter continued meandering through various and curious tales. The group indulged in this, as the fire waned in soft pulsating embers, before turning to another.

Bombay, 7th July 1762

My Dears,

My relatively recent appointment in Bombay has allowed me to partake in experiences which I could only otherwise have imagined or known through the pages of a book. It is my honour to have become acquainted with a rich cultural heritage, replete with the arts, music, a vibrant society, and curious religions.

However, will you permit me to confide some concerns to you? I do not wish to burden you, but it is no trifling matter. Do not be alarmed; I am quite well. My concerns to which I have alluded in the past pertain to my business here, and more particularly the general conduct of the Company and the pursuit of its interests.

Whilst some Indian producers are growing rich from our trade, I fear our negotiations are encountering challenges. Indeed, I must confess that I find myself not quite at ease with the current circumstances. The politics have intensified, and I have observed many exploitations, with which I cannot agree – dishonourable and unworthy of the values and principles of a gentleman. I desire to temper my communication to you on this matter, mindful of your feminine sensibilities. The abuses are of such complexity that I shall not do them the disservice of presenting them here; suffice to say they are grievous.

I have made close acquaintances whom I hold dear, and upon whose trust I have come to place great reliance. I must confess, the internal struggle is becoming harder to bear, and I am unsure that I can continue. I had intended to reside here one year more, but I would be most grateful to seek your opinion on whether I should alter the duration of my sojourn.

Lady Thornbury was visibly perturbed to read that her husband's concerns had only grown since his previous communication. Too far removed from the issues raised and the complexities not quite comprehensible to her, she could only wish ardently that her husband would return and expressed as such to Isabella. 'I shall assure your father that it is not only our fervent wish that he should return home, but shall also beseech him not to continue where his conscience does not permit. In this, he has our complete and unwavering support.'

Bombay, 14th July 1762

My Dears,

It is my pleasure to enclose a gift of various silks, to provide you with an essence of this beautiful land, and so you can admire the exquisite artisanship of this region.

These textiles are from Seth Pestonji Rustom Bomanji, a cherished Indian companion. The ladies of his house, so familiar with these fabrics, have kindly designed some fashion plates, which they hope will inspire you and breathe new life into British fashions.

I am aware you may have little use for such opulent clothing, given Isabella is not yet out; but as I have mentioned many times, I would have no objections. Indeed, it may be beneficial for her to experience the excitement of London or Bath.

The ladies have provided measurements in gaj, which I understand is approximately a yard. Thus, allowing eleven yards per gown, I trust there will be sufficient fabric to produce nine of the most splendid quality.

I can only be at ease if I give my friend a fair price in exchange for his high-quality goods. I regard this as an exploratory attempt to comprehend if these, at a fair price, may become the rage and serve as a method to regain trust and political trade stability in a just manner. Indeed, it is a modest recompense.

Recently, I have been made aware of a company of missionaries. They have attempted to advocate for a fair exchange, relief of punitive taxes and arbitrary seizure of property, which, amongst other egregious actions, have sadly characterised our rule. There is some discussion in Parliament, yet I know not what will come of it, given our own lamentable state of affairs and, moreover, the influence of the East India Company.

This gift marks the commencement of my efforts to redeem what scant honour may remain, however futile such attempts may seem in the face of the monopoly. However, I have assured my good friend I would endeavour in this process.

I am making the necessary arrangements for a tea chest to be shipped from Canton, filled with the usual Bohea and Young Hyson leaves, as I recall, you were so delighted with this in the past.

I must close for now. Pray convey my warmest regards to our dearest friends at home, most especially to the Reverend Fernsby. I do miss our conversations.

With all my love,

Your devoted husband and father,

P.S. Should you deliver to me a sample of the new designs, I would be most grateful, so my friends and I may assess the outcome.

Lady Thornbury placed the final letter down, sighing, 'I do hope he heeds me this time and returns home.' Then brightening, she said, 'However, let us not allow this to dishearten us; instead, shall we explore these delights?'

They lifted the heavy cedar lid together and the thin, light-yellow fibres of straw, dried in the heat, were pressed aside in the chest and the protective sheathes of waxed cloth removed. Lady Thornbury drew the first piece of silk brocade with a swift and delicate upward sweep. As the cloth caught the air, it billowed softly in a great balloon, displaying the beauteous vibrancy of a powerful cerise, shimmering with a translucence revealed to full effect by the milky light streaming through the room before sinking softly to the ground.

Upon this action, the faint scent of spices from distant places was released and mingled with the oaky smoke of the room; a balm to the London grey.

As they unfolded each fabric, mother and daughter explored the intricate weave imbued with gold and silver, tracing their fingers over its rich qualities. An opal spectacle transformed the room, as if in celebration of Holi. Colours ranged from rare deep indigo to clear cerulean and the reds of the madder roots, which brought hot pinks, crimson, and turmeric with its apricots and yellows.

They could not help but conjure images in their mind's eye of Sir Nicholas Thornbury, and piece together any evidence they could glean from the gift, as though once again playing with a piquet pack of Indian card, as he had taught them.

Gathering the fashion plates, which had been placed within the chests, the ladies formed a plan to secure an appointment with a modiste for a fitting, with all despatch. Indeed, the receipt of this consignment could not have arrived at a more opportune moment than that of the beginning of the London season.

As they mused on this charming plan, with the fabrics all tumbled about the room, Heloise entered, desiring conference with Isabella on a private matter.

Without a lady's maid of her own, the dowager was often attended upon by Heloise, who had done so this very morning. In celebration of what she deemed a triumphant evening, the wise widow had permitted herself the rare indulgence of taking her breakfast within her bedchamber, with the secondary motive of restoring her vigour for the anticipated exertions to come. However, having seen to the lady's comforts, Heloise made a discovery of an alarming nature which had persuaded her to interrupt Isabella's joyful morning.

In the passage beyond the morning room, she confided to her mistress, 'Last evening, you entrusted me with a pocketbook for safekeeping, which I placed upon my bedside table. Yet, upon returning to my quarters after this morning's duties, I discovered it had disappeared.'

Isabella, in all earnestness, had all but forgotten the book in the midst of the morning's languor and diversions. However, as their eyes met in shared acknowledgement of the situation at hand, she sighed resignedly. There could be no doubt, for this was not the first occasion that Mary had pilfered from their home.

'Though, do keep this from Mother,' Isabella requested. 'She has been in such good spirits this morning, for we received a delivery from father, and she is now reading some of his more tender billets-doux.' She concluded, 'Could you bring Mary to me, so that I may enquire. If you can, I suggest you search her quarters whilst I do so, to see whether you can locate the book.'

Isabella was waiting within her bedchamber when Mary entered. 'Mary, I have a delicate question to ask you,' Isabella commenced hesitantly, feeling as though she were on the verge of reprimanding a cruel aunt and did not believe herself equal to the task that had fallen upon her. 'Last evening, I handed Heloise a book and I am answerable for its return to its rightful owner. Do you happen to know where it might be found?'

'I must say, I am at a loss. I know not what you mean, Miss,' replied Mary, simply and unmoved.

'A book – a small leather-bound pocketbook?' coaxed the young lady.

'No, Miss, indeed I have seen no such thing,' came the reply – not insolent, but self-possessed.

Understanding the bounds of her capabilities, Isabella resigned herself to concluding, 'I see… would you be so obliging as to inform me if you should happen upon it?'

At that moment, Heloise strode into the bedchamber, book in hand. The lines on Mary's face altered, growing slightly deeper. Her jaw tightened, and she pressed her lips into a thin line. Her eyes narrowed as she fixed her stare on Heloise. Indeed, she appeared as though she retained a rancid oil in her mouth, rolling over her tongue, which she could not remove. Then she averted her gaze with a tight sniff, the grease still present.

Now flushed, Isabella sought to draw this most uncomfortable episode to a close. During the strained trialogue which ensued, Mary, now cornered, admitted, perhaps with a mix of resentment or bitterness, that she had accessed Heloise's sleeping quarters, browsing her personal belongings.

Indignant, Heloise glossed over the flagrant intrusion to enquire directly, 'And why did you take the liberty of retaining this particular book?'

'You evidently have not taken the liberty to read its contents. If you had done so, you would have your answer,' said Mary, with barely suppressed anger as she stalked towards the door. Pausing for a moment without glancing back at them, she said, her voice acerbic, 'If I were you, I would consider very carefully into whose hands you deliver that book. You know not what you may provoke.' With that, she flounced out of the bedchamber, drawing the door to a close with exaggerated gentleness.

This was a striking blow to the remaining pair, with Isabella feeling oddly reprimanded, even threatened, yet uncertain how to proceed. Indeed, Mary's bitterness exceeded reason, given the context. In fact, on one previous occasion, Mary's guilt had not incited such a reaction. Perhaps there was an underlying connotation which currently eluded them.

They exchanged glances before regarding the book which, once seemingly innocuous, now seemed to hold a new significance. Their moral perplexity soon became evident and occupied their thoughts.

'We cannot come to a sound decision about how to proceed without first comprehending its contents, but I am uneasy with the prospect of reading someone else's private documents,' deliberated Isabella.

Heloise countered these simplistic sentiments, as she had a distinct feeling that there was something greater at play. 'Though we distrust Mary,' she said carefully, 'there may be something to her admonition. Now that I consider it, the nature of this book is yet to be discerned, and we could be held accountable for having it in our possession.'

The final awareness impacted the pair like a chilling wave that washed over their skin and it was this that was perhaps worst of all. If Mary's enigmatic retort were proved correct, should the book fall into the wrong hands, indeed they did not know what they might provoke. Mary's last utterance lingered in the air, resonating.

Whilst the pair brooded, Lady Thornbury, now fully satisfied with her letters, entered glowing. She was accompanied by Pudding, who matched her elation, and summoned them for a turn about Hyde Park.

As Isabella made preparations, she entrusted Heloise to place the book within the concealed alcove in her bureau for discussion, during their usual nightly collation of sweetmeats, which they so often enjoyed.

CHAPTER 4 – STRAWBERRY HILL

The small oak wherry boat shuddered as it hit the banks of the River Thames. As it rocked gently, two passengers stepped over the hull and crunched carefully onto the crisp, white frost of the bankside meadow at Twickenham.

Across the expanse of green, with its hoary sheath, rose a picturesque vision of a striking white castle. The prevailing winter wind howled eastward towards London, undoubtedly a reason for the stronghold's pleasantly positioned setting. Its battlements coursed across the uppermost reaches of the rectangular structure, yet its walls were oddly stark and unblemished, as though still in its youth and yet to be tested in battle. Though pleasing to the eye from a distance, upon drawing closer, it became increasingly apparent to the observer that there was something most peculiar about the building.

As the gentlemen in their dark greatcoats traversed the meadow, their breath rose in clouds like cannon smoke. The arched medieval windows with mullions came into view. Further fine adornments and artifices protruded from the folly's crown, creating a romantic aesthetic.

The gentlemen were drawn to this magnificent edifice, not solely by their curiosity concerning its recent developments, but also by their shared artistic interests with its owner. Yet, they harboured an ulterior motive – to observe another guest.

At the moment of their admittance, their host, Horace Walpole, had been guiding a Mr David Garrick up the bright entrance hall staircase, a replica of that in Rouen Cathedral, to admire the armour situated on the second floor. Upon hearing the footsteps of the new arrivals, he poked his head over the balustrade and, flourishing a wrist of foaming lace, he called, 'Greetings, greetings, gentlemen! Dashwood, Fitzwilliam, come, come in and join the tour.'

The speech had a theatrical flavour, and yet, he was not the thesp. Garrick, the pre-eminent Shakespearean actor, could lay claim to that title.

The gentlemen convened in the library, where the light streamed through the lancet windows, striking the embellished glass and illuminating the jewelled constellation of rubies, emeralds and sapphires.

'Most intriguing, Horace. You truly live in your art,' mused Garrick, as he contemplated his surroundings. 'You deserve your nomenclature: The Abbot. I am astonished you did not make this a scriptorium. Pray, I trust you do not intend to stray from your natural disposition.'

'I thank you. That is most kind. This is but a mere indulgence of my own imagination,' Walpole said, with a sweep of his hand to indicate the room. 'However, the castle is still undergoing enhancements, so that I may display my collection of curiosities to full effect.'

Once supplied with a glass of port wine by the footman, the four gentlemen took their ease. Sir Francis Dashwood stood with Mr Henry Fitzwilliam by the intricate mock-lithic library fireplace, which unbeknown to the guests had been crafted out of wood. Separating himself from the new arrivals, Garrick began wandering about the room and resumed his questioning of The Abbot of Strawberry Hill.

After observing the pair for some time, seizing the opportunity whilst alone with Henry, Dashwood broached the subject of Garrick and said with an amused smile, 'So, what do you think? Will he do?'

He took Cardinal Wolsey's wide-brimmed hat of red felt, which was resting upon a table, and placed it upon his companion's head.

Mr Fitzwilliam, unruffled and accustomed to Dashwood's pranks, left it there as he pondered the question, almost as though the hat were made to grace his head, before delivering his assessment. 'Well, Garrick and Walpole are of similar temperaments. They each share a fervent devotion to the arts. However, you know Walpole would never subscribe. He does not approve. What is he always saying? "I would rather be nobody here, than somebody there." No, no, he is far too reserved.' Then he paused before finishing with, 'But the crux of the matter is that I doubt Garrick would join us either, nor align himself with our members' philosophy.'

'In that case, we shall cut him – from the list,' said Dashwood, as he carved his hand high in the air and across Henry's throat in a mock execution. Henry indulged his friend's act, and, bowing his head, allowed the hat to fall to the ground.

'Indeed, one cannot find fault with Walpole in matters of the arts. He is most steadfast in his devotion,' mused

Dashwood, 'and that is precisely why I am so exceedingly fond of him, despite our differences.'

Walpole's voice drifted into the library as he passed through to the adjoining staircase, laughing, 'Indeed, a gothic architecture. I confess, I begin to be ashamed of my own magnificence.'

'Are you not envious, Dashwood? Such discourse might well tempt you to pursue an attainder from Bute on your very behalf,' smirked Henry.

'I assure you, I am exceedingly delighted with the results of my own architectural triumphs, even if they are not so visible to the general populace,' replied Dashwood, with a playful smile.

Then, leaning towards Dashwood confidentially, Henry murmured in a hushed tone, 'Let us attempt to be serious for once, Dashwood. Tell me, are there any other prospects on the list?' As he said this, Henry thrust his hand into Dashwood's coat pocket, only to draw out an unexpected Egyptian ushabti figurine, and he gazed upon it quizzically.

Dashwood, unperturbed and accustomed to these antics, continued, 'No, I have it not with me, Henry,' before delicately retrieving the figurine from his companion and placing it back into his pocket. 'That puts me in mind,' he hesitated, as if weighing whether it were worth broaching the subject, before continuing, 'I appear to have mislaid my pocketbook containing the list. I have not seen it since Lord and Lady Bute's salon, and Bute cannot seem to place it either.'

Henry, seemingly unperturbed and also accustomed to his companion's pranks, retorted, 'You are in jest, surely?'

'No, no, I assure you, Henry, I am not,' replied Dashwood, soberly for once.

'You are not serious, man, are you?' retorted Henry, his face dropping. 'Come, come now, how so? It has all the –'

Dashwood, desirous of pacifying Henry, who appeared to have forgotten to lower his voice, cut him off with a soothing whisper, 'Henry… Henry… I am sure it will be discovered; it has just been mislaid.'

'Well, if by the next meeting you do not have it, I am evidently going to summon Le Chevalier,' burst out Henry, visibly rattled.

Fortunately, Walpole had been discoursing with Garrick at that moment, who had been refining on the nascent aspects of the tromp de l'oeil on the adjoining staircase, so this passed unheard.

'Oh, do not be so melodramatic,' said Dashwood serenely, before diverting the conversation. 'On to candidates, let me see… as I recall, Richard Hastings.'

'You cannot possibly entertain the thought. That man is beyond us; I think he is beyond himself,' said Henry, horrified. 'Like yourself, I derive pleasure from theatrics, but not at the point of lunacy. Anyone else?'

'Cheltenham's son,' mused Dashwood. 'I had thought to include him on the list.'

'Ah, Lord Augustus. Well, I am aware he was eager before the war. Indeed, now that he has recently returned, let us present our proposal once more.'

'His father would approve; I am sure of it. It should support him in his intended path for his son.'

Meanwhile, Walpole and Garrick, who were situated on the staircase, were engaged in a very different discourse. The following words were heard from Walpole: 'And all at once there it was, a gigantic hand in armour. It was of the supernatural; the most fantastical nightmare, I assure you.'

Garrick replied, 'Well, perchance it betokens something weighing upon your mind? One can "count oneself a king of infinite space, were it not that I have bad dreams," and all that. What are you guilty of, Walpole? I would not have thought it of you.'

'No, no, not at all, Garrick, I assure you, though I agree, "The mind is its own place, and in itself Can make a Heav'n of Hell, a Hell of Heav'n."' Then he paused. 'I confess though, it is my frustration, dear fellow, I feel that, "Something is rotten in the state of Denmark," – or rather here, on this very isle and there is little I can do.'

With that, they rejoined their companions in the library.

CHAPTER 5 – MISAPPREHENSIONS

A smart, black barouche adorned with a coat of arms glided to a halt outside the Thornbury's London residence and a tall, distinguished gentleman, cloaked in a dark greatcoat, wrapped against the elements, stepped out. Isabella caught but a glimpse of his imposing figure as she took her ease in the drawing room with her mother on the first floor. His bicorne hat obscured his face from her view as he strode up to the door with a commanding grace, breath forming plumes in defiance of the winter.

The ladies had received several calls from new acquaintances in the few days since Lady Bute's salon. However, one crucial visitor had yet to make an appearance, leaving Isabella with a sense of lingering uncertainty. She had begun to question whether she had any right to anticipate a visit from Winterbourne. Perchance his singling her out that evening was but a figment of her imagination, and by all means other ladies were accorded the same treatment.

In the recesses of her mind, the book and its rightful owner also lurked, and she found herself wishing she had read its contents, so she could anticipate who may shortly be upon her. At this moment, she was equally brimming with a mixture of excitement and trepidation, unable to discern which feeling pertained to which circumstance.

She caught the sound of the front door open and shut as the housekeeper admitted the caller, and the low tones of the gentleman floated up. As the moments passed, Isabella saw in her mind's eye the housekeeper accepting his greatcoat and the gentleman removing his hat, revealing the visitor, yet to her, still indistinct. Then the footfalls of both housekeeper and guest struck against the wood of the stairs as they made their ascent. Isabella's heart thudded once; she briefly clutched her chestnut locks and drew in her breath, preparing herself.

Her mother, oblivious to Isabella's existential crisis, savoured a few final, precious moments with Thomas Grey before reluctantly hinging the book shut. She placed it on the console table by her side as she exhaled, though retained her index finger upon the book a moment longer than was required to achieve its placement, releasing it just as the visitor was announced.

The door swept open as, 'Lord Augustus Kant, son of the Earl of Cheltenham,' was announced.

Augustus presented a dashing figure with his frock coat befitting him and his smooth, black, polished high boots. His natural light brown hair had been powdered and queued and had not yet been subject to its customary tousling.

'Ah, Gussie, what a surprise,' said Lady Thornbury, delighted. 'Mrs Mills, could you please bring in the tea and cakes,' she requested of the housekeeper.

'I do not suppose you happen to have any macarons to complement the tea?' Augustus asked. 'It appears I have quite a weakness for them, but do we not all harbour a fondness for something sweet?' He smiled mischievously before claiming a seat. He remembered the Thornbury's confections well, and had not sampled them these seven years.

'You seem well. Are you in good health, Lady Thornbury?' enquired Augustus.

'Yes, very well, and how are your father, mother, and siblings? I rarely see them except in the formalities of church – if you can call Reverend Fernsby's services formal.'

As the bosom friends engaged in laughter, Isabella's participation was under the pretence of amusement but was in fact in relief of her previous anxieties.

Augustus replied, 'I too rarely see my father beyond the formalities; you know his inclination. My younger brother is at Oxford and hopes, upon being conferred his degree, to embark on the Grand Tour. My younger sister, Lady Catherine, resides in Henley, but is eagerly anticipating her first season in the following year.'

At that moment, Pudding presented himself at the door.

'Ah, Pudding, do come join us. You must have overheard us speaking of Reverend Fernsby. Are you anticipating the small cakes?' asked Lady Thornbury.

Unacquainted with this particular dog, Augustus seemed bemused by the formalities maintained by the family.

Before he could enquire, Lady Thornbury resumed, 'I understand you attended Lord and Lady Bute's salon and were so kind as to provide comfort to my dear Isabella during her most unexpected swoon.'

'I was pleased to be of service and to see Isabella once again,' replied Augustus, glancing over at the young lady with sincerity, before addressing her with a significant smile, though it did not reach his eyes this time. 'Prior to our conversation, I observed you were making a new acquaintance.' He said this with an undercurrent of scepticism in his voice, almost indiscernible.

'Indeed, the Duke of Winterborne did me the honour of introducing himself,' replied Isabella.

Augustus raised his eyebrows, 'Indeed, His Grace introduced himself.' He emphasised the last word, reflecting on the audacity.

'Are you acquainted with His Grace?' she continued, undeterred.

Augustus looked deep in thought, before he offered, 'Before I went abroad, I knew him well. Our views were even, dare I say, aligned before we parted.' At that juncture, he faltered for a brief moment. 'Although I must confess, the fault likely lies with me. It is I who have changed, not he. How did you find his conversation? I suppose it was his extraordinary humour which led to your unfortunate turn?'

'In the essentials of discourse, he was amiable, but I cannot comment on the particulars,' said Isabella. She thought her old friend's line of questioning was somewhat presumptuous.

'How interesting,' said Augustus, passing his hand across his lightly powdered hair, aggravating it somewhat.

The conversation subsided momentarily. Then, catching a glimpse of the book by Lady Thornbury, Augustus leaned towards Isabella, remarking, 'Oh, I see you are reading Thomas Grey.'

'That is not Isabella's; I was enjoying it just before you arrived,' said Lady Thornbury. 'Are you familiar?'

'Only mildly, yes, *Ode to a Favourite Cat* is my preferred,' he mused before apologising to Pudding, stationed at his foot. 'Although on the face of it enjoyable, one must not forget that it reminds us not to take what is not rightfully ours. How does Grey term it?'

Lady Thornbury nodded, quoting, "'Nor all that glisters, gold.'"

She glanced knowingly between Isabella and Augustus, discretely hinting, in the hopes of unity between the pair.

At Augustus's comment, Isabella had visibly flushed and was now touching her chestnut locks to comfort herself, whilst her thoughts flew to her own transgression – her withholding of the book.'

Augustus, noticing the change in her disposition, believed that he had awoken her emotions in his favour. Encouraged, he contemplated how else he could present his suit further to his advantage whilst the company pondered the poem.

Then, turning the conversation, the lieutenant colonel asked, 'Lady Thornbury, how has the war affected you?'

'Well, I know it has affected my husband's trade routes, but he has shown great fortitude in the face of adversity,' replied Lady Thornbury. Just as she was about to provide him with a platform to exhibit his own military prowess, to his surprise and disappointment, the housekeeper entered with the tea and the requested macarons, prompting a frenzy from Pudding, which diverted everyone's attention.

The irony was by no means lost on the unfortunate lieutenant colonel. Following a delightful tea and further exchanges of pleasantries, he resignedly took his leave, so as not to intrude on the Thornbury's hospitality further.

CHAPTER 6 – REVELRY

Beneath Medmenham Abbey, Sir Francis Dashwood

The revelry is at its height tonight, though only the privileged and chosen few may partake. Here, under cover of darkness, the powerful are gathered, as in a second parliament. Yet, it is more than this. In these our underground caverns, many of the most noble may enjoy a carnival; a temporary abandonment of inhibitions and all power structures, where humour and chaos reign.

It amuses me. I embrace the merriment, the jollity, and the theatrics of it all. I leave business to those whose persuasions are that way bent. Indeed, there are some who come not for the gaiety, but to advance their strategy, ambition, and to build their empires further. If any place were suited, it would be this.

Following the opening ritual, each of us, in our milk-white robes, with our new appellations, winds our way through the murky, stoney passages carved into the hill beneath the abbey. Snaking through the passages, one must beware not to lose one's way. Be sure to watch and not to fall. Ah, I hear a voice floating down the passage, chanting the secret rhyme:

*"Take twenty steps and rest a while,
Then take a pick and find a stile,
Perhaps to hide this cell divine,
Where lay my love in peace sublime.""*

It tickles me to know that this will lead them to a further hidden room of my creation, known only to my Inner Temple nine – the privileged of the privileged, a jest in a jest. One can only wonder what they wish to do there.

I am the architect and all is as I have planned. Room upon room, each designed for pleasures and festivities. Let us not miss the Buttery – that is most important. It is a cavern of barrels where the rivers run red with the finest wine that members can provide as a form of offertory. Yes, yes, like indulgences in penance for past and future sins. These members do indeed indulge. Some, I confess, more than most.

I can hold my cup, but Henry, oh, Mr Fitzwilliam, he does take things too far. Always predictably unpredictable, he is usually found… somewhere. Tonight, I observe he is already in the Buttery with his head bathed within a wine barrel. Good God, man, your cravat is entirely dyed red. I leave him to his overindulgence.

As I pass into the Banqueting Hall, there is a hive of activity and greater indulgence. The tempting nectar is lavishly arrayed on the elaborate table, with vine leaves intertwined between the overflowing dishes. Turtle soup, meats of all kinds, and an abundance of pies. An assortment of confections, syllabubs, tarts, fruits piled high, and at the pinnacle, a pineapple crowning the centrepiece. It is perhaps our equivalent of another apple, but for the ambitious. I have in mind an overreacher who is inclined to reach for that. Good Lord, I think he oversteps his bounds, but who am I to pass judgement?

I glance across the Banqueting Hall and am content. It is exactly as I have planned.

As I meander down the passages, having taken my fill, I catch voices from each chamber that I pass.

'Did you attend Bute's? Fairfax, good man, did not even flinch.'

From another chamber I hear, 'It was Fitzwilliam, yet again. He rolled him up in a carpet and bowled him down the stairs.'

'He found himself in the waters of the Thames, nearly frozen.'

'Too far, too far, I agree. Though the fellow was alright once we had warmed him up.'

Yes, I have often meditated on Fitzwilliam. The dear fellow is on his way to losing himself to drink and more, but I cannot stop him. Whilst Walpole and Garrick are not aligned with our philosophy, Henry takes it a little too much to heart. Leave such behaviour at the door on the way out, my man. Do not bring it into polite society. That is what this place is for.

Our motto, our credo, is etched above the abbey entrance. It serves as a reminder to abandon our cares at the door. There is a new set of rules here: *Fais ce que tu voudras. Do what thou wilt.*

Indeed, Fitzwilliam is not the only one to take it too far. There are others of a different variety – more strategic and certainly more sober – who use this place for their own gain and carry it to the pinnacle.

I continue meandering through the passages, on and on, passing more chambers. I pass a nun with a friar who both bow to me, and then I come to one last chamber where sits the Earl of Sandwich, his play in pause, regaling the company with his stories.

'And so, in order not to disturb my game, I request meat between two slices of bread,' says Sandwich. 'I recommend it, gentlemen, in order not to break one's winning streak.'

I chuckle seeing him in his element, for whilst he plays high stakes – a true profligate – I believe he understands his limitations, and yes, his fortune is vast.

'It has been so convenient that I have also taken to doing so at my writing table,' continues Sandwich.

'What, man, the gaming?'

'No, fool, I mean the collation,' they laugh and clink glasses.

I take this as my queue to enter. 'Gentlemen, will you deal me in?' I say, and take my seat next to the Earl of Cheltenham.

After some play, I turn to Cheltenham to broach the subject of prospective members, specifically his son.

'Hmm... Augustus?' he rumbles, hunched over his cards, which he holds in his left hand. Then slowly and deliberately, he replies, 'Yes, yes, my son. At one time, I believed him to be amenable, but he has since changed, and not for the better. Indeed, you may find him not so agreeable to this society.' His right-hand rests upon the green baize of the table, as he manoeuvres his stack of tokens, picking them up and letting them drop, one... two... three... before he continues, in measured tones, 'I believed the war would make a strategist of him. You would think a lieutenant colonel would cut through any emotion like butter, but I can see in his eyes that he is weak. I shall work on him some more, now that he has returned.' He continues with his game, muttering, 'That is critical.'

CONSEQUENCE OF POWER

Beneath Medmenham Abbey, Mr Henry Fitzwilliam and Le Chevalier

In a further chamber deep in the abbey's underground passages, sits Henry Fitzwilliam, now with his head out of the wine barrel and his person installed on a chair at table, with wine bottle in hand and engaged in an intense and desperate conversation with Le Chevalier – desperate at least on Henry's part.

'I tell you; it has not been recovered,' he cries, moving his face close to Le Chevalier, who withdraws a little, repulsed by the fumes emanating from Henry, but remains listening silently. Henry continues, 'Bah, Dashwood does not care a fig. He is in it for his own delight. His reputation will remain intact. Nay, he may become a legend in society for it, but I,' almost weeping now, 'I would be ruined, ruined. So much have I done; so many transgressions.'

Le Chevalier considers this and says quietly, 'C'est vrai? À quel point est-ce sérieux?'

'Serious enough for me to flee,' Henry weeps, his face crimson and damp. He pulls out a kerchief and begins wiping his visage with it. Then he seizes Le Chevalier, pulling even closer, and whispering as though he desires not to wake the devil, 'It is my conscience that keeps me awake throughout the night. I see visions of both the past and a dreaded future. The torment is ceaseless.'

Le Chevalier disentangles from the man's grasp, and sighs, 'Quel dommage.'

'And so, I beseech you to come to my aid. I beseech you to trace it. You are truly peerless in your domain, and I fear the only one who can come to my aid. I dare not approach the authorities,' Henry concludes breathlessly, for he has spent every ounce of his strength.

'I must confess, I am curious about this book and its possessor. They must be daring if they mean to trifle with so many in seats of power,' replies Le Chevalier.

Medmenham House, above the caverns, Lord Bute

I stalk the corridors of Dashwood's House. The others, fools, are already underground, revelling with St Francis. I take my pick of the festivities, as, unlike Dashwood, I am not by any means here solely for amusement. I shall join them, grace them with my presence when I am duly ready. Just as His Majesty would, I am the last to arrive and the first to leave. That is my notion of a jest. And yet, it is no jest at all.

I continue to advance along Dashwood's gallery. Good of him to allow me to use his library for some administrative affairs of state before I join them. However, this has also afforded me an opportunity to wander the corridors... and to allow my mind to wander.

Indeed, I have more responsibilities than most, who idle away their time within their estates and occasionally attend Parliament to partake in debates. Some are worse and degrade themselves with gaming and debauchery. I have not the leisure for such matters, for, as their prime minister, I have taxes, negotiations, and treaties to navigate. It is not true that I do not find pleasure in gaming. On the contrary, I employ myself in pursuits of a strategic nature – a supreme game to secure the influence of the highest.

Ah, now there it is, Dashwood's jovial portrait. He has a rounded, cheerful countenance. With a beaming smile, he lifts his glass to offer a salute. His joie de vivre shines out and his hospitality is legendary. It is evident why he is so well-favoured by many, given his easy manners. My manners may not be so easy, and though I may not be as well-favoured by so many, the King's favour is of far greater consequence.

There is no occasion for haste. Whilst they indulge beneath, I shall permit myself a while to muse and compare our portraits further. Similar to my own portrait in my London residence, Dashwood too dons a robe, though his is only trimmed with ermine. Mine is layered with it, signifying closeness to the throne.

There are various other distinctions. I flatter myself that mine is a regal countenance, conveying an air of great condescension to the viewer, whoever they may be, and that they are privileged to gaze upon me and despair.

How does that political philosopher term it? "The vulgar crowd is always taken by appearances and the world consists chiefly of the vulgar."

Aye, therein lies the difference. I have a strategy and a keen understanding of my own worth. Instead, Dashwood descends to their level to indulge in a blurring of the lines and friendships, rather than in cultivating strategic alliances.

Now that I find myself here, alone and in a measure of peace, I shall draw up a chair and permit myself this small indulgence – to reflect upon the strategy that secured my success... step by step. It has indeed been a protracted endeavour, demanding considerable sacrifice, and it is far from over.

I have studied that most esteemed philosopher and been a devoted pupil of his teachings. I am by no means surprised that his book was forbidden to the populace. The formula is all too easy and were it known it would no doubt lead to revolt.

When, by mere fortune, I made the acquaintance of the late Prince of Wales at Ascot, I seized the opportunity to apply my lessons. In time, I attained the position of tutor – to his son, no less, the little prince who is now

King himself. From that point onwards, the path lay smooth, for the too-young Sovereign was, and is, malleable to my will and easily guided. No truer words were spoken: "everyone sees what you appear to be, few really know what you are."

I marvel now at how, just a few short years later, I find myself in my position today. It was study and design that made me, not Dashwood, prime minister, and more besides. Indeed, now that I am here, I am entirely convinced that "the ends justify the means."

I executed what was required, and would act now without hesitation to maintain hold or respond to any challenges. It is for this very reason, this discipline in adhering to the philosophy, that I am the true power, the influence behind the throne.

CHAPTER 7 – INTO THE FLAMES

Since Augustus's visit that morning, a growing sense of unease had lodged in Isabella's mind. She recalled the vivid image of the barouche drawing up and the dark figure in a greatcoat stepping out. The sound of boots tripping up the stairs echoed in her thoughts, as though they were drawing nearer and nearer every moment. A heavy closeness in the air built, bearing down upon Isabella. Vibrations coursed through her veins – her nerves were on a knife's edge. It was whilst she was deep in these reflections in the drawing room that a voice said, 'Isabella,' making her jump sharply.

'It is too beautiful a day for you to wear such a dull countenance,' came Lady Ingram's matronly tones. 'Come, we shall take a turn about Hyde Park. You never know whom we might encounter,' she continued with a knowing sparkle.

Finding herself at a loss for an excuse and faced with these rather daunting yet reasonable words, Isabella reluctantly agreed to step out with her.

As she promenaded through Hyde Park with Lady Ingram on her arm, she reflected upon the book and that she had no certain idea of its contents. In her mind, she saw Mary's tense countenance, as she stalked towards the door and heard her acerbic retort, 'You know not what you may provoke.'

As she walked with Lady Ingram, lending the elder lady an arm, a feeling of being followed overcame her, and she persistently glanced around distractedly. She became increasingly concerned when she perceived a black barouche with a crest passing them. It then slowed and came to a sudden halt. Isabella drew in a breath and paused momentarily, causing Lady Ingram to be pulled back abruptly.

'Isabella, are you quite well?' enquired the dowager incredulously.

Isabella remained silent; her eyes fixed upon the door of the barouche. It opened slowly, and two elderly ladies in black stepped out of the carriage, taking no note of her. She exhaled, before continuing their perambulation.

This weight to her existence escalated over the course of the day, heightening to a moment of crisis by the evening. By the time Heloise came into her bedchamber to assist her in preparing for bed and to partake in their nightly collations, Isabella could stand it no longer.

'Heloise,' she cried. 'Thank goodness you are here. We must resolve the matter of the book.'

Moments later, the pair stared at the book in silence, as it lay upon the bed. It was a small, leather-bound pocketbook, without inscription upon the cover, though somewhat worn at the edges. Heloise eventually broke the silence, saying, 'I believe we know what we must do. We are left with no alternative but to read some of it.'

Isabella nodded in agreement. With apprehension, they turned to the first page, where they found a list of names, none of whom either lady recognised, except for the last two:

Mr Richard Hastings
John Fox-Knowell, Baron of Hollinsbury, MP
Maximillian Upshur, Earl of Dullington
Mr Benjamin Franklin, Diplomat for North America
Lieutenant Colonel Augustus Kant, son of the Earl of Cheltenham
Mr David Garrick, actor

This list of seemingly miscellaneous names meant little to the ladies. There appeared to be no discernible connection, except perhaps that they appeared to be notable figures. Both ladies found it perplexing that Augustus was mentioned.

They proceeded to the next page, which appeared to contain notes from the minutes of a meeting dated only two weeks prior. With it was a list of nine council attendees. Sir Francis Dashwood was listed as the Chairman. Lord Bute was also mentioned. Another name that Isabella thought she recognised was Henry Fitzwilliam, as she had a vague recollection of Lady Ingram noting the gentleman to her during Lord Bute's salon. Finally, a name with which she was undoubtably acquainted was the Earl of Cheltenham.

In silence, the ladies each took their time to peruse the meeting minutes and understand the meaning of the detached and rather disjointed esoteric comments.

The agenda began with an appeal for views on the repair of an abbey interior door, which had sustained damage during a session. There was debate regarding whether Henry Fitzwilliam – the likely culprit – should pay, or if it should be covered by the general funds.

Mr Fitzwilliam, present during this discourse, appeared to object to paying, arguing that the damage was part of the general deterioration expected during such sessions. The vote concluded unfavourably for Mr Fitzwilliam.

There came raised eyebrows from Isabella, though Heloise, having heard of something similar in the White Hart in her home village, bore the comments with equanimity.

The agenda turned to a more personal matter as they proceeded to items mislaid and recovered. An appeal was made for the return of Mr George Whitehead, who seemed to have disappeared. Again, suspicion appeared to have been cast upon Mr Fitzwilliam, who vehemently denied the allegation of theft. Sir Francis Dashwood then proposed dispatching a note to all members, stating that if Mr Whitehead were left at the door of the abbey before the coming week, at the prankster's convenience, no further mention would be made of the matter.

Isabella wondered first what Mr Whitehead would make of the matter, and second, whether Mr Fitzwilliam was, indeed, as eligible a gentleman as Lady Ingram had professed.

Under the following agenda item was the question of whether to replace or refurbish the nuns' religious habits, for they were showing signs of serious wear.

At this juncture Isabella broke into a smile of palpable relief, albeit still somewhat uneasy, and looked up at Heloise, saying, 'Of course, this is just a play. That would account for the list of cast members and their costumes. I wonder what production this could be, though? Mary was evidently toying with us, though she has taken it too far this time.'

Heloise did not look at all convinced. They continued reading as the notes turned to politics and wider issues.

Whilst neither had any real understanding, it appeared that the Earl of Cheltenham had put forth a proposal, urging members to pledge their support for the East India Company and the suppression of a Bill, which was contrary to its interests and currently making its way through Parliament.

Isabella was aware of Cheltenham's interest in the Company and that he was a Member of Parliament. Dashwood had swiftly dismissed the notion, rebuking Cheltenham for raising such an issue during the council meeting, as this political matter was not the concern of the general assembly. He preferred that Cheltenham address the relevant members directly, rather than broach the matter during the council meeting.

Now, Lord Bute himself took issue and professed it to be a key item, declaring that he would convene a meeting to address this with members.

This was merely the beginning of issues raised over many pages, which culminated in a most lamentable portrayal of the self-interest exhibited by numerous Members of Parliament who seemed to be affiliated with the group.

Isabella, clutching the book as they read, at length let it fall into her lap, as she came to the realisation that this was no mere scene from a play.

Heloise retrieved the book cautiously, and read further, turning the pages slowly, as her expression gradually changed to one of shock. Isabella, studying her, could not help but ask with impatience, 'Well? What is it?'

Heloise became transfixed. Her eyes darted across the pages, and with her mouth slightly agape, she raised her hand, as if to request a moment to absorb what she had just read. Then, suddenly, she snapped the book shut with both her hands clasping the covers as if in prayer.

Her eyes wide, were drifting and lost, as though she were searching for a response to Isabella.

'Well?' repeated Isabella. 'Is it more politics?'

'I do not believe you should read more than is necessary,' Heloise replied. 'We cannot allow this to corrupt our minds.'

'How? How bad can it possibly be?' exclaimed Isabella.

Heloise, at first pursed her lips, reluctant to divulge more, before disclosing, 'If the contents were known to general society, it would sow further distrust in the very fabric and, who knows, cause a revolt. Yet, these individuals are amongst our general acquaintance.'

'Yes, and supposedly so respectable,' said Isabella slowly. 'Let us not forget, very influential, too. Dare I say, I have seen four or five of these gentlemen at Lady Bute's salon alone.' Then her thoughts turned. 'And Augustus, how could he be involved? This is such a departure from his character, though he did mention that he had changed.' She reflected privately too, with relief that at least Winterbourne had not been amongst those listed.

They sat in silence, though their minds were each in a maelstrom.

In sudden impulse, Isabella seized the book and hurled it into the fire, which was at a low flame, though the embers emitted a red and orange glow. The book lay on the cinders, surprisingly without further fuelling the fire. The light white and grey ashes, which had been stirred upon impact, slowly descended onto the cover. Isabella enlivened, with an anxious command, looked back at Heloise with an unmistakable appeal for approbation, which was not met.

Rather, Heloise sprang up, grabbed the poker, and began jabbing it at the book in an attempt to retrieve it before abandoning the tool with a clatter, and pulling the book out with her bare fingers and dropping it upon the stone hearth. The book smouldered, but was not aflame.

'Your hands, Heloise,' exclaimed Isabella, for they were burnt.

Heloise, ignoring Isabella's remark, but with hands shaking said quietly, 'Let us not act on impulse.'

CHAPTER 8 – A RARE DAY AT THE MANTUA-MAKER'S

'Kindly extend your arms, Mademoiselle Thornbury, and I shall begin with your sleeve length,' requested Madame Noyer, one of the pre-eminent mantua-makers in the capital.

Isabella, her mother, Lady Ingram, Heloise, and Mr Thornbury were enjoying a rare day at the mantua-maker's. Whilst Isabella was being attended to by Madame Noyer, the seamstresses stood to the side of the fitting room, studying the fashion plates provided by Sir Nicholas Thornbury.

Absorbed, these masters of their art were discussing the intricate techniques required to craft specific folds and the blending of these inspirations with their own flare to achieve the desired aesthetic.

In the preceding days, Lady Ingram had been hard at work as usual, utilising her connections to the full. To her delight, these efforts had borne the most magnificent of fruit that very morning. The Duke and Duchess of Harringshire, no less, had requested the honour of Lady

Ingram's presence, accompanied by members of her esteemed household, at a ball to be held at their Graces' residence on the nineteenth day of February at eight o'clock in the evening.

That Lady Ingram no longer had her own establishment was, in her mind, of little consequence, for she assumed that her residence with the Thornburys would naturally mean the invitation extended to them.

The prospect of a ball of any kind was excitement enough for the ladies; it was a welcome distraction for both Isabella and Heloise from their concerns about the book.

Lady Ingram was a natural barometer for the significance of any event, and her elation was far beyond anything that the other ladies had ever witnessed in her. Indeed, the news had prompted Lady Ingram to expedite their appointment with the foremost mantua-maker. It was anyone's guess how this was possible, as Madame Noyer was usually engaged a month in advance.

However, it may be attributed to the fact that prior to the loss of her fortune to her husband's third cousin, as she frequently reminded them, the countess had been one of Madame Noyer's most cherished patrons. Now Lady Ingram found herself once more in her proper sphere, preparing for a ball and, with the anticipation of being able to do her utmost for Isabella's future happiness.

Given that the well-intentioned lady was not blessed with offspring of her own, Isabella represented a single chance to express her maternal instincts in her own unique manner. The dowager also felt deep within her heart, that by dedicating her talents to the service of the Thornburys, it would be a manifestation of her gratitude for their generosity, for she had been all but cast out by her husband's kin and the late Lord Ingram appeared not to have considered providing for her in the event of their having no sons. It was, therefore, with these sentiments that Lady Ingram oversaw every detail of Isabella's gown with assiduity.

Lady Thornbury, understanding where her own talents lay, and that Isabella was in capable hands, embraced the opportunity to repose with Mr Thornbury and Heloise at the little tea table with bonnes bouches set before them by the mantua-maker, as they observed the entertainment.

For a lady who devoted so much of her time to sampling cakes, Lady Thornbury maintained a figure of remarkable elegance and, if anything, the regular consumption of exquisite delicacies added an appealing softness to her appearance. However, it might also be supposed that many of those confections were lost to Mr Thornbury, who had his own persuasive talents, but whose own form, alas, could not boast the same refinement, despite his relative youth.

In this most inviting setting, the ladies enjoyed a memorable afternoon together, offering Isabella and Heloise much relief and distraction from the previous night's concerns.

'Miss Thornbury will require this piece with the gold embroidery for her bodice,' mused Lady Ingram, caressing the material with fondness.

'Very well, make a note, Mademoiselle Ainsley. Mademoiselle Thornbury, would you kindly turn about?' requested Madame Noyer.

Lady Ingram had insisted that Isabella don a striking ruby silk brocade at the ball to distinguish her and leave a lasting impression. It was a departure from Isabella's favoured delicate light blues, but in Lady Ingram's view, she would not allow her charge to squander her best opportunity to date, and withdraw into the background, like a sconce.

'You will be enchanting, my dear,' came the dowager's voice behind Isabella, who imagined her friend's lined countenance softening in unison with her visions.

'She will indeed,' came her mother's sigh.

'Yes, she will indeed...' Then after a brief pause, Lady Ingram's thoughts shifted instantly to business, in that dexterous flexibility of mind so natural to her. 'Oh, but you must not outshine your hostess or her daughter. No, no, that will never do. It will certainly not endear you to them,' said the widow with concern. Then, brightening, she pronounced, 'I have it! We shall gift them a gown each. They would surely appreciate receiving such a rare and exquisite offering.'

'Thank you. You may rest, Mademoiselle Thornbury,' said the good mantua-maker, before turning to Lady Ingram. 'Indeed, we have her Grace and Her Ladyship's measurements,' she said, well-informed previously by Lady Ingram of the event, the hostess and all manner of speculative details.

Satisfied, Lady Ingram then turned her attention to discussing with Madame Noyer the materials to be used for the esteemed hostess and her daughter. To outshine Isabella's chosen materials was indeed a challenge, given the embellishments of fine gold thread with tiny beads planned for the young lady, which added a touch of opulence without overwhelming the delicate artistry.

However, Lady Ingram possessed a discerning eye, adept at balancing refined luxury, while skilfully avoiding the excesses of ornamentation that might veer into the realm of the vulgar. The forbearing Madame Noyer, not only skilled in her trade, but in diplomacy, indulged her patron's strong opinions.

'No, no, we cannot use gold embroidery for the entire gown. They are not royalty, only near-royalty. There must be a distinction in rank and it is incumbent on each of us to exhibit the suitable degree of condescension,' came the dowager, with a note of pleasure.

Finally, after a great deal of consideration on the widow's part and patience on Madame Noyer's, the design and materials of the gifts were decided and Lady Ingram could join the vastly entertained idlers on the settee.

'I am certain you are much anticipating the prospect of dancing, Isabella,' her mother ventured after some intervening moments, during which fresh tea had been provided to replenish Lady Ingram. 'You have so seldom had the opportunity.'

'Indeed, I am,' reflected Isabella, her thoughts wandering to whom might offer her to dance. With few acquaintances in town, she privately feared that none of the gentlemen would solicit her hand, before a more pleasant thought sprang forth. Perhaps she might dare to imagine that Winterbourne would seek her. She betrayed herself with a coy smile and gentle blush at the prospect before pushing the notion aside. She had to confess to some disappointment, as he had not called upon them. It was entirely possible that she had made too much of the encounter with the duke.

'Indeed, we must endeavour to secure you suitable dance partners prior to the ball,' came Lady Ingram, revived by her refreshment and ready to embark on the next stage of the design. 'It will not do to have an empty dance card, and to be engaged for the first two dances would be a promising sign. Hmm... the next opportunity to seek partners shall be at Vauxhall Gardens in the ensuing week.'

Despite Lady Ingram's efforts, the invitations to large gatherings had not been as forthcoming as she had hoped, and there were many evenings when they were obliged to create their own amusement, which admittedly in such a household as theirs was relatively easy.

However, the dowager secretly reflected that efforts must be doubled. It would not be amiss to permit it to be known that Isabella's dowry was a considerable thirty-thousand pounds and that she was the sole heir of the Thornbury family fortune. This knowledge would no doubt offer the gentlemen a measure of additional encouragement. The dowager knew from having long observed the drawing rooms of society that, sadly, beauty and spirit alone rarely constituted the necessary inducement.

Setting these thoughts aside for the present, Lady Ingram turned the company's attention to another delicate matter: that of Isabella's dancing. 'Whilst we await the ball, and we are at leisure in the evenings, I have taken the liberty of engaging Monsieur De La Fontaine, to assist in further refining the steps and graces required.'

'Oh, but Mr Watley has instructed me so admirably. I feel quite equal to the contradance,' exclaimed Isabella, her countenance lighting up with a smile. She had delighted in the relative freedom and lively spirit afforded by the country dance, which permitted a true expression of her vivacity.

Predictably, this was not acceptable to Lady Ingram. 'Pray, I beg you not to consider such a bold and, dare I say, audacious step as engaging in the contradance,' the dowager cautioned. 'I advise you to remain with the more formal minuet and gavotte until your standing in society is more firmly established. You would not wish to incite gossip of an unfavourable nature, and believe me, gossip abounds at such events.'

Lady Ingram understood just how powerful gossip could be, either in one's favour or against, and she had privately vowed that she would work to turn the tide to Isabella's advantage.

'And as for Mr Wately, he is all well and good for a country assembly, but for the Duke and Duchess of Harringshire's ball? What an idea! You might as well have engaged Reverend Fernsby,' the widow sighed. 'I think you must be teasing me.'

Mr Thornbury raised his head briefly at his favourite's name and licked his lips, before settling his head back upon Isabella's foot, where it had been resting.

On that note, Isabella assented, whilst helping herself to the fruitcake and marvelling at the complexities and pitfalls of navigating society. She thought to herself that she would try to make a conscious effort to appreciate her well-meaning friend's advice, however perplexing it may appear. Lady Thornbury, nibbling on a macaron, had similar sentiments, but each lady maintained a reserved silence.

CHAPTER 9 – TEMPTATION

'We still are no further advanced in our decision,' said Isabella despairingly to Heloise as they promenaded out of Hyde Park on a crisp January afternoon.

The afternoon at the mantua-maker's had considerably diverted Isabella and Heloise from the concerns surrounding the book. However, by the following morning, it had begun to occupy them once more. They were agitated from their confinement indoors, as they could not freely discuss the matter without fear of being disturbed, and so by that afternoon they found themselves on a walk with Mr Thornbury.

Lady Ingram had announced that she would be engaged most of the day, making calls to personal acquaintances. However, she refrained from disclosing the nature of these, or the information with which she intended to endow them. Though not one to gossip, in her own mind, a minor infraction in this case was justified for the greater good.

Lady Thornbury was also occupied, but in writing replies to Sir Nicholas Thornbury's billet-doux.

Therefore, a walk provided the young ladies with the perfect freedom to discuss their dilemma – not that they had made much headway.

'What do you suppose we should do, were we to encounter an acquaintance listed in the book?' Isabella asked Heloise covertly whilst coming to a halt on the path.

Heloise, also coming to a stop, collected her thoughts before disclosing, 'I believe we have a duty to maintain composure, so as not to betray ourselves,' she replied.

'And what do you suppose the lists mean?'

'The council attendees' list is clear, but I cannot account for the names on the first page of the book. Could they indicate those absent from the council meeting? I am uncertain, but they evidently have some connection,' Heloise surmised in discrete undertones.

'There is also the question of what the council is striving to achieve. Additionally, to which abbey are they referring?' pondered Isabella furtively.

Heloise remained silent as two gentlemen passed, lunting, not wishing the strangers to overhear their enigmatic discourse. Isabella studied the two gentlemen who were receding into the distance, trailing smoke from their pipes and then glanced at Heloise, as though to suggest that any gentleman might be subject to their review.

However, Heloise shook her head, applying an appropriate level of scepticism to her mistress's abstraction, before resuming, once they were beyond hearing. 'Of those seated at the gaming table at Lord and Lady Bute's salon, which gentlemen also appear on the lists?' she enquired.

Isabella whispered conspiratorially, 'Well, Sir Francis Dashwood, the Earl of Cheltenham and Mr Henry Fitzwilliam. However, I believe we can deduce that the book surely must be Dashwood's, as I found it close to where he had been seated.'

Whilst the day had a cool freshness about it, and a dusting of snow still clung to the street, the sunlight had broken through the white clouds and their warm pelisses and fur-lined stoles were more than adequate for the winter. Isabella often presented Heloise with her gently worn attire, which was more befitting a companion than a lady's maid. In truth, Heloise performed the duties of both.

Therefore, so snugly attired and desirous of extending their peregrinations, they resolved to avail themselves of a new, longer route home and permitted Mr Thornbury to lead the way.

It was upon one of these unfamiliar streets that they passed a shop, from which a sweet, rich and inviting aroma floated towards them irresistibly. Isabella paused and, glancing up, saw a wooden sign with the words *Mrs Grey's Chocolate House*, as Mr Thornbury investigated the crack at the base of the door with his delicate snout.

Neither lady had sampled chocolate before, as Sir Nicholas Thornbury's chests from China and the East Indies did not contain cocoa. Henley, too, was unable to provide the opportunity, as it boasted neither coffee nor chocolate house.

The sweet aromas which drifted from the premises and towards the young ladies were a luxuriant heavenly temptation, and one could detect subtle hints of what might be vanilla and caramel. Both ladies attempted to resume their walk and discussion, but the tempting scent of the chocolate house remained with them.

The name "Mrs Grey" justified their choice, for who could object if such an establishment were under the management of a lady? In truth, they were merely seeking a reason to allow themselves an innocent pleasure. That is, however, in spite of the fact that as a young lady with a reputation to uphold, Isabella would not customarily visit dining establishments, even when chaperoned.

They stepped into the darkened shop, which had the ambiance of a bygone era. It had rich wood floorboards, tables dotted here and there, and a counter towards the far end, behind which a matronly-looking lady in widow's garb was reaching for a jar amongst those stacked on shelves.

Presently, a waiter attended to them and guided them to the table by the bay window, which both afforded them a prospect of the street and the opportunity to survey the shop and its customers.

'I find it remarkable that Mrs Grey is managing such a delightful establishment herself,' observed Isabella to the waiter. 'I was unaware that ladies could engage in such business.'

'Yes, ma'am,' replied the rough-hewn waiter. He hesitated, his eyes first wandering to Isabella's fine garments, then to Heloise's, lingering with indiscrete appraisal, as his countenance progressed to bemusement. 'Tis rare to find fine ladies such as yourselves here, but you are welcome, I am sure. What might I fetch for you?'

Heloise regarded Isabella with a look of alarm, given his remarks and examination, but astonished herself that she felt oddly gratified and accepting of his good graces. However, her mistress so close to the indulgence, could not bear to have it snatched away, by obscure formalities and countered Heloise's regard by commenting, 'Now that we are here, I am certain that sampling just one dish of chocolate, would be acceptable, and after all, I am chaperoned.'

They each requested a dish of chocolate, which came thick, dark and frothy. As they brought the cups to their lips, the steam began to warm them and the aromas to play more intensely. Upon taking their first sip, a warmth flooded them, as the smooth, luxuriant taste, velvet and slightly viscose coated their palates with its sweet nutty tones. When they inhaled the intense aroma, they could affirm the presence of the vanilla notes that had been added to the cocoa.

This was truly unlike anything they had tasted before. Even the French macarons and cream cakes of home could not compete. This was a most novel and sumptuous nectar from heaven. Both ladies, closing their eyes, sank back in their chairs with a sensation of great indulgence and relaxation.

Whilst the ladies were resting languidly with their libations, unbeknown to them, at the rear of the house, Horace Walpole was in animated discourse with another gentleman. It would be more accurate to say that Walpole was the sole maintainer of the conversation, as his companion sat back in his chair with a silent and composed demeanour.

'It is a disgrace; I cannot bear it,' came Walpole's voice with intensity. Placing his palm upon his forehead in despair, the foaming lace of his wrist came down over his eyes. 'Truly, I cannot stand by and watch operations which are so morally... well, there is but one word for it – corrupt!'

'Steady on, Walpole,' soothed his companion.

Arms flailing now, Walpole remonstrated to drive home his point. 'Do not suggest I overstep the mark. I do not. Think of their influence on Parliament. Their contributions so evidently sway decisions in their favour, to the sacrifice of everything, even human dignity and our reputation.'

Overcome, Walpole could no longer remain seated, and he sprang up abruptly, crying, 'They know my disposition, and I am not afraid to speak out on this matter. Nevertheless, you need not fear; even I acknowledge the importance of discretion regarding the particulars.' Leaning on the table with his hands, with great tension he pressed forward impassioned, 'This behaviour is unbefitting of gentlemen, and I cannot – nay, I cannot – stand by in silence.'

Then, with an exasperated huff, he took up his elegant silver-topped walking cane and with an air of grace and fashionable sophistication, he strode with palpable tension out of the chocolate house.

Towards the latter part of this discourse, his animated voice had become apparent to the young ladies, and Isabella opened one blue eye to steal a glance as Walpole whisked past her. Then her eye moved to his companion. All at once, she sat up. Could it be?

Heloise heard the rustling of Isabella's silk skirts and too opened her eyes, to discover what had caused her mistress to move so suddenly, whereupon the movement of both women drew the attention of the remaining gentleman.

The Duke of Winterbourne espied them and, with the commanding presence and noble grace of a gentleman, he advanced towards their table. Bowing to them once in their presence, he then addressed Isabella with elegance. 'Good day, Miss Thornbury. How do you and your companion fare this fine afternoon?'

'I am very well. I thank you, Your Grace,' replied Isabella, astonished at her composure.

'Pray, do excuse my friend. He finds pleasure in lively conversation and tends towards the theatrical,' explained Winterbourne. 'I must confess to being somewhat surprised to find you here. Conversations in such an establishment often feature political discourse, and when impassioned, they may not always adhere to the civility to which a lady such as yourself is likely accustomed.'

Isabella laughed now with understanding, 'Yes, I am sure it could not be helped.' She had always held the view that it is preferable to live embracing one's passions and expressing oneself openly, so she could easily overlook this of his friend.

Directing the course of the conversation, Winterbourne commented, 'I trust you are enjoying the delightful sunshine on this crisp winter's day.'

'Yes indeed; I find it also renders the indoors all the more inviting,' replied Isabella, continuing to marvel at the admirable composure with which she was conducting this interaction. Even Heloise appeared somewhat impressed, though also intrigued, being entirely unaware of Isabella's apparent familiarity with so distinguished a gentleman – a duke, no less.

'Indeed, and a dish of chocolate is deliciously warming,' observed Winterbourne. 'Do you often visit chocolate houses?'

'Oh no, Your Grace,' Isabella laughed.

'Ah, so you are open to new curiosities, I see,' he mused. Then, pausing, he glanced at Heloise before looking back at Isabella, 'I advise you procure the spiced Spanish-style chocolate, and thus you can indulge privately in the comforts of your own home, away from the clamorous discourse of the common public.'

'I thank you, and shall gladly take your advice, Your Grace,' said Isabella. Then, turning to Heloise, she said, 'Would you be so kind?'

Heloise regarded Isabella for a moment, then assenting, made her way to Mrs Grey's counter towards the rear of the shop.'

Adapting his tone, Winterbourne expressed in a velvet purring quality, 'Tell me, Miss Thornbury, how did you find your first taste?'

'It was an experience I have not had before, and the cocoa is so rich and sweet, I can hardly describe the sensation.'

'Yes, I would agree,' he intimated, leaning closer and positioning himself to ensure she received his meaning. 'One's first taste is always the sweetest.'

Isabella stared at him, somewhat bewildered, and though she could not fathom why, she flushed.

'And once you have experienced it, you will be tempted to surrender to it once more,' he resumed. 'Ah, but it is important to manage temptations. I strive to govern mine, yielding only in circumstances where indulgence is permissible.'

He drew back from Isabella as Heloise rejoined them. Then, in a lively tone, he straightened himself and said, 'I am sure your mother will enjoy such a luxury. Now, I must bid you good day, ladies,' as he bowed.

Before Isabella could bid him farewell, Heloise, perceiving a gentleman in the street passing by the window on foot, exclaimed, 'I declare, is that Lord Augustus?'

Isabella and Winterbourne directed their eyes away from each other and towards Augustus as he walked by. Isabella impulsively raised her hand to greet him. The lieutenant colonel, seemingly catching sight of her, paused momentarily, and, without any acknowledgement, continued on his way. Isabella lowered her hand slowly, in some perplexity and could not help but utter quietly, 'I do wonder… perhaps we did not draw his notice.'

Winterbourne enquired with immediate curiosity, 'Are you well acquainted?'

'Yes, he is a dear, old neighbour from my childhood, but has only recently returned from extended service in the military, so our acquaintance of late has been rather brief,' Isabella replied. Then, glancing out of the window once again to watch Augustus fade from her sight, she murmured, 'Perhaps I have offended him?'

Winterbourne countered, 'I know him well, and unfortunately the war has affected him greatly. I would not take it to heart. Our relationship is not what it was. He no longer desires to associate with me, though we were such dear old friends and so alike in our youth.'

Isabella glanced up at Winterbourne, somewhat disturbed, and asked, 'How so?'

Winterbourne continued, 'He seems to detach himself more and more from our society. I would even go as far as to recommend being discerning in your acquaintance with him, as much as it might pain you to do so.'

'Well, he does engage in society. I renewed my acquaintance with him at Lady Bute's salon and I understand he will also attend the Duke and Duchess of Harringshire's ball,' replied Isabella.

'Ah, then we are likely to encounter him, though we may endeavour to avoid him,' he said in an affable tone.

Isabella contemplated whether this was an indication that Winterbourne's own attendance could be expected. She recalled Lady Ingram's aspirations of engaging dance partners in advance and she briefly entertained the faint hope that His Grace might ask her. However, Winterbourne concluded, 'Now, I really must take my leave. I bid you good day, ladies.' Bowing, the duke left the chocolate house.

CHAPTER 10 – THE QUEEN TRAP

'Why must you insist on playing?' said Augustus, as he appealed to his father for a moment of conversation uninterrupted by strategic commentary or diversions.

The Earl of Cheltenham responded only with a familiar expression of authority, positioning his strut arm towards the chessboard, assuming a level of condescension and sequestration.

'A gentleman can reveal many of his virtues and faults through the manner in which he approaches the game,' instructed Cheltenham, 'and only once you have engaged the most challenging minds within our society, might you evaluate your own temperament.' His demeanour conformed to the polished oak décor, which panelled the gallery where they sat, and the alabaster statues surrounding them. 'Lord Bute, for example, embodies the art of strategy,' Cheltenham continued. 'He positions his pieces to secure advantageous proximity to the King. You can learn much from him.'

Augustus, turning squarely towards his father, ignored this and listlessly made his opening move. 'Father, I wish to speak to you concerning my future, and particularly the feelings I hold for Miss Isabella Thornbury.'

The earl, unmoved by this request, and determined to begin his own game, took it upon himself to reach over to execute Augustus's move for him and positioned one of his son's white pawns on the chessboard. 'There, I see today you are favouring the King's Gambit,' stated the earl. 'Unfortunately for you, I shall adopt a Classical Defence and decline your gambit in favour of my own central position.'

Undeterred, Augustus pushed his suit further, saying, 'I have fulfilled every request you made of me, having joined the conflict and distinguished myself by rising through the ranks. I now desire to turn my attentions to Miss Thornbury, if she will have me.'

The earl's cold eyes shifted from his own move to Augustus with a measured air of disdain. 'This is most uncharacteristic of you. Perhaps you have another motive at hand, which you have not disclosed? However, if not, such an appeal does not distinguish you at all, rather it lays bare your weaknesses,' he remarked, before positioning one of his black pieces with deliberate care, fully aware this strategic placement would serve to his own advantage in due course. 'It should not be necessary for me to repeat the instruction on matters so self-evident, but you appear to have forgotten them in recent years,' Cheltenham continued. 'It is of paramount importance to maintain appearances and one should never lay bare one's vulnerabilities; if any such flaws exist, they should immediately be expunged.' He articulated the final word with great emphasis upon each syllable and strength in the last letter.

Augustus stared down at the board as much to avoid his father's gaze, as to gather himself. The earl continued his attack. 'Again, I should not be required to reiterate what is self-evident. That girl is manifestly unsuitable for a son of mine, possessing to my knowledge neither fortune, rank nor connections – not that I have been taking note of that house's movements, for they are wholly unworthy of our consideration. Need I elaborate any further?' He drew breath following this lengthy speech, before continuing. 'I anticipated a level of maturation on your return, I believed war would make a strategist out of you, ready for the next phase. Instead, you return driven by sentiment.'

'You may have manoeuvred me into position,' replied Augustus, 'but for all your strategising, you failed to foresee the events which would unfold on the ground, on the battlefield. You gentlemen may discourse on such matters within your clubs and in Parliament, but you were not there.' He hesitated before delivering his final challenge. 'Have you ever truly considered the ramifications of your actions on those who bear their consequences, or is it merely a game to you?' said Augustus, now white as his chess pieces, the blood drained from his face.

'By what audacity do you challenge my decision!' seethed the earl. 'I understood entirely, but it was the gambit I resolved to pursue, to maintain the appearance of honour and standing. This is merely the beginning; you will not withdraw at this juncture.'

Then once again, picking up one of his son's white pieces, Cheltenham collected himself and remarked with a more serene composure, 'One must think three steps ahead of one's opponent. Given your inability to think effectively for yourself, I shall have to do so for you.'

'The trials of war, the intrigues of society, the clubs, politics, what purpose does it all serve?' said Augustus, despairingly and staring into the board.

Pausing, the earl examined the board himself, before taking hold of one of his black pieces and resuming, 'What do you think? Power!' before knocking Augustus's bishop off the board. Then, after once more orchestrating his son's move, the earl affirmed his instructions. 'I do not grant my consent for you to consort with that hoyden. Yes, yes, I perceive you well,' he said, fixing his son with a penetrating look. 'You have frequently been swayed by a fair face, yet now you must turn to the serious business of securing an alliance.'

He struck the table with his fist, causing the court's defence to shudder. 'In due course, you may consort with her as much as you desire; with due discretion, naturally.' Almost as if timing his chess moves with the conversation, Cheltenham knocked the white queen off the board. 'No, an alliance with the Thornbury's is evidently not the strategy I have so meticulously devised for you,' he concluded with steely resolve.

'Well, what lies ahead for me then, Father?' conceded Augustus.

Observing that his efforts were yielding their customary results, his father resumed, 'You shall join me at the next meeting of the Order of the Friars of St. Francis of Wycombe, at Dashwood's place in Medmenham. There, you shall build upon the vital political and business alliances, that I have worked tirelessly to secure for our house, Lord Bute amongst others.'

Having achieved checkmate, his father rose from his chair and stalked out of the oak-panelled gallery. Augustus bowed his head and closed his eyes with a great intensity.

CHAPTER 11 – SCANDALISED

The aroma of chocolate rose from the dish and as she breathed deeply, it filled her senses with the sweet, rich notes of the cocoa and accents of vanilla, which had been blended with the thick creamy liquid. 'It is indeed luxuriant,' uttered Lady Thornbury with indulgence.

Isabella had proposed that they include the beverage as part of their breakfast table and her mother evidently embraced the change with visible bliss. Lady Ingram, too, was ready to partake in the decadence, but not without some measure of inquiry into its provenance.

'Oh, Heloise and I procured it from *Mrs Grey's Chocolate House* during our journey homeward from the park,' came Isabella's unconsciously innocent reply.

'You procured it?' she squawked, for such was the sound that came from the alarmed dowager. 'Procured it? At a chocolate house? Heavens above! Pray, do not tell me you ventured inside?'

Isabella dropped the lightly toasted, buttery brioche that was almost at her lips. 'It was Mrs Grey's,' she stammered.

CONSEQUENCE OF POWER

'The identity of the proprietor is immaterial,' cried Lady Ingram in dismay. Though severely ruffled, she sought to soften her tone as she observed how shaken both her companions were. She was a lady of great compassion, despite her formidable demeanour.

As she beheld Isabella, she sadly reflected that shielding her from the truth might cause her to unwittingly stumble into social peril, wholly unprepared. Comporting herself, and gazing across the table towards Lady Thornbury, Lady Ingram had a great conviction that it was her duty to intervene.

She continued, 'I realise you may not be entirely versed in all the protocols of town that befit ladies of our station, but you must understand, Isabella, we do not frequent chocolate houses. A lady such as yourself must be more prudent. One cannot be certain whom one may encounter, which is a cause for concern.' She drew in a long breath, deliberating how to contain any ensuing repercussions, given that the incident was now an inescapable fact.

'Well, we encountered the Duke of Winterbourne,' replied Isabella, praying the revelation of this news would smooth her friend's feathers. It did indeed have the intended outcome.

'Oh, heavens,' Lady Ingram exclaimed, striving to maintain a composed tone. She considered that this could be favourable, but acknowledged too that this may not be without complications. Outward appearances frequently hold as much consequence as truth. 'Your reputation could still have been compromised. Had others observed you?'

'Not at all, I assure you,' replied Isabella, momentarily forgetting that Lord Augustus had passed by. 'His Grace advised me to procure some chocolate, that I might enjoy it at home in comfort.'

'Yes, well, it was entirely proper for him to offer such advice. Though, I am certain he would have found your appearance most unexpected,' the dowager mused. 'One can only hope he did not perceive your presence there as too forward. Oh, how mortifying, a chocolate house!'

'He was somewhat surprised,' reflected Isabella, 'however, he engaged me in conversation at considerable length and appeared notably amiable.'

To the matron, this did not seem to portend calamity and may, in fact, have provided an opportunity for good. 'Hmm... as I observed before, I believe we may be setting our sights too high with His Grace. However, we must place trust in his discretion, despite your indiscretion,' she considered before raising a hot dish of the velvet liquid towards her lips, whilst sinking back in her chair.

After taking a sip, Lady Ingram could not quite conceal a subtle smile. Gently touching one corner of her mouth with her napkin, she drew the matter to a close, proclaiming, 'From henceforth, one of the footmen will attend to the purchase of the chocolate.'

CHAPTER 12 – CLUB DE VIN

'Would it not be delightful to have Lady Ingram and our two new acquaintances join us today, Carter?' mused Mrs Stoughton. Then, casting her eyes about the library, she remarked, though not unkindly, to her newly appointed first footman, 'I take it you are withholding the additional seating in order to cultivate an atmosphere of suspense?'

Mr Carter, now conscious of his mistake, thanked his mistress for the prompt and returned with the required chairs, in a manner both remarkably elegant and refined for a man of his position.

Lady Margaret and Mrs Wilkes had arrived early. The latter was wife to John Wilkes, the Member of Parliament for Aylesbury and a prominent journalist. The trio of ladies were in high spirits at the prospect of admitting new members to their literary circle, as their presence promised to infuse the gathering with new opinions and a fresh vivacity.

Upon the arrival of the newcomers, it was Mrs Stoughton's great pleasure to welcome the honoured guests and the ladies soon made themselves comfortable, seated in a circle with some refreshments.

'We have been grappling with Milton's *Paradise Lost*, though this is somewhat subversive of us, as it is in fact a prohibited book…' explained Mrs Stoughton with a twinkle. Lady Ingram almost choked on an almond macaron, flavoured with rose blossom and had to be supplied with a dish of tea, whereupon Carter, attending to the ladies, left the room to replenish the pot.

'I should elucidate,' smiled Mrs Stoughton, 'it is currently restricted by the Roman Catholic Church, not Britain itself. However, Milton did not coat himself in glory with his other tracts, some of which were seen even in England as traitorous and burnt, earning him a spell in the Tower of London. Thankfully, a century later we have progressed and live in very different times, where such a severe punishment would seem utterly ridiculous.'

This provided little comfort to Lady Ingram, so it was fortunate that Mrs Stoughton professed it to be too heavy a tome for discussion at present and allowed Mrs Wilkes to turn the conversation in another direction.

'Very well, shall we proceed, now that Carter has left us?' said Mrs Wilkes, as she shut the book. 'Have you heard the latest scandal concerning Mr Henry Fitzwilliam?'

'Pray, do divulge,' cried Mrs Stoughton, her face lighting up.

'Well,' continued Mrs Wilkes, extending her head towards the centre of the circle, seeking to deepen the confidential exchange. 'I have it on good authority that he entered into a wager with Mr Robert Hastings, that he could advertise in the London newspapers a most implausible endeavour, and not only find enough simpletons in London to fill a playhouse, but that they would pay generously.'

'Indeed, and what was this performance?' asked Mrs Stoughton animatedly.

'He claimed the audience would behold the spectacle of a man squeezing his entire body into a common-sized wine bottle. Can you imagine?' laughed Mrs Wilkes, before turning a trifle more serious. 'The worst of it is that, not only did a vast gathering attend the performance, but when the act failed to materialise, it sparked a riot.'

'Has he no shame?' cried Mrs Stoughton. 'He should be thrown out of every withdrawing room in London. I certainly shall not admit him, particularly following the carpet rolling incident.'

'Ladies, I find myself bewildered,' said Lady Ingram, somewhat perplexed and casting a glance towards Isabella. 'I was under the impression that we had gathered here to discuss literature.'

'And indeed, this was the original purpose of this club,' said Mrs Stoughton soothingly. 'I do require satisfaction of my romantic sensibilities. That reminds me, I must lend some of my novels to Isabella. However, in truth, since the founding, our activities have since deviated considerably.' She raised her glass of Madeira. 'The gentlemen have their clubs and so why should we not have ours?' said Mrs Stoughton with a wink and her usual twinkle.

'Indeed, we are at liberty to discuss any topic of our choosing. We are most eager for light-hearted discourse and delightful intrigues over a glass of wine,' said Lady Margaret, sipping her own Madeira.

Lady Ingram could not entirely conceal her disappointment, as she had been preparing Isabella all morning to exhibit her knowledge of *The Whole Duty of a Woman*.

Conversely, Isabella brightened upon realising she was likely now exempt from any scrutiny. However, one could look slightly askance at the dowager, as despite her efforts to maintain outward appearances, even her moral superiority was not unassailable. Therefore, when Isabella expressed an eagerness to know more, it was intriguing that Lady Ingram for once remained silent.

After one or two comments of insignificance, Mrs Stoughton, as though reminded, cried out, 'The ball!' startling the party.

'I have it on good authority from the Duchess of Harringshire herself that you ladies generously bestowed upon her and her daughter the most splendid gowns for the ball. Indian silks, I dare say,' she declared in her broad, magnificent manner. Then, turning to Isabella, she continued with exuberance, 'I am most intrigued to hear what you will be wearing. Indeed, with a bloom like yours, you will undoubtedly be the most admired, enchanting all the gentlemen and capturing their hearts.' She sang the final phrase melodiously, pressing her hand upon her own heart.

'Well, we have no desire to outshine anyone, least of all the Duchess of Harringshire,' cautioned Lady Ingram.

Mrs Stoughton dismissed her ladyship's suggestion with a wave of her hand. 'It would be delightful to see the dear girl captivating hearts, but perhaps she has already won the admiration of one or two gentlemen? I shall keep a watchful eye at the ball,' she added with yet another mischievous wink at Isabella.

Isabella blushed deeply in response, further confirming Mrs Stoughton's suspicions. Fortunately, the good lady had the grace not to expose Isabella further and somehow succeeded in restraining herself, satisfied with her findings.

CONSEQUENCE OF POWER

Lady Margaret, perceiving Isabella's unease, diverted the company's attention. 'Ladies, I have some new intrigues from the palace.'

As lady-in-waiting to the young king's mother, the Dowager Princess of Wales, Lady Margaret held a privileged position to witness events at the palace. 'As you are well aware,' she continued, 'Lord Bute, being favourite of the King, has succeeded in securing court positions for many of his own friends. The latest is Mr Fairfax.'

'Are you referring to Mr Fairfax, who so delighted us at Lady Bute's salon with his sensational, and most gracious defeat at the Faro table?' asked Mrs Stoughton.

'The very same,' replied Lady Margaret. 'And that is not all. I am fully convinced that it is he who assists Lord Bute in his nightly conversations with the Dowager Princess of Wales.'

'No!' gasped Mrs Stoughton, visibly thrilled and nearly leaping from her chair with excitement. 'An intrigue of my favourite variety!'

'Indeed, no, that cannot be,' rebutted Mrs Wilkes confidently. 'Mr Fairfax is too noble.'

'Indeed,' said Mrs Stoughton, a little more soberly, 'That does not sound like a man with such a public backing of his honourability. It must be tittle-tattle, and we should not aid the tarnishing of Mr Fairfax's good name.'

'Why would it be dishonourable for our Prime Minister to have nightly conversations with our Dowager Princess of Wales?' queried Isabella innocently.

'Isabella!' Lady Ingram exclaimed, remembering her charge and causing Isabella to start. 'Mrs Stoughton, perhaps you have a piano-forte?' the dowager enquired. 'Isabella is most proficient, and would be glad to perform for us a rendition of one of Handel's pieces.'

'Yes... yes, I suppose she could. Yes, that would be delightful. What a wonderful suggestion, Isabella,' said Mrs Stoughton, catching Lady Ingram's intent. Then, on Carter's well-timed re-entry into the drawing room with the tea, she said, 'Ah, Carter, would you be so kind as to show Isabella to the music room so she can delight us?'

Carter bowed his assent and escorted Isabella to the adjoining room, where the sweet sounds of her playing would soon fill the air, allowing the older ladies to continue their conversation discreetly.

Whilst finding pieces for Isabella, Carter enquired politely, 'Are you enjoying Milton, madame?'

'Milton?' asked Isabella, somewhat confused.

'Were you not savouring the delights of that most lyrical of epic poems, *Paradise Lost*?'

'I suppose we were to begin with...' mused Isabella. Then, briefly seeking his perspective, she said, 'The discourse turned to something about a conversation between Lord Bute and the Dowager Princess of Wales, but it was concluded that Mr Fairfax is too honourable to help them. I am most confused.' She sighed, before turning the leaves of the music to find a suitable piece, as tasked.

Carter hesitated before offering, 'I do not know the particulars, Miss Thornbury. However... no, it is not my place to say...,' his speech fading.

Isabella surveyed him questioningly, as though prompting a response, whilst she began playing an aria from Handel's *Giulio Casare*, providing him cover for any disclosures he might have. 'Pray, do continue, Mr Carter,' she urged.

'I fear Mr Fairfax is not all that he may appear to be,' he ventured.

'Oh? Do continue, I entreat you,' Isabella persisted.

Carter, somewhat emboldened by her prompting, began his disclosure, almost as though resonating with the theme of the tune. 'I regret the need to broach such a subject with a young lady of such virtue, but I must confess that I am in a state of utter desperation, with little hope of any other opportunity to express my sentiments.' His countenance had changed to one of anguish.

Intrigued, Isabella ceased playing.

'I am, in truth, Mr Thomas Fairfax, the most unfortunate younger brother of Mr Fairfax, the head of the House of Fairfax,' he admitted.

Isabella was astonished and said, 'I am surprised that Mrs Stoughton would permit a gentleman of your stature to serve as a footman within her establishment.'

'No, no, she is unaware,' replied Carter, 'but this is the only means by which I can determine why I lost my estate in Surrey.' Casting a furtive glance to confirm that no other ears were prying, he continued to explain his history. 'A life estate was in fact granted to me according to my late father's will. Since I was old enough to comprehend, this has always been the understanding. The legal ownership remains with my brother, but I may reside there for the duration of my life. As recently as last month, when I was preparing to settle there, unaccountably I was refused.'

'That is dreadful,' said Isabella.

'At a loss of any other recourse, as my allowance was immediately discontinued at the moment of my father's passing, I have come to London in an attempt to understand the situation, though my brother has invariably refused me admittance, whenever I have endeavoured to communicate with him.'

'But why select the role of a footman?' enquired Isabella. 'Why are you concealing yourself?'

'It provides me with shelter, whilst permitting me to make enquiries through servants as to what happened. The doors of society have slammed shut, as it seems my friends have been influenced by my brother and taken against me.'

There was an underlying look of hurt, but predominantly also of resolve in his eyes. Then he continued, 'I have lost everything and am cut off entirely. As this was so unforeseen, I lack training in a profession, so there is little else I can do, whilst I seek to understand what happened.'

'Why do you not tell Mrs Stoughton?' Isabella asked. 'She is a generous lady, and would no doubt assist you or could make enquiries on your behalf.'

'First, I would not wish to burden her, and second, Mr Fairfax is so esteemed, and London is his domain. He possesses connections in the highest echelons. I would require a solid standing before anyone will lend credence to my claims.'

'I am so sorry, Mr Fairfax, I truly am.' Isabella's voice was full of compassion, for the man appeared truly downcast. She was silent as she pondered, before she resumed slowly, 'I must say, since I arrived in London, I am beginning to understand that society here is not all it appears to be.'

The sounds of laughter permeated from the adjoining room. Isabella resumed playing, to provide Mr Fairfax with further time to discuss and she was conscious that she could provoke comment from the ladies were she to pause for too long. 'Is there anything at all that I can do to be of service?' Isabella asked.

'I thank you, Miss Thornbury. Will you be attending the next literary club?' asked Mr Thomas Fairfax.

'Yes, I intend to.'

'Perhaps, if you hear anything that could aid my cause, you could share this with me then?' he said quietly, with despondence. 'But in no event, would I wish to compromise your position.'

She nodded and turning the page, continued her piece, until its last refrain.

CHAPTER 13 – DARK VELVET

'Heloise, have you ever experienced or beheld anything so charming and rich? We ought not to have found ourselves there, but I was swept away by the most unexpected moment. Though I should have resisted with greater resolve, I must confess, I truly have no regrets. I have never felt anything like it. Have you?' asked Isabella indolently, as her maid brushed the powder from her chestnut locks in her lady's dressing chamber in preparation for retiring for the night.

'Well, there was once a gentleman of my acquaintance. I cannot say he was rich, but he was exceedingly charming in my eyes. Oh, yes, I remember...'

'Gentleman? Heloise, where is your mind? I was referring to the chocolate at Mrs Grey's,' countered Isabella with a smirk, as she took another sip of the dark velvet, which had become a crucial addition to their nightly collations.

'Isabella, what were your true impressions?' asked her companion with grace.

She caught Isabella's involuntary sentiments, which seemed to betray her affections, and provided Heloise with all the response she required. Continuing to brush Isabella's hair, Heloise raised her eyebrows very gently, before pressing her next question. 'Did he, by chance, engage you to dance at the Harringshire ball?'

'He did not,' said Isabella, mildly disheartened, before brightening with, 'but His Grace provided every indication that he would. Indeed, perhaps this is the customary approach for gentlemen of his standing.'

Heloise retained her own thoughts and swiftly changed tack. 'Perhaps you are right and what do you make of Lord Augustus's appearance?'

'I am uncertain what I must have done to displease him, but Winterbourne seems to imply that Gussie has become so disagreeable since his return. Do you think it is necessary that I should distance myself from him?'

Heloise considered, 'I would be guided by your own experience of an individual, rather than be persuaded by a gentleman with whom you have been so recently acquainted. Let us consider what we know.'

Isabella was quick to reply, 'Well, Augustus appears in the book, does he not? And we both understand that his father maintains a central position in the meetings referenced by Dashwood.'

'Does it follow that he is all bad?' asked Heloise.

'Both Augustus and indeed Winterbourne, have acknowledged that he has changed, and possibly for the worse...' reflected Isabella, concluding the remainder of the essence.

Changing course, Isabella ventured on a topic which had been weighing on her mind since the literary circle that afternoon. 'Heloise, does Dashwood's book mention anything about a gentleman named Mr Fairfax?'

Heloise considered for a moment before retrieving the book from the bureau, and proceeding to read Dashwood's notes. Presently, she replied, 'It mentions others whom we recognise: Lord Bute, Sir Francis Dashwood, the Earl of Cheltenham, Mr Henry Fitzwilliam, Augustus.' She ticked them off on her fingers as she listed the individuals, before continuing, 'However, Fairfax is not mentioned in either of the lists. There is a minor reference to a Fairfax later in the book. Let me read the passage to you: "Lord Bute has graciously brought with him an exquisite selection of wine of the most esteemed vintage, generously donated by Mr Fairfax, for the pleasure of all." Why do you ask?'

'I had a most curious discussion with a rather distressed gentleman by the name of Mr Thomas Fairfax. He is seeking justice, as he seems to believe that his elder brother is unfairly withholding a life estate, which is rightfully his.' Pausing, Isabella reflected further. 'It was an estate in Surrey and if memory serves, Mr Fairfax lost his Surrey estate at cards during Lady Bute's salon. Perhaps that was the elder brother.'

'If this is true and it is the same Fairfax, this is scandalous,' said Heloise in dismay. 'However, we lack sufficient evidence, and I am at a loss as to how we could use the book as proof, as we have yet to fully comprehend the matter at hand and we should not even have it in our possession.'

'Oh, Heloise, I wish I could bring him some solace, yet have no apparent means to do so. I promised that I would inform him if anything should come to light by the next literary circle.'

'When I have the opportunity, I shall endeavour to converse with as many of the servants as possible during my attendance at your social gatherings,' said Heloise, concluding her own warming beverage.

CHAPTER 14 – GARDENS OF ENCHANTMENT

The glow of flickering candles dotted intermittently guided the ladies along the path, illuminating it in the cool February nocturne and providing a mystical ambiance. Above them were strings of colourful lanterns, radiant emeralds, rubies, ambers and sapphires, swaying gently in the breeze, as though charming them, as they drew nearer and nearer the festivities and the strains of the Hornpipe from Handel's *Water Music Suite No. 2 in D Major* began to build.

Though undetected by Heloise beside her, Isabella felt a tremor of anticipation for this grand celebration of The Treaty of Paris, the first of many to mark the close of the Seven Years' War. The celebrations at Vauxhall Gardens promised to unveil wonders, which she had never before beheld. Dazzling illuminations and a spectacle of fireworks were but a few of the marvels foretold.

However, Isabella's angelic mask of feathers and gilding, which Mrs Stoughton – also present at the event – had so graciously provided her, concealed a faint blush, for this was to be a masquerade. Isabella was conscious that her rosy cheeks were not due to the chill of winter's breath, but from the thrilling prospect of perhaps encountering a different, more beguiling kind of winter altogether. Whether she would discern him beneath his guise, if indeed he were wearing one this evening, or if he would identify her, was yet to be revealed.

Leading the way as was her custom, Mrs Stoughton already in raptures over the orchestra, trilled, 'You are entering a realm of enchantment and intrigue, a truly picturesque setting for those of romantic sensibilities. I fully intend to be transported by the magic of the event,' she sighed dreamily, with a sweep of her rich crimson, gold brocade gown and sable fur cape, as the white feathers in her pomaded hair swayed gently with her movements to the music. 'Keep by my side ladies, I do not wish for you to be entirely swept away into the maze or the hidden alcoves, no matter how alluring,' she said as her eyes twinkled at Isabella.

Mrs Stoughton had generously invited the Thornburys and Lady Ingram to join her in the box that she had reserved and had promised an array of delightful delicacies, for this was a shared passion among all the ladies. Thankfully, Pudding was none the wiser, or he would surely have been quite vexed at having been excluded from the festivities.

As they found themselves at the heart of the event, they were greeted by brightly lit tents, draped in vibrant patterned fabrics. Artists danced and fire appeared to flame out of their mouths spectacularly, like dragons, as others juggled fire batons, throwing up their orange flares into the blackness of the night's sky.

The music had turned to a mystical tune, luring the party into a dreamlike state. Other dancers, ethereal in swathes of cloth that billowed in the night air, moved gracefully to the rhythm of the music. Crowds gathered, chattering in merriment, many with their faces concealed by masks, which further enhanced the mystical air of the venue, as though there were opulent, gilded creatures amongst them from another world.

The scene reminded Isabella of a brave new world, or an island such as that of *The Tempest*, but she was not afraid, rather enthralled, spellbound. The words came to her:

"Be not afeard; the isle is full of noises,
Sounds and sweet airs, that give delight and hurt not.
Sometimes a thousand twangling instruments
Will hum about mine ears, and sometime voices
That, if I then had waked after long sleep,
Will make me sleep again: and then, in dreaming,
The clouds methought would open and show riches
Read to drop upon me than, when I waked,
I cried to dream again."

So mesmerised was Isabella, that she would be content to believe that she was in such a dream and earnestly longed to prolong these fleeting moments, desiring to linger, indeed revel with the many in the enchantment of the experience.

Naturally, her thoughts turned to whom she may encounter, possibly another reason for her desire to capture these moments, should they prove themselves to be auspicious as the evening progressed.

Many were in full masks, but even with only half, Isabella wondered how she would ever recognise acquaintances. Unbeknown to her, she was at that moment in close proximity to at least five key participants of Dashwood's group. Their identities, as with others, were concealed by masks. However, on this evening of the Treaty celebrations, they were engaged in pursuits far more sensible than their usual entertainments. Yet, Isabella was infatuated by a notion entirely more agreeable, and this clouded her judgement regarding the dangers that Dashwood's book might present.

As they lingered by the fire eater, Mrs Stoughton requested the ladies' maids to first ascertain the location of their assigned box and then procure refreshments. Heloise volunteered to find an usher and ventured forth to navigate the throng.

As she meandered between the figures, Heloise overheard various fragments of intermingling conversation, as is customary in the gossiping crowds.

'I shall be on the lookout for her tonight.'

'Most lamentable terms for the Treaty, I must confess. A celebration may be well and good – I enjoy a convivial gathering as much as any man – but one cannot deny it was a dubious affair. I place the blame for this disarray squarely upon Lord Bute.'

'Do steady yourself, my good man.'

Then, moving further through the crowds, Heloise overheard a most relevant snippet as she passed by, which piqued her attention. 'Yes, the Thornbury damsel, have you heard? The news is the talk of the town this week – a dowry of no less than thirty-thousand pounds. Most beguiling.'

'Truly, I had scarcely regarded her, for she is so demure; yet, perhaps I shall become more attentive henceforth,' replied another voice with mirth.

'Well, allow an old chap to have a chance too,' retorted another.

She continued to meander through the vibrant multitude, when she heard a voice say, 'Are you aware of this, Your Grace?'

Then came the unmistakeable and familiar rich tones, 'Most intriguing, I agree.'

Heloise halted briefly, and turned to glimpse a stately gentleman clothed in red burgundy, in a dark half mask burnished with accents of gold. Hoping to remain unnoticed, she then hastened on to seek an usher who might show them to their box.

On her return to Isabella, she whispered, 'He is here.'

Isabella required no further indication as to whom Heloise was referring, and though subtly thrilled, a squeeze of Heloise's arm in thanks was all that betrayed her, and her mask continued to do her service.

Once the ladies had been comfortably and safely installed in the pavilion box, Mrs Stoughton felt at liberty to wander and greet a few of her acquaintances.

The music continued to drift upon the air, and the ladies spoke enthusiastically about the anticipated fireworks. Heloise sought to solicit Rose, Mrs Stoughton's lady's maid, for her opinion, as she had promised Isabella, and so followed her towards the refreshments.

She had only progressed a short way from the company when, to her surprise, her path was intercepted by Augustus. He had no mask to cover his countenance and seemed wholly to have neglected to don a costume in keeping with the event. Rather, he was simply attired as his own character.

'Augustus, I am astonished to see you here. I should not have thought that this event would be to your liking,' said Heloise, who could not help but cast her eye over his garments.

'Indeed, you are quite correct,' replied the young gentleman. Then, with a dim shadow of hope in his voice, he ventured, 'However, I hoped that, given the chance, I might seek Isabella's – Miss Thornbury's forgiveness for not greeting her when I passed the other day. It was below me.'

After a pause, he said, 'Ah, I see that she has made the acquaintance of Mrs Stoughton. That will no doubt put her in good stead in this arena.' He nodded towards the company, where Mrs Stoughton had already rejoined the group. She was evidently concluding her introduction of a gentleman of advanced years, whose ample girth and dignified air bespoke a life of leisure and indulgence; his well-groomed moustache was a distinguished grey.

Heloise glanced over at Mrs Stoughton's prized gentleman, pursed her lips and chose not to respond to the latter remark.

Instead, she responded to the former. 'Forgiveness? Is that all you seek? Perhaps your desire extends beyond that? If that is the case, do you believe it is wise considering your father's disposition?'

They both gazed over at Isabella, in time to glimpse a statuesque figure approaching her with all the self-assurance of His Grace, Winterbourne.

They continued to observe the scene before them in silence, as Isabella's countenance brightened visibly. Then, following a brief remark from Winterbourne, they witnessed the couple in union, sharing a moment of mirth, followed by conversation brimming with affection.

After observing this, Augustus turned slowly to Heloise and said with despondence, 'Perhaps you are correct. I can see that Miss Thornbury is happy with her new acquaintance.' Any former flicker of light had now died in his eyes. He continued, with restrained emotion, 'It would be sensible to withhold our conversation from Isabella. I do not wish to interfere with her evening,' said Augustus, before bowing abruptly and formally taking his leave.

CONSEQUENCE OF POWER

Heloise continued to wend through the crowds, allowing enough time to ensure that she would not interrupt the couple's discourse. She pondered the significance of her conversation with Augustus, and weighed this with the comments expressed by Winterbourne and even those prior remarks from Augustus himself. Would withholding disclosure of her encounter with Augustus have any influence on her mistress? She rejoined Isabella after some time, once she had procured some refreshments.

'Did I observe you conversing with our favourite duke?' asked Heloise playfully. 'And did any other titles take your fancy?'

'Oh yes,' came Isabella's joyful reply. 'Though, there were one or two gentlemen who were clearly more captivated by my father's shares than in investing in my own company,' she laughed, but then managed to comport herself on Lady Ingram's account. Then she revealed, 'That was until Winterbourne presented himself.'

'Was he agreeable?'

'He was... more than amiable.' Her subtle glance at Heloise fortified just how enchanted she had become. 'He promised to introduce me to his sisters, and you will never guess: he engaged me for the first two dances at the Harringshire ball. This is truly the most delightful evening.'

Lady Ingram appeared overcome with emotion, as though she had accomplished all that she could have wished for, and her efforts had finally come to full fruition. The triumphant notes of *Rule Britannia* rose, in mark of the Treaty of Paris, though to Lady Ingram this ranked second to her own victory of that moment.

At length, having satisfied themselves, the ladies rose from the pavilion box and made their way towards a clearing within the gardens in anticipation of the forthcoming display of fireworks.

In the centre, Lady Thornbury, Lady Ingram and Mrs Stoughton gathered in lively conversation, as Isabella animatedly shared further with Heloise her discussion with Winterbourne.

The area was softly illuminated by scattered twinkling lights, casting a warm, gentle glow that gave the appearance of a circle fading into the surrounding darkness. Paths meandered through the dimly lit, secluded groves of the garden.

As Heloise began to respond to Isabella's remark, her mistress's attention was momentarily diverted. Isabella's eyes narrowed as if perplexed, as she peered over her companion's shoulder into the shadowy recesses of the park beyond. Casting her gaze in the same direction, Heloise observed a solitary dark figure obliquely departing from the warmth of the sphere, slowly roaming from the crowd.

He bore no festive garments, attired only in his customary garb, though his head was heavily bowed, reflecting a profound internalised sense of private loss. His steps had an air of a valediction and repressed grief, as though forbidding mourning. Yet momentarily he paused, fleetingly, as though the spectre could scarcely bear to press on into the black, before continuing, gradually becoming a shadow, melting silently into the encroaching darkness, as he disappeared in its final embrace.

CHAPTER 15 – ENTOURAGE

In an uncommon turn of events, neither Lady Ingram nor, perhaps most surprising of all, Pudding, made an appearance at the breakfast table the very next morning, despite the distinct wafts of bacon floating throughout the house, beckoning them. Therefore, mother and daughter were unencumbered by the canine's demanding paws that so frequently tugged at their skirts when bacon graced the table. This also granted them a measure of tranquillity, free from any assignments that the dowager might thrust upon them.

Indeed, Lady Ingram had ended the prior evening at Vauxhall Gardens in splendidly exuberant spirits, and had hummed lively tunes to herself during their journey home. As she did, Isabella quietly speculated with amusement, that the dowager must surely have overindulged in the Madeira – most inappropriate!

The soft February sunlight passed through the large windows of the morning room, bathing the ladies in its glow and bringing a deep sense of comfort. Isabella leaned gently towards the table and took a satisfying bite of her lightly toasted bread, which crackled with the accompanying fire. The interior exuded warmth with an edge of sweetness, the enticing aroma of which blended with the creamy, slightly salted melted butter, which had seeped into the crumb.

Lady Thornbury had finished her portion of bacon, savouring its salty, sizzling slices that were imbued with subtle sweet undertones and caramelised to an exquisite crisp. Its tantalising aroma mingled beautifully with the smoky essence of the fire.

'My dear, shall I serve you another dish of chocolate?' came Lady Thornbury's gentle, soothing voice. 'It is especially rich and creamy today. It seems that I am becoming somewhat too liberal with the quantities of grated chocolate, I might have to part with the keys to the chest. Do you think Heloise can be trusted?' she tittered; eyes sparkling. Then she poured the frothy liquid from the chocolatière into Isabella's Famille Rose cup, musing fondly, 'I concur that we ought to continue using cream in our preparation, rather than milk.'

Whilst they were indulging in the chocolate, Lady Thornbury asked, 'Pray, how did you enjoy your time at Vauxhall, my dear?'

Isabella still relishing the memories of the evening's events had at the forefront of her thoughts the conversation with Winterbourne, though she moderated her expression with, 'I must confess, I was honoured that Winterbourne engaged me to dance at the ball.'

'Indeed, my dear, that is an honour. He is certainly an impressive gentleman. And the other gentlemen that Mrs Stoughton introduced to you, I thought they too had lively conversation and appeared just as agreeable,' came her mother's sensible reply.

Isabella chose not to respond to this, and rather at that moment, lifted the froth to her lips for a delicate sip.

CONSEQUENCE OF POWER

'It is a great pity that we have not had the pleasure of Augustus's company of late,' continued Lady Thornbury, with a sigh. 'I am surprised that he was not at Vauxhall.'

Meanwhile, Lady Ingram had resolved that a celebratory breakfast in her bedchamber was more than deserved following her extraordinary success at Vauxhall Gardens. She regaled Pudding with the events of the prior evening and allowed herself to fully indulge in conjecture as to future developments, in the comfortable knowledge that the little spaniel would keep her confidence. Indeed, he was utterly absorbed, likely drawn by the enticing aroma of savoury morsels that emanated from her plate, even as the venerable lady recounted her success.

It was fortunate that both Lady Ingram and Pudding were engaged for most of the morning, for they avoided the advent of Monsieur De La Fontaine, the dancing master and what one might refer to as his entourage.

The gentleman embodied his art, and with a slender, whip-like grace, glided into the Thornbury's withdrawing room, where the furniture had been moved to the walls, in preparation for Isabella's lesson.

To her astonishment, a veritable parade of individuals followed in his wake. Two poor fellows entered, grunting with effort as they wrestled with a grand, gilded mirror, presumably for the purpose of scrutinising dance postures. Others strolled in nonchalantly, with an assortment of instruments: two violins, a French horn and a cello, no less. Another sauntered in and began racing feverously through scales on the piano-forte, as if preparing for a grand performance. A further two appeared to have no discernible employment, except to observe their master's every movement with unflagging enthusiasm, occasionally attempting to replicate his posture with impressive precision.

Altogether, this assembly numbered ten, including a diligent artist who was employed in sketching Monsieur De La Fontaine.

After allowing some time for the crowd to settle, the dancing master clapped his hands and cried out in a Parisian accent, 'Alors, we shall begin with the formal presentation,' and swept a low bow.

Isabella gave her customary graceful curtsey in response. 'Ah, ah, what is this?' the dancing master exclaimed. Then, flinging himself almost prostrate on the floor, he examined Isabella's silk slippers. 'C'est totalement inacceptable! Do you wish to clomp around the floor like a clod hopper?'

Upon recovering his stance, he expounded with an air of authority, 'Take note, you need Pierre-Joseph Chaussard. You can commission a pair of slippers when you are next in Paris. Until then, I cannot allow you to disrupt the rhythm with those. Remove them, s'il vous plaît.'

Isabella was somewhat put out, but complied with the instructions in order to placate him, sensing that he was of a delicate constitution when it came to matters of his art.

Then he cried, 'Le minuet,' signalling to his orchestra to strike up. Isabella commenced with the first steps, before being interrupted almost at once with, 'Non, non, non, et non!' from her teacher, who was already slightly perspiring. 'My coat, my coat, vite, vite,' he commanded in a shrill voice, and as he extended his arms either side, two of the gentlemen sprang to assist in the removal of this garment.

'Alors, regardez-moi,' commanded Monsieur De La Fontaine. Now unencumbered by his justaucorps, he incorporated a jeté and then proceeded to perform a series of intricate courtly movements in triple time with impressive precision.

Whilst, in theory, this might indeed have been of benefit to his pupil, choosing to perform the entire four-minute routine with an imaginary partner, resulted in the exercise being somewhat redundant.

'And now, proceed,' he directed Isabella, once he had completed his dance, flourishing a kerchief and wiping his now florid brow. She hesitated. 'Mademoiselle, please proceed; we have but trente minutes, and I am bound for another appointment thereafter – there is no time to waste,' he exclaimed, clapping his hands twice.

Isabella began with her opening steps once more. She had scarcely passed beyond the point that she had reached on her first attempt, before she found herself interrupted again.

'Alors, you were not attending, regardez,' cried Monsieur De La Fontaine, before starting another, this time different, four-minute dance with truly matchless exuberance.

'Et voila!' he declared at the conclusion, and the two gentlemen who had been attempting to mimic him in the corner of the room broke into applause. 'Formidable!' they called.

'Formidable, indeed!' Isabella cried out in frustration.

Heloise had peeked into the room, only to be met with this spectacle and Isabella caught her eye with an expression of appeal. In response, Heloise raised her eyebrows with resigned bewilderment and, with a subtle shrug, quietly crept sideways out of the room.

'Ah, mon Dieu! C'est fini!' shouted Monsieur De La Fontaine in a most shocking manner as he glanced at his pocket watch.

'No, Monsieur De La Fontaine. This is quite unacceptable! Monsieur De La Fontaine! Monsieur!' came Isabella's raised voice, her hand held aloft, in an attempt to gain his attention. However, the luminary had already swept out of the room.

Now battling her emotions, Isabella cast her gaze about the assembly, as they packed away their instruments before filtering out of the room. 'Utterly ridiculous,' she said in a tone of exasperation, her azure eyes aflame as she paced the room in agitation.

Taking compassion on her, one of the gentlemen offered, 'Monsieur De La Fontaine is a true master of his art. He perceives the world to a degree that others cannot appreciate, and that is what distinguishes him.'

'Yes, but that does not help me. What am I to do!' she said, turning to him, with a mixture of frustration and irritation. 'I have the most important ball of my life next week, and I am more confused now than before breakfast.'

'Well, I am certainly not nearly as proficient as Monsieur De La Fontaine, but should you wish, I would be pleased to guide you through a few steps. Music would not be required,' replied the kind gentleman.

'Would you? Oh, I would be so grateful,' said Isabella in relief. 'And what of my slippers? They are not so inappropriate, are they?' She held up the discarded pair, appealing to the gentleman.

'Not at all,' he reassured her. 'They will do very well, I am certain.'

The gentleman proceeded to guide Isabella through various routines, though he raised only the occasional comment or encouragement, as she was already familiar, under Mr Wately's instruction in Henley.

'Indeed, that is correct. Now, do remember to attend to your ankles,' advised the gentleman.

Isabella followed his direction with diligence and focus, gradually allowing her frustration to dissipate.

Heloise entered the room bearing refreshments, which offered a welcome respite from the exertions. As they took their ease, he continued to offer Isabella further guidance. 'The success of the dance is greatly dependent upon self-possession. You already have a gracious presence. My advice is to express yourself, allowing your character to radiate.'

She was surprised that such sagacious advice regarding the depth of feeling and candour should be revealed to her by a stranger, almost as though it were a divine message delivered by the Reverend Fernsby.

'It is not my place, but may I be so bold as to enquire if you have received any invitations to dance?' he ventured delicately.

'Yes, I have indeed. The Duke of Winterbourne has engaged me,' replied Isabella, her countenance illuminated with delight as she forgot herself. This soon gave way to a conscious blush, betraying her own eagerness.

'Upon considering the prospect of dancing with this gentleman, what feelings arise?' the dancer enquired.

'Indeed, I must ensure that the routine is executed flawlessly,' she considered.

'Ah, but instead of considering the accuracy of the routine, embrace the dance and let your emotions guide you. Consider the gentleman and attune yourself to his spirit. If you are content and at ease, it will be reflected in your dance and this will distinguish you. Consider Monsieur De La Fontaine today. He was brimming with passion – truly beautiful to behold. His emotions refused to confine him to a routine, rather he was wholly absorbed in the moment, as unpractical as it might seem.

This passion cannot be conveyed through words, but must be felt.'

Isabella considered this new perspective.

The gentleman continued conveying his philosophy, 'I advise you to consider your affections for your dance partner, and to channel those sentiments. A dance is a connection between two individuals and an expression of emotion, a symbiotic exchange of feelings. Together you are in harmony, in balance.'

'How is it possible to discern one's feelings for another when one has spent so little time in their company?' asked Isabella.

'This is not something that one can explain with mere words. One will simply know when one encounters it and under the right conditions. How would Monsieur De La Fontaine express it? A certain je ne sais quoi. In truth, the dance may be the true test.'

Isabella comprehended the theory, yet she knew that true understanding would only be revealed to her through her own experience.

'Finally... indeed the very last piece of advice I can impart, which I hope will come naturally, is to smile.' He bowed to Isabella with a flourish of his hand, content that she now had all that she required.

Isabella stood transfixed, her countenance aglow with a newfound light, as if a veil had been lifted and the truth had begun to be revealed.

CHAPTER 16 – A WINTER'S TALE

The anticipation for the Duke and Duchess of Harringshire's ball was palpably mounting throughout town amongst those fortunate enough to have received an invitation. This sentiment was no more keenly felt than in the Thornbury household.

Numerous gentlemen had called upon Isabella since the Vauxhall Gardens celebrations, thanks to Mrs Stoughton's introductions. Her dance card was soon filled, save for one pair of dances, which she had left available should Winterbourne request to stand up with her once more.

It was thus only a few days before the ball that the Thornbury ladies, and Lady Ingram, stepped into Madame Noyer's to collect their finished gowns.

Arrayed in exotic silks of vibrant colours, the ladies were most striking, and none more so than Isabella, enrobed in a ruby-silk gown, with a gold-embossed bodice.

'You are most charming, my dear,' smiled Lady Ingram. 'You will indeed have many admirers.'

Isabella was gazing modestly at her gown in the reflection of the looking-glass, and turned to admire the most remarkable train. Her neckline was adorned with exotic trim and beadwork, complemented with elaborate flowing drapery cascading from her shoulder, inspired by the designs of Sir Nicholas Thornbury's friends in India.

Despite her reserve, she could not entirely resist the allure of her exotic costume's dreamlike appearance, which she in turn hoped might enchant a certain gentleman.

Those inspired words came to her: "For she is a spirit of a higher nature" and "We are such stuff as dreams are made on." Dreams indeed, she mused, as her thoughts drifted.

'Mademoiselle must needs have an admirer already,' said Madame Noyer, with a knowing glint in her eye.

'What leads you to say that?' enquired Isabella, momentarily taken aback, as her thoughts returned to the present, a warm glow spreading across her features.

'Well,' commenced Madame Noyer, pleased that she had the opportunity to impart such an encouraging tale, 'a few days past, a noble gentleman made enquiries about the colour and style of your gown. He professed a desire to match your outfit.'

'And what of the gentleman's appearance?' asked Lady Ingram authoritatively and suddenly alert.

'He had a powdered queue wig, which perfectly framed his dark intense eyes,' Madame Noyer considered. 'His coat, made of the richest dark velvet and adorned with exquisite embroidery, bore the unmistakable mark of Mr Harrison's craftsmanship.' The mantua-maker continued to marvel, hands clasped in delight, her voice crescendoing as she reflected. 'He truly did justice to his tailor, as his statuesque presence filled the shop, commanding attention with an air of remarkable distinction.'

'Was it the Duke of Winterbourne?' cried Lady Ingram, unable to remain discrete for much longer.

'It was indeed. His Grace is not a gentleman whom I would wish to deny, so I took the liberty of confirming Miss Thornbury's gown to him, in the hope that this would in turn be acceptable to you,' Madame Noyer responded gleefully.

The ladies were quite overwhelmed with euphoria upon receiving this news, though Lady Ingram and Isabella, perhaps more so than Lady Thornbury. Mr Thornbury, who had accompanied them, sensing the excitement, began barking joyously and took it upon himself to take a zestful turn about the room.

The words "I am amazed, and know not what to say!" flew into Isabella's romantic mind – she could not restrain herself. With satisfaction, she glanced back into the looking-glass. Indeed, it seemed as though her dreams were materialising in a manner most divine.

Across the street at the shop of Mr John Harrison, Purveyor of Fine Garments, Tailor to the Nobility and Gentlemen, the Duke of Winterbourne was at that very moment being dressed in his ensemble for the ball and admiring himself in the looking-glass.

He had indeed a statuesque silhouette; the envy of many.

'Are the cuffs to Your Grace's liking?' enquired Mr Harrison, gently pulling the sleeves to ensure the placement was perfectly achieved.

'Indeed, they are, I thank you.'

'I have long been aware of your discerning taste and exacting standards in matters of dress, and it is rare indeed to witness any deviation from your customary style. Thus, I must confess that I was truly delighted to have the opportunity to incorporate new embellishments into your attire.'

His Grace's attire was indeed in complement to Isabella's, though not excessively so; merely enough to render her a suitable compliment. The hue of his waistcoat was an exact match to the shade of ruby in her gown and although the silk was of the same Indian origin, it was not of the same consistency. Nevertheless, the gold embroidery and trim undeniably echoed the details of Isabella's gown.

'You have indeed surpassed yourself, Mr Harrison, with the inclusion of these impeccable accents at the last hour.'

'I thank you, Your Grace. The lady is indeed most fortunate to have your attentive consideration,' said Mr Harrison, adjusting Winterbourne's sleeves once more and observing the alignment.

'Indeed, she is,' confirmed Winterbourne with a satisfied grin. After a moment's reflection, he continued, 'London society is much given to idle gossip, my dear sisters included amongst them. I had heard that the design of Miss Thornbury's gown was most singular, and I wish for her not to feel in any way isolated, rather comfortable in the presence of the company. She shall undoubtedly be both striking and charming. There will be fashion journalists present, so this is an opportunity for her to make an impression in society, though she has already been the subject of much discussion.'

'Indeed, I too have heard remarks concerning the lady from other customers; however, in truth, I do not believe any could rival you,' the tailor felt free to remark.

'Well, I have ever been able to rely upon you,' replied Winterbourne, with grace. Then, elaborating on his previous thoughts, 'I can assist her in society by extending my support. Furthermore, I believe it might be to the host's pleasure, for the Duke of Harringshire is an old companion. He is known to have a keen appreciation for such visual elegance, a matter of particular significance given that His Majesty will be present at this event.'

'That is indeed a consideration,' mused Mr Harrison. 'In all the years I have had the honour of serving as your tailor, I do not recall having received such a personal request, nor ever having been privy to your admiration for a lady. Dare I say, you are a changed man? Might I have the pleasure of offering my congratulations ere long?' he suggested.

'I can assure you that I remain steadfast in my character. However, with regard to your congratulations, should all proceed as desired, it may indeed be within the realm of possibility,' came Winterbourne's stoic reply.

CHAPTER 17 – THE KING DOTH KEEP HIS REVELS HERE TO-NIGHT

The Ball at Harringshire House, London, Isabella Thornbury

The long-anticipated moment had arrived. We had all made meticulous preparations for this grand occasion and at last, I was standing in the ballroom of Harringshire House, adorned in the most auspicious, resplendent ruby gown of my father's silk.

Hundreds of candles glowed, casting a shimmering radiance, as they exhibited the brilliance of the chandeliers with their cascades of crystal. It was quite possibly the most opulent room I had ever entered. The very skirting boards were marble veined, and as I raised my eyes from the ground to the fresco ceilings, raging across the space was a celestial battle still in fierce contest, framed by the asymmetrical gilded coving.

The ballroom was adorned with numerous grand gilded mirrors gracing an entire wall; resplendently reflecting and amplifying the room's majestic depths and dimensions. As I traversed the threshold, with deliberate and slow step and all the elegance I could muster, a profound sensation took hold, as though the ballroom itself were a setting for a precious gem, elevating the grandeur of my gown. I was enveloped in a sensation of almost regal magnificence, as if this very moment were preordained to enable me to radiate with all the splendour of that rich fabric, accompanied by a warm and inward joy that glowed.

In contrast to Lord and Lady Bute's salon, I made this entrance with what I trusted was an assured poise, buoyed by the spirited demeanour of Lady Ingram, whose presence, with that of my mother, lent me considerable support, as though combined we had become The Three Graces.

On this occasion, the many eyes which turned towards us – including those whom I now recognised – were not merely expressing curiosity, but rather that we were eagerly anticipated and belonged. It was, indeed, Lady Ingram's moment of triumph as well; I could sense it keenly. Moreover, the confidence I felt was greatly bolstered by the invaluable assistance rendered by Monsieur De La Fontaine's gentleman, which assured me that I might dance with Winterbourne with grace. This all boded well for a most splendid evening.

Almost the moment we entered, we were greeted by Mrs Stoughton and Lady Margaret. However, it was not long before others paid me compliments, including those who had called upon me since Vauxhall Gardens, as well as the gentleman with his grey moustache, who greeted me. However, I could not yet discern the whereabout of Winterbourne – enigmatic as ever, I concluded, though perhaps it was precisely this that magnified my fascination with him.

'My dear, your gown is most resplendent; how romantic. We have all been in anticipation of it and it has indeed surpassed all expectation,' sighed Mrs Stoughton, as she greeted me. 'What a curiosity to behold!'

'Is Mrs Wilkes in attendance this evening?' enquired my mother, considering that all the literary circle were present except for this lady.

'Ah, you may well ask,' replied Lady Margaret in a confidential tone, 'but the truth is that her husband, Mr John Wilkes, the journalist, as you know, is presently at severe odds with Lord Bute.' Then, with a flourish of her fan, she concluded, 'Thus, power prevails, and he is not welcome here.'

At the name Lord Bute, my eyes flashed up.

'That sounds most severe,' my mother responded with evident concern.

'Indeed, one must not take it lightly; one might say that Wilkes plays with fire. Are you not familiar with his newspaper, *The North Briton?*' said Lady Margaret, with circumspection.

'No, indeed,' my mother replied with keen interest, her eyebrows arching in curiosity.

'Many speculate that he launched it solely to criticise Lord Bute, having commenced the paper merely a few months following Lord Bute's accession to prime minister.'

'That is most bold,' commented my mother, 'and indeed, it is no wonder that the Wilkes stay away.'

Amidst listening to these comments and greeting some passing acquaintances, I found leisure to cast a sweeping glance across the ballroom, searching for Winterbourne with resolute boldness.

By chance, Lord Bute and Sir Francis Dashwood attracted my attention across the ballroom and as they conversed with each other, I felt an involuntary chill. I ought to have anticipated that these individuals would honour the ball with their presence, as would many others listed within Dashwood's book; yet these considerations had eluded my notice for several days, overshadowed by other priorities.

This ballroom, after all, was an arena reserved for the highest in society, many of whom wielded power – those who ruled this kingdom, quite literally. Those who could in a sense decide on life and death, to behead or not to behead. I reflected on all senses of that final word: the removal of one's title, power, standing in society, or indeed the ultimate…

Certainly, the King could exercise magnanimity and pardon, but those in power could, I had no doubt, also advocate for their own ends. In truth, it was I who had stepped into their realm, and I was but a guest. I was distinctly aware that my admittance was chiefly by virtue of my father's recent elevation, as well as Lady Ingram's skill and connections.

Yet, observing at a distance these two gentlemen of power for the first time since reading Dashwood's pocketbook, caused me to shudder and I could easily have yielded and turned out of the room. However, I assured myself that I should be safe within this ballroom, surrounded as I was, by numerous witnesses. Had they any suspicion that I had the book in my possession, they would surely already have taken action.

Resolutely, I beheld them now, the Prime Minister and Chancellor of the Exchequer, no less, conversing as old acquaintances. I could not disassociate them from Dashwood's scandalous book. Indeed, why should I? Now I knew to some extent at least who they were, beneath the appearance which they chose to present to society.

Dashwood's book… a book of which the most egregious contents I knew had been shielded from me by Heloise. I required no further details to discern that such matters, to put it mildly, were wholly unworthy of gentlemen, much less those who govern this realm. I averted my gaze, uncertain how to contend with such feelings, and well aware that I was, in any case, powerless.

Burying these concerns in the deeper recesses of my mind, I continued my search for Winterbourne. However, another caught my attention, the Earl of Cheltenham. Pray God, that Augustus be not present, for what could I possibly say?

I proceeded, and to my dismay, there stood the worst of them all: Mr Henry Fitzwilliam himself. Granted, he appeared as any other gentleman might. A glass of Champagne wine in hand, composed and presumably anticipating a lively evening of dancing. Let us hope he does not incite a riot this time, I thought to myself, with secret and guilty amusement.

Then came an unmistakeable voice behind me, rich as velvet, 'Good evening, Miss Thornbury.'

I could not refrain from starting in surprise, yet I quickly composed myself as I turned and encountered his dark gaze. Boldly this time, with daring assurance, our eyes met with mutual understanding. In that instance, I could meet him with all my faculties intact; if not as an equal in rank, at least the disparity between us seemed less pronounced than before.

'Good evening, Your Grace,' I replied, sweeping a curtsey.

Thus did the evening begin, with all proceeding smoothly. Winterbourne was exceedingly attentive and gracious to my mother and Lady Ingram, and they had ample opportunity to converse, indulging in the customary pleasantries. I deemed this a good sign.

Then, those fateful and long-anticipated opening strains of the minuet from a solitary violin drifted towards us. The exquisite moment had arrived, when we would be alone to converse and engage in the silent, unspoken poetry of dance. The ballroom floor would be the space where the harmony of our souls might intertwine and our emotions merge in tender communication.

He presented to me his most gracious hand and as if within a dream, I found myself slowly reaching out, placing my cold fingers into the warmth of his palm. Then, with a gentle, yet assured firmness, whereby I could feel his strength, he guided me out onto the floor for our first dance. The particulars of the room became a mere blur, and I was wholly immersed; my entire world was encompassed by this dance.

As the minuet commenced, and the full orchestra joined in harmony, with my newfound self-possession, I seized the opportunity to break the silence that had fallen between us. 'Your attire fortuitously complements my gown.' I ventured, not wishing to be too presumptuous. Yet privately, I could not help but feel flattered by the attention.

He appeared amused. 'I took the liberty of making enquiries of your mantua-maker,' he said as he extended his hand. 'Madame Noyer has no doubt mentioned my recent visit.'

He was clearly not one to suffer fools. Our eyes met once more, and I sensed his candour. As the sweet, yet rhythmic melody continued, he commenced the next turn of our discourse.

'Your mother clearly dotes on you. You are fortunate.'

'I am indeed.' His interest in my mother was another most favourable sign.

'And your father has achieved considerable success in the East?'

'He has indeed,' I affirmed, before taking a turn.

'But you have no siblings?' He said this as he faced me once more, extending his hand as I placed mine lightly upon his.

'That is correct,' again I reflected on his attentiveness to my family. 'However, you are fortunate enough to have sisters. Are they here this evening?'

'They are and most eager to meet you.'

We continued on with elegant flourishes. I sensed eyes observing us, yet our conversation would remain solely ours.

'You chiefly reside near Henley?' was his next turn of discourse.

'I do indeed.' My heart leapt at the thought of home.

'I have done so all my life, until my London season,' I replied.

'Could you envision yourself settling in London in the future?'

'I do not find it to be my natural home, yet I must confess that it is growing upon me,' I replied.

'You will discover that with each passing day in London, your fondness will undoubtedly deepen,' he reassured me before he turned. As he faced me anew, he offered, 'I possess a great many acquaintances whom I wish to introduce to you.'

We turned once more, as I pondered this.

'Indeed,' he continued, 'Since your arrival, I have observed that you have undergone a marked change.'

True, and upon reflecting on my naivety only a few weeks past, I found myself unable to comprehend why he had singled me out from the moment of my entrance into society.

All too soon, the dances were over. After his bow in my direction, and my curtsy in response, I placed my hand in his, as he led me gracefully from the floor, to a side where we could converse further.

'I trust you have observed that all eyes are upon you this evening,' he remarked.

'Yes, and some are clearly more captivated by my father's standing and fortune than with me,' I retorted. 'However, you bestowed your attentions long before there was any understanding of my situation, and for that, I must thank you.'

'Thank you,' he replied.

'I have often pondered why you chose to address me during Lord and Lady Bute's salon?' I asked.

'For the simple reason that you appeared so refreshingly unburdened by the concerns of society and politics. Your novelty assuredly contributed to this, and your innocence was most appealing,' came his exceedingly bold reply.

He offered his hand once more, and as I placed it, now more firmly in his, he guided me across the ballroom in an endeavour to introduce me to his sisters, as promised.

We walked across the room and into an expansive adjoining reception room, with further adornments, this time with alabaster statues poised in eternal stillness, flanking two opposite walls of the room, which had a marble black and white chequered flooring. Once more I glimpsed Lord Bute and Dashwood, who were now joined by the Earl of Cheltenham.

Clearly, beneath the formality of the ball, an ominous undercurrent was emerging. Like rooks they seemed to be gathering one by one, their increasing number resembling a foreboding portent of ill omen.

Whilst Winterbourne introduced Isabella to his sisters, in relatively close proximity, three gentlemen conferred, as a conspiracy of ravens engaged in council.

The Earl of Cheltenham was circling, fixed steady as ever on his prey, ready to strike. 'I cannot emphasise this enough: it is of utmost importance that the Company secures its dominion over Bengal now that the Treaty is concluded. We must seize this critical juncture with all possible resolve,' he said.

'The Company already has my administration's support in this. Indeed, this solidification of our sovereignty is reflected in the Treaty,' replied Lord Bute.

'So, you will procure Parliament's absolute and unyielding support in this next step. I have garnered support from many others, including Secretary of State, George Grenville. Yet it would carry greater weight if it were to come directly from the Prime Minister.'

'Indeed, you will have it,' replied Lord Bute, before his attention took sudden flight.

A hush had descended upon the room. It was not only Lord Bute's, but all beady eyes were imperatively drawn, like magnates, almost in an inquisitive unison, to the entrance of the late arrivals. In his regal magnificence, the young King George III had arrived, with the new, even younger Queen Charlotte, delicate and graceful.

In support stood the King's mother, the formidable Princess Augusta, Dowager Princess of Wales. Every person in the room dipped and curtsied in homage to their majesties.

Lord Bute then swiftly took his leave of Sir Francis Dashwood and Lord Cheltenham. The latter gentlemen observed the Prime Minister as he advanced across the chequered expanse towards the regal party.

'That is most characteristic of Bute! Indeed, we must bide our time for the King to find his way to us. As for Bute, he forges his own course,' came Dashwood's jesting display of vexation.

'The consummate strategist in action,' mused the earl, continuing to scrutinise the situation, as he would a chessboard, anticipating Bute's next move.

'Indeed, he is most fortunate in his friendships,' replied Dashwood.

'Fortune does not play a part in this. He has secured intimate allegiances that others cannot hope to come close to forging.'

'Ha! How droll! That is indeed most amusing of you, Cheltenham. I had no notion you possessed such a gift of jest,' came Dashwood's laugh.

'I most certainly do not,' retorted the earl with stony demeanour.

Dashwood's voice lowered to a quiet coo, as he drew nearer to his companion, 'Perhaps you are unaware of Lord Bute's intimate allegiance to Princess Augusta – his most intimate allegiance. But I trust you will keep this matter to yourself.'

'Naturally,' replied the earl, alert and curious, slowly drumming each of his fingers of his right hand against the glass that he held, as he meditated. 'Thus, he discreetly assails from beneath, approaching from multiple angles.'

'Ah, indeed, multiple angles. You are doubtlessly informed that Queen Charlotte's elder sister was once considered a prospective bride to the King. Pray, who do you suppose was the guiding hand behind the change of strategy?' teased Dashwood.

'Bute,' the earl cawed monosyllabically.

'A more subdued disposition is considerably malleable,' mused Dashwood, observing the quiet figure of Queen Charlotte.

'I have carefully examined his moves,' said the earl, himself honing in on Bute, 'I know what he is and concur: "the ends justify the means."'

Dashwood was somewhat diverted, having relayed this titbit of gossip, and was keen for something of more considerable amusement. Therefore, as the Earl of

Sandwich and Henry Fitzwilliam approached to join them, he greeted them with, 'My good fellows, our forthcoming assembly at Medmenham is scheduled for next week, and it promises to be most delightful. Bute has procured the most divine wine from Fairfax – good fellow, lost his estate, yet still provides for us all.'

'Good fellow, Fairfax. Indeed, I have partaken of the vintage already; it possesses an exquisite bouquet,' replied Sandwich with an edge of satisfaction.

'Are you aware whether Le Chevalier shall be in attendance?' enquired Henry, gesturing with a new glass of Champagne wine in hand, chilled to perfection.

'Ah, indeed, Le Chevalier traverses at will, emerging from the shadows at whim, appearing at any moment, and vanishing into the obscurity from whence we know not,' said Dashwood mysteriously.

A silence fell upon the group, before Sandwich broke it with a jovial, 'Well, well, my dear fellow, you do have a knack for roguish mischief!' raising his own glass of the crystalline Champagne wine, which shimmered as it caught the candlelight.

'Ha, ha, I fear I may be laying it on rather heavily, perhaps,' Dashwood said with a playful twinkle in his eye, 'but I speak from some experience.'

Then casting his gaze across the room, Dashwood said, 'That puts me in mind. I have not had the pleasure of seeing Lord Augustus this evening. Have you been successful in persuading him to honour us with his attendance at Medmenham, Cheltenham?'

'To my chagrin, he has chosen to absent himself this evening, though he shall indeed be present at the next club meeting,' replied the earl in a deep voice imbued with unshakeable assurance.

To this, Dashwood himself raised his glass of chilled Champagne wine and announced, 'We shall set him upon the proper path,' whilst the effervescent bubbles danced playfully on the surface of his rare beverage.

In that instant, Winterbourne and Isabella's striking presence was felt as they glided past the company, prompting the Earl of Sandwich to comment, 'Miss Thornbury is making quite an impression.'

'Indeed, with thirty-thousand pounds and more, what do you say Cheltenham? You should secure her for one of your sons before Winterbourne has the chance. What a most sensational gown,' remarked Dashwood.

'I have no need for such pecuniary considerations, and do not trouble me with discussions of frivolity,' retorted Cheltenham in his usual stony manner, concealing a rising ire at the suggestion.

'One ought to examine more closely, Cheltenham,' whispered Dashwood in his ear, 'rather than dismiss her as you have. My riddle to you is: what significance does the frivolity hold? You must be aware of her father's prominence in the East Indies and his dealings with the Company.'

Then, realising that Cheltenham was in fact unaware, Dashwood continued his jest, goading him. 'Good heavens, man, you let your upper hand slip. Her home practically borders your estate! How mortifying,' and he laughed theatrically before turning to Sandwich to comment on his most shameful loss at the gaming table the prior evening at White's. Sandwich took Dashwood's comments in his stride and displayed no visible distress; it was merely a trifling matter.

Lord Cheltenham considered Dashwood's comments as he watched the Duke of Winterbourne lead Isabella out of the chamber, and his usual stoic expression faltered for a moment. A mere flicker of recognition, fleeting as it was, alone betrayed the workings of his mind.

Winterbourne and Isabella passed into the opulent, gilded ballroom for their second and final pair of dances together that evening. This afforded the many spectators a second view of the now renowned pair.

'With his statuesque presence and her grace, they complement each other admirably in style,' remarked an elegant lady adorned with a long white feather in her headdress, standing on one side of the ballroom.

'I shall not prolong my observations, Sarah, but her gown is so exquisite,' commented her younger sister, Carlotta, herself adorned with an emerald gown and the most sensational diamonds at her neck.

'I observe the Harringshires are pleased to have garnered such attention, for had they not received her gift, Miss Thornbury would assuredly have outshone the dukedom,' remarked white-feathered Sarah.

'Ah, but she will be a Duchess ere long, mark my words. One can discern this even in their dance,' replied her sister, Carlotta.

The two ladies, with the rest of the assembly, observed the enchanting pair moving through the minuet.

'They are indeed dignified in their attire, yet I would not wish to be unkind, but they do seem somewhat out of harmony,' remarked Sarah.

'Nay, you must be envious, Sarah; for shame!'

'Not at all, I assure you. Observe for yourself before passing judgement, Carlotta.'

At this, the younger sister did sincerely observe and, with a thoughtful nod, slowly raised her hand to adjust the diamonds at her neck. 'Yes, I perceive it now... I understand your meaning. Indeed, I have witnessed Winterbourne perform far more in harmony with a partner on previous occasions than this evening,' she conceded.

'There is a certain disparity which I cannot quite place,' mused Sarah.

'Ah, but they are likely nervous at present. They perceive themselves to be the focus of the ball,' said Carlotta with a wave of her fan, and a smile. 'Indeed, so would I, were I of their youth.'

Having concluded their final dance, Winterbourne led Isabella from the ballroom floor, whereupon they were approached by a gentleman in a periwig, holding a small notebook and pencil.

Winterbourne acknowledged him with a nod and greeted him with, 'Mr Jackson, splendid to see you. May I have the honour of introducing you to Miss Thornbury?'

They exchanged bows and curtsies, after which Mr Jackson said, 'Indeed, it is an honour and Your Grace, as ever, you are a man of your word. I see you do not disappoint.' Then, turning to Miss Thornbury, he asserted, 'You cannot be at a loss why I am approaching you, for you have created a sensation this season.'

'Indeed, I am at a loss,' replied the young girl modestly.

'Indeed, such modesty will be noted, and is oh, so endearing to the readership, to be sure.'

Isabella was still none the wiser, but glancing up at Winterbourne, he gave her a reassuring look.

'Now, may I ask you for the details of your gown? It was displayed to full effect, as you danced just now. Indeed, we have our artist observing from the corner, over there, hard at work.' He indicated a fellow nearby who had escaped Isabella's notice. Having drawn up a chair, he was discretely sketching.

Isabella executed a slight double take upon recognising him as Monsieur De La Fontaine's artist. She presumed that he must be an independent practitioner. Turning back to Mr Jackson she said, 'I must apologise. Might I enquire as to the purpose this is intended?'

Mr Jackson smiled and explained, 'I am a journalist from *The Gentleman's Magazine*. Whilst we primarily feature news, essays, and literature, we do on occasion cover events and esteemed individuals, who we believe will appeal to our readership.'

As he said '*The Gentleman's Magazine*,' Isabella grew alarmed, at which point Mr Jackson clarified, 'Are you not familiar? How surprising. We have a wide readership, including both ladies and gentlemen, despite our nomenclature.'

Isabella glanced up again at Winterbourne for some guidance, hoping that he might intervene at this juncture.

'I can assure you of all propriety and indeed, even Lady Ingram would approve,' Winterbourne replied with assurance. 'Perhaps you can enlighten Mr Jackson on your gown; its materials and design.'

'Indeed,' replied Isabella, now reassured.

She began to elaborate upon the materials, the intricate beading and the drapery which cascaded from her shoulder.

Meanwhile, Winterbourne took a moment to survey the room, observing that many eyes were still upon them, some peering curiously from behind fans, or glancing sideways whilst whispering to their neighbours. Isabella then remarked that several other attendees were also adorned in gowns fashioned from fabrics imported by her father.

'And should our esteemed readership wish to procure such extraordinary fabrics for their own attire, might they be made available to them?' asked Mr Jackson, pausing from his frantic scribbling in his notebook, with his pencil poised mid-air.

'Indeed,' replied Isabella, 'I am certain my father would be most pleased. He was keen to understand how the materials would take. If your readers were to correspond with Madame Noyer, I am confident we could come to an arrangement.'

Mr Jackson looked quite gratified with the information he had gleaned, not least by the fact that Isabella offered to provide him with some of the fashion plates, should he call upon her the following morning.

With evident satisfaction, Mr Jackson inclined his head in a bow, saying, 'And might I venture to say, you make a most charming couple. I thank you most sincerely for being so obliging.' He then proceeded to seek Lady Thornbury and Lady Ingram, whom Isabella had confirmed were likewise adorned in gowns of the most exquisite silk.

'Bravo, Miss Thornbury.' Winterbourne's voice conveyed warmth and approval, which brought a most agreeable sensation to Isabella's heart. It leapt as he continued, 'I believe you have now firmly established yourself at the pinnacle of the London season, and achieved a resounding success.'

CHAPTER 18 – FAIR IS FOUL, AND FOUL IS FAIR

Lady Ingram had declined the invitation in protest, judging it to be most improper. She would not encourage such notions, and neither, in her view, should Lady Thornbury. 'Isabella, I have no wish to revisit the matter, but your escapade at the chocolate house was quite sufficient, and now this,' she rebuked her young charge.

'Surely it cannot be as dreadful as that,' said Lady Thornbury, 'and we have quite exhausted the books which we brought with us from Sir Nicholas's library.'

'A circulating library, indeed. Most inappropriate,' replied the dowager before turning back to Isabella. 'Moreover, you shall befuddle your mind should you indulge in any more romantic novels; and Shakespeare, though perhaps deemed tolerable, still requires moderation, young lady.'

With a sigh of exasperation, she inclined her head to her friend most graciously, uttering in a resigned tone, 'Well, I leave the matter to you, Sophia, but you know my views.' At this retort, Lady Ingram flounced from the morning room in a manner that she felt was most dignified.

Isabella was somewhat frustrated; Lady Ingram's, or perhaps society's restrictions, were becoming in her view, increasingly onerous, even as the allurements of London grew. She had plucked the apple and savoured the excitement of the town, and now, she found herself unable to forsake it; rather, it had kindled a temptation for further indulgence.

That very morning, the ladies had once more reflected upon the Harringshire ball which had occurred but a few nights past – another truly remarkable soirée, with Winterbourne at the foremost in each of their thoughts.

Indeed, soon after that most auspicious evening, His Grace had called upon Isabella. To the ladies, it was evident that Isabella's path was unequivocally on course towards a future with Winterbourne.

However, the morning's discourse eventually moved to the day's pursuits. Isabella had invited Lady Ingram to accompany her, along with her mother, Heloise, and Mary, on a visit to subscribe to the nearest circulating library. The ladies, undeterred by the dowager's sentiments, resolved to set out almost immediately after breakfast.

Thus, the ladies, sans Lady Ingram, found themselves upon a bustling London street, on that cold, but brisk February morning, taking the short walk to that most accessible of institutions, home of the erudite pursuit of which they were all most fond: reading.

'What do you seek, Heloise? Should it be a volume that piques my interest as well, perhaps we might share it and later discuss our reflections,' suggested Isabella.

'I was curious about *Pamela* and I noted you did not bring it from Henley,' replied Heloise.

'Oh, indeed, it is rather dramatic in certain respects; I wonder you have not yet read it. I am inclined to attempt *Candide* by Voltaire. I began reading the initial pages after Reverend Fernsby returned it, and I regret that I did not bring it with me to London.'

Lady Thornbury halted before them as she surveyed a cross road for any notable buildings or names that might indicate which way they should proceed.

This pause, afforded Isabella a closer scrutiny of the busy, grey, even sooty London streets. It was not mist as she was accustomed to, or an air of dewy freshness. Instead, this was suffused with a heavy smog which hung and clung, with a thick murkiness, which Isabella reflected, "hover[ed] through the filthy air." The buildings, too, had a veil of grime that seeped up their walls.

At that instance, advancing towards them through the haze, Isabella noticed a remarkably smart gentleman on horseback. The equestrian had a periwig and tricorn hat of the highest fashion, and a heavy brocade riding habit, trimmed with sable, with a high collar. His supple boots were of a rich gloss, deep ebony. The thoroughbred horse was remarkably well-bred; its well-groomed physique shone in a lustrous sheen. Its bridle of beautiful leather, an elaborate design embossed with gold buckle ornamentation on its headstall, gave all the indication that this was a most refined and expensive steed.

However, it was not this but the visage of the rider that gave rise to Isabella's whispered aside to her companion. 'Pray observe over there. That is Mr Thomas Fairfax, Mrs Stoughton's footman,' she said softly.

Heloise glanced up and appeared somewhat bewildered. This did not resemble any footman she had ever encountered – and there had been many. The impression he made certainly did not suggest a gentleman fallen on hard times.

Heloise turned to Isabella, whispering, 'I should follow him to see where he goes. Perhaps we can discover the matter. Would you make an excuse for me?'

'Indeed, excellent idea, Heloise,' replied Isabella, before calling her mother who was pondering the street ahead of them. 'Mother, I require some new pink ribbon for one of my bonnets. Heloise will procure some at the haberdashers and meet us at the circulating library.'

Mary appeared to suspect that there was some silent communication between Isabella and Heloise and intervened with, 'Oh no, do not trouble yourself, Heloise. I have plenty of pink ribbon in my basket at home. You should have asked.'

Heloise glanced from Mary to Isabella and pursed her lips.

'I find that I am in need of blue as well,' replied Isabella quickly and firmly.

'I have blue available too, all various shades. Indeed, you need not trouble yourselves,' Mary replied with a smile, which did not reach her eyes.

Lady Thornbury looked at Mary fondly, sighing, 'You are so thoughtful and organised. What would we do without you?'

Isabella, now desperate, observed her chance slipping away as Fairfax turned a corner and cried out, 'A surprise! I have a surprise for Mother, which Heloise is assisting me with. It was intended as a surprise, but now you have forced my hand,' she said pointedly in Mary's direction.

Lady Thornbury appeared thrilled at this prospect, and said, 'Very well, Heloise. Shall we rendezvous at the circulating library when you have completed your errand?'

Without reply, Heloise lifted her skirts and hurried down the street.

'She is most eager!' Lady Thornbury remarked, whilst Mary looked quite vexed.

Once Heloise had caught up with Mr Thomas Fairfax, she was able to walk behind him at a distance and observe. In a short while, he halted outside a palatial residence with six colossal Corinthian columns, above which was a pediment of Minerva, standing tall with her spear, flanked by an owl. Engraved were the words: Honestas, Integritas, Exemplo.

He dismounted, assisted by a stable hand, who promptly appeared to lead the fine steed to the stables. Fairfax then climbed one of the symmetrical double staircases of Portland stone leading to the front entrance, and was immediately admitted by a footman, in a most distinctive livery of purple and gold. Heloise could recognise that livery anywhere, and indeed was further assured as she perceived the footman to be James Heydon – belonging to the household of the Earl of Cheltenham.

There was no doubt that Mr Thomas Fairfax was an official visitor to that family. However, what purpose could he possibly have for his visit? Heloise was quite positive that Isabella had mentioned that were it not for his employment with Mrs Stoughton, Mr Fairfax would be on the verge of destitution, and that his acquaintances in town were influenced by his brother.

She waited across the street for over a quarter of an hour before Mr Fairfax re-appeared. However, instead of calling for his horse, he proceeded to walk further down the road. Heloise pondered how intimately acquainted Mr Fairfax must be with the Earl of Cheltenham, if he could leave his horse stabled there. It was even conceivable that he had borrowed the earl's horse. If so, he clearly had friends in town, however unsavoury.

She continued to follow the gentleman as he meandered through the streets, including several smaller side streets. He appeared wholly absorbed in his thoughts and did not turn around. Indeed, thought Heloise, why should he? Thus, it was relatively simple for her to follow him to Holborn and eventually to the door of a building, into which he vanished. Unable to proceed further, Heloise ventured to the steps of the door and observed a brass plaque affixed to the side, inscribed with the following:

Mr George North
Attorney at Law Chambers
At No. 279 Lincoln's Inn

This was most confounding, yet Heloise was convinced she possessed enough intelligence to relay to Isabella. Moreover, time was slipping away, and the ladies might already have concluded their visit to the circulating library. What she knew with certainty was that there would be much for Isabella and herself to deliberate upon during the evening's collation.

Then, as if struck by a sudden revelation, it dawned upon her – could there be a connection to the book? Cheltenham was indeed a notable figure within its pages and the society or club it described. Even Mr Thomas Fairfax's brother was mentioned therein, though, she speculated, as his first name was not mentioned, it could well have been either brother.

With such explosive revelations, it seemed inevitable that someone might be hunting for the book, tracking it with the tenacity of hounds scenting out a fox in a hunt. Whether to safeguard their own reputation or to protect the interests of their associates, the pursuit would surely be relentless. She did not wish to challenge the earl's ruthless reputation, yet it appeared that they might already be ensnared in his trap.

In light of this, Mr Thomas Fairfax's true intentions were now suspect. It was clear that she and Isabella must deliberate whether they should indeed bring this matter to the attention of Mrs Stoughton, and the literary circle – at least with respect to his identity.

Then another disquieting thought occurred to her: could anyone be trusted? From the highest echelons to the humblest of servants, treachery may lurk in every shadow; not all were as they appeared. For the first time, the true weight of the book and its implications pressed upon her. She and Isabella were entangled in a perilous hunt, far more dangerous than they had realised. Were they to be the hunters or the hunted? Or was it merely a contest of who would yield first?

CHAPTER 19 – THE WINTER OF DISCONTENT

Beneath Medmenham Abbey, Lord Augustus

I float slowly through the engulfing darkness, descending, deeper and deeper, inexorably through the tunnel; like an oesophagus, swallowing me up whole. My thoughts are consumed with death, which has claimed, and is ingesting me. Death, whose cold and withered fingers reach out towards me like wisps of smoke.

I extend my own fingers from beneath the folds of the robe, brushing them against the enclosing walls barely a foot away on either side of me. As I make contact, the cold, rough stone, like him, scrapes along the tips, lightly tearing at my skin.

This is my "winter of discontent." I shall engage my father in his game for now, his game of strategy, of which he is so fond and which alone resonates with him. What options are left to me? I am dead to him unless I play it. And yet, from within, I feel that I have already perished. A fire died out some nights prior, a flicker of hope in an otherwise weary and empty world devoid of meaning now.

I follow what they allege to be a member, clad in a milk-white robe; yet, to me, he is a spectre and it is as if I were trailing Death himself. Yet, I am his very likeness, clad in my own chalk attire, hood raised. Such cowls hide our visages, so they cannot be seen, as though they are erased. Here, my name is also dead, and I have been given another, befitting of the destination – the inner chambers and bowels – where we shall ultimately arrive, and I shall become as they are. Here they revel.

Many of us, including the meagre remains of my being, come to rest in one of the larger chambers, as others continue on, deeper. They are like wandering milky spirits in search of I know not what, to satiate themselves with their sins.

Here beside me in this great cavity, my father stands in his white robes like an alabaster marble statue. He is as immovable and unyielding in emotion, heart or requirements, that all eventually yield to his will, as I have done.

'I present to you my son, Friar Augustus of Henley, the future Earl of Cheltenham,' he announces to the gathering. 'As such, you will treat him as an extension of myself, so long as he does justice to the name. If he should not, his punishment of me is far more grievous than any that you might contrive, for I know his soul.'

I hear one gentleman whisper to his companion, a young lady, who wears a long black nun's habit and is so in the shadows that I cannot wholly see her face, 'Cheltenham, he plays the man.' He proclaims this with the air of one who had said it many times before, as though it were a habitual refrain to other young ladies.

I glance around the room with its walls of coarse dark rock, carved as a cave deep within the stomach of the hill and which is dimly lit with candles. It has many darkened corners and recesses, with chairs and small tables to take one's ease. Though most notable are the numerous white-robed figures as columns gazing at me, steady and unnerving, fresh from the inaugurating rituals, the mesmerising effect of the chanting, not yet faded from their aura. It is as if their spirit lingers as in the newly dead, some moments longer, before it is snuffed out for eternity.

All at once, as though the enchantment has been broken, there comes a cheer and another and another, rising up. The revellers and their chaos break out in tumultuous gaiety, and their voices, so clamorous and abrupt, are a torment to my soul. I, who above all else crave peace, tranquillity, so shattered are my nerves. Their screeches pierce the cold, turgid air of the cave, and the echoes enhance the raw and primal cries, harsh and grating, just as the rocks that surround us, as though the very essence of the cavern had been given voice.

I bow my head in solemn resignation, akin to a hawk lowering its gaze and spreading its wings, which quiver at the very tips of the quills, before the final, fatal embrace. I close my eyes tight, in hopes of shutting the tumult out, but that, of course, is in vain.

I know not how, but I manage to make my way to a recess and take a seat in a chair, my perch for the evening. An onlooker of the revelries, under duress. Though, death as a captor never releases its prisoners, buried so deep in its underground cells.

Servants have begun to bring glasses of wine for the participants, and this raises spirits further, as they cast off their costumes. My father takes his place across the room, undoubtably to confer with Lord Bute on their favoured pastime – strategising on I know not what. I am aware that I must, at some juncture, rise and at least feign engagement in the society, as directed.

I settle, as much as I am able, in my upright chair for the evening, ensconced within the blackened recess, where few can perceive or concern themselves with my presence. This is as I intend it. However, it is not long before I am aware of two voices engaged in low murmuring conference, within the neighbouring secluded recess, and I, finding little else to occupy me, direct my ear towards them.

'Is it indeed true what I have heard? Did you indeed fight and kill Le Comte de la Corbeau at the Battle of Leuthen?' comes Henry Fitzwilliam's voice, as I hear him sip his first glass of... let me guess... brandy. It is entirely characteristic of him to already indulge in strong spirits.

'Voyons... Le Comte de la, ah oui, oui, il était un adversaire redoutable. Ee was most dangereux pour le roi. Though bereft of his sword ee was an even greater peril,' Le Chevalier mused. 'Owever, Le Comte was nowhere to be found on ze Battlefields of Leuthen. Évidemment, he did not make it from his chambre à coucher.'

'But if you had met Le Comte, you would no doubt have emerged victorious. It is said that you possess the ability to vanquish any adversary with ease,' enthuses Henry, with widening eyes.

'Who has claimed that I did not encounter him on that day?' comes Le Chevalier's enigmatic reply.

'Good heavens, did you strike him down before he had even reached the field?'

'Well, I am not certain. The accounts suggest that he choked on une pomme, but it seems to me more plausible that it was an almond – at least, that was the scent that lingered. I shall let you make... how would you say... votre propre évaluation.'

Henry looks deep in thought, before speculating, 'How can a man who is able to assassinate Le Comte de la Corbeau, with arsenic in his own bedchamber, not be able to find a damn pocketbook? I am beginning to believe you were the one that took it. What kind of man are you?' he exclaims, before hesitating and finishing with, 'are you even a man…? There are rumours that you were the lady-in-waiting to the Empress Elizabeth of Russia,' he says, before bursting into a drunken laughter.

'I do not deny it. I have been a maid, a footman, a king's advisor and an empress's lady-in-waiting. You should learn to appreciate people for who they are. They each have their part to play. Incidentally, how is your newly appointed scullery maid, Eliza?'

'What? You are asking me about a scullery maid? In what world would I interact with a scullery maid?' Henry scoffs.

However, Le Chevalier continues, 'If you had asked her, she would have been able to inform you that she removed a red wine stain from your silk, duck egg blue under sheet, but one day ago, and was happy to replace it only this morning.'

Henry, now quite shocked, clasps his hand to his chest, appearing to feel his heart tremble with the realisation that Le Chevalier had materialised into his scullery maid, and had been in his bedchamber that very morning.

Then Le Chevalier, not allowing him time to recover, continues, 'But I digress. You were questioning my skills in the art of espionage. Continuez, s'il vous plait.'

I am listening to these attendees and have at this juncture, transitioned from a languid despondence and a sense of doom, to curiosity, and I am suddenly alert to the unfolding discourse. The obscurity of the conversation compels me to continue to listen with growing intrigue.

'You have made your point. Pray, tell me, what have you discovered thus far?'

'Et bien, I am proceeding methodically to examine tous les invités du salon de Lady Bute, commencing with ze most suspect and proceeding to ze least, including your esteemed self, bien entendu. Cette entreprise requires time, but it is thorough, and I can assure you of its succès éventuel.'

Henry appears relieved, but with a slight note of impatience, says, 'Indeed, but how long will it take? I cannot afford to let certain matters escape. Once loosed from Pandora's box, it may never be put back within.'

'Might I remind you that you are not the sole person interested in discovering the whereabouts of this book. There are others who are making their own inquiries. I would just say, patience… patience, mon ami.'

Henry, sweating, takes a large swig of the remaining liquid from the abbey's crystal glass, before smashing it on the table – shards fly across the cavern. I see the fragments as they pierce the air, catching the candlelight, mimicking the oh so familiar French grape-shot. Then his chair, with a discordant screech, scrapes across the floor as he rises. To my frayed nerves, it is akin to the nails of a phantom raking across the blackened rocks, and a dagger through me.

I watch that reprobate pass by me and trudge out of the cavern. A few spots of darkened liquid remain on the floor, of blood, brandy or wine, I cannot tell.

This excruciating moment draws the attention of the entire room. Even my father, engaged in a deep discourse with Bute, lifts his gaze sternly from their conversation to regard the darkened chasm that has swallowed up that delinquent, yet tormented soul. Then, from the tunnel emerges, in place of Henry, the form of Robert Hastings entering the room, now the Friar of Pembroke, or perchance it is Petersfield, as I recall from the ritual, though I must confess, I am in no condition to heed such minutiae.

'Hastings my man, I have something for you,' rumbles my father, then in a commanding voice, 'Come, Martha, you are required.'

The lady who was in receipt of Winterbourne's confidence earlier in the evening, steps forward towards my father. I recognise her as one of the household maids and am quite astonished to see her there, but watch for what might unfold.

'Hastings, I have brought a most sweet delight who will assist with your inauguration,' he says, indicating Martha, who still wears a wimple and habit. 'Ah, ah… but remember this favour I have rendered you.'

Anticipating the conversation, I avert my gaze to face into the inky recess, to the wall, anything, and even squeeze my eyes shut once more. I cannot bear to endure such as this from members of my own household. I cover my ears to shield all my senses from this dreadful, unnecessary nightmare, allowing them to be obscured for many moments, almost as if to find sanctuary. As those moments pass in silence and darkness, I allow myself to feel. What I feel is a profound sense of frustration and anger beginning to spread within me, like slow-moving tar finally spilling, thick, molten, hot, the liquid no less deadly for its slowness.

Finding my current recess unbearable, I resolve to rise and move to another on the other side of the chamber, furthest away from my father. I compose myself once more in the obscurity of the darkness, seeking some measure of comfort in the quiet of my thoughts.

However, I am scarcely settled before rich, velvet tones come drifting from the neighbouring recess.

'I beheld a most enchanting young lady and immediately felt compelled to secure her acquaintance. Fortuitously, she was not only possessed of a pleasing countenance but, upon closer observation, I discerned her innocence – a country girl, most assuredly – quite ideal.'

At this moment, my curiosity is aroused. He continues, 'Both the Duke of Harringshire and I noticed her comely presence as she entered, and he jestingly wagered that I could not persuade her to be nunnified. "To what end?" I enquired. He proposed a bottle of venerable cognac. While it was not of considerable value, it was a rare quality absent from my collection.' It is unmistakably the voice of Winterbourne.

'Pray, which cognac might it be?' comes the Earl of Sandwich's voice.

'A rare Montclair Grande Champagne Cognac, which I had not previously encountered,' remarks Winterbourne.

'Ah, I see why you might be tempted to make the effort,' Sandwich replies. 'Almost too facile, a triumph indeed. I am astonished His Grace did not suggest you also attempt for the mother, Lady Thornbury, or even the dowager countess – what is her name? Ingram, is it? By Jove, we are speaking of a rare Montclair. You fortunate fellow. I ought to seek Harringshire's counsel more frequently.'

Winterbourne responds, 'Indeed, the challenge required but little persuasion, for it was all in the spirit of amusement. From the simplicity of her almost country attire, I inferred she was either unacquainted with such refined company in town, or of modest means, thus likely to be amenable to my attentions. I was attired in my faithful red velvet justaucorps. Truly, it seemed an effortless conquest.'

'And yet, despite the justaucorps, you still failed to bring her here?'

'Well, that was prior to my discovery of her fortune and her father's esteemed position. At that moment, I cast aside the Montclair.'

To this the Earl of Sandwich chuckles.

'I am now resolved to secure her as a bride,' resumes Winterbourne, 'and making a most commendable effort to that end, if I might say so – indeed, you were present at the ball.'

Sandwich replies, 'Indeed, we were all astonished, but now it all becomes clear.'

At this juncture, I find myself seething once more with ire, scarcely able to contain my vexation, for it is all too manifest to whom the gentlemen allude.

'And you shall scarcely credit it, but I even arranged for a journalist to come and interview her, ensuring our presence as a couple in society is noted. I deemed it a most excellent touch. She was, of course, entirely taken in. I truly hold high hopes; I do not believe it shall be long before I make my proposal. Naturally, I shall continue in my customary way of life, yet more wealth is never unwelcome. And, perhaps Harringshire will award me the Montclair as a nuptial gift.' Winterbourne cannot suppress a chuckle.

I erupt in a fury, and as I spring up, I hurl the chair to the ground with a crash, screaming. 'I shall not let this stand!' Every fibre in my body shakes, 'No! I shall not let it stand. Stand up at once. You insult one who is dearest to me. Rise this instant!' My screams echo through the cavern and reverberate down the passages.

Initially, both the Duke of Winterbourne and the Earl of Sandwich are struck with astonishment, but as I stand towering over them, their shock gradually gives way to laughter, which begins to ripple throughout the cavern, with other onlookers joining in.

At this moment, my entire form is visibly rigid; hands clenched, face ashen with fury, and trembling with perspiration and anger – a wrath such as I have never before experienced – even in battle, for this was most profoundly personal.

Winterbourne regains his composure and, slowly rising, proceeds to retrieve the chair which I had hurtled aside. 'I must commend you,' he remarks, 'a most theatrical display for a first appearance.' He calmly restores the chair to its former place. 'Who would have imagined, when we were once friends, that it would come to this over a mere lady?'

At this, nearly in tears, I utter softly, 'I challenge you.'

'And with what, pray tell?' enquires Winterbourne with overzealous delicacy and accentuation.

I proceed with deliberate purpose to the crested decorative shield mounted upon the wall, beneath which are displayed two pristine and finely wrought small swords, neither of which have ever been intended to be used in battle. I seize them both and cast one across the room towards Winterbourne, where it collides with screeching sounds of clashing metal and stone at his feet.

Two gentlemen rise to intervene and appeal to my father, 'Cheltenham, good god, you must put a stop to this. Your boy has gone mad,' exclaims one.

Winterbourne remains standing with the weapon lying by his feet. All eyes are now drawn to my father, who remains firmly in his position.

To my surprise, my father replies, in a slow and deliberate manner, 'I shall not intervene. My son has made his choice.'

Unsatisfied, members of the party now appeal to Le Chevalier. The unparalleled practitioner, observing from a recess and leaning against the rock in a stance denoting ease, replies in a slow, measured tone, 'If Winterbourne accepts the challenge, no one shall intervene. Je vous assure.'

Nothing now lies between Winterbourne and me, save for his assent. Experience overtakes me, refining my focus and mastering my emotions in this pivotal moment. A stretch of silence ensues, during which my gaze remains fixed and unwavering upon Winterbourne's countenance. I perceive it is his pride that is at stake, rather than any material prize. My adversary seems to appraise me intently, and at length, he meets my gaze as he descends slowly towards the ground, reaching for the sword which I have cast across the room to rest at his feet.

Without exchanging a word, Winterbourne paces backwards and, so predictably, flaunts a grandiose en guarde with a shallow angle parry prime. I am well aware of such classical training, to which all aristocrats are accustomed and which defines their distinction. It surely pleases the onlookers, who must so delight in the optics of such an artistically wielded sword, and he no doubt takes great pride in this display. Indeed, so distinguished is he that this performance sets him apart. Yes, he is apart – from one who has truly engaged in the harsh realities of battle, where life hangs in the balance and where practicality, rather than theatricality, is paramount.

I survey his stance more closely, noting the weight he places upon his left foot. This detail informs me precisely about his intended approach, which provides me with considerable comfort.

At this, I adopt my preferred stance; septime, with a choked grip and a single finger resting upon the blade's ricasso – so versatile for countering the assumed attack. Reliable, it has never failed me in necessity. Had it, I would not be here. Let him persist in his display; I will permit his theatrics and allow my success to speak for itself.

With a sudden flourish, Winterbourne endeavours to execute an advance. Yet, with a flick of my sword, I cast his to the ground, disarming him with remarkable ease, as one might pluck a flower. It is all too effortless.

Winterbourne freezes in shock, as though the hilt remains within his grasp. I could draw his darkened soul from his body there and then, and liberate Isabella from the taint of his vile designs. Yet, for such a man, my task has been all too easy.

Observing his insignificance and the paltriness of his skill, I deem him unworthy of the grave consequence of my hand. The contest has been so disproportionate it borders on injustice, and as my wrath diminishes, I find myself moved with a measure of pity. My point has been duly made; he will cease his pursuit of Isabella. Her honour has been safeguarded, and could she truly wish to be with one who is a murderer? Moreover, I have vowed to the Almighty that, henceforth, I shall seek peace.

Just as I lower my sword, Winterbourne looking into my eyes steadily, though with some shadow of fear, appears to search with his right hand for his sword. I can scarcely conceive what he is doing. Indeed, it seems he cannot bear the loss... the humiliation.

Suddenly, Winterbourne leaps to his feet, unleashing his full might and fury in wild, unpredictable arcs, slashing at the air towards me with unbridled abandon, as if to splatter my blood across an imaginary canvas. His strikes, devoid of precision, come from every conceivable angle, as though it is a matter of all or nothing. The room reverberates with the thunderous clash of metal against metal. I counter, striving to maintain my precision and press forward relentlessly, until, in a swift moment, his back is driven against the rough-hewn wall, and my blade is poised at his throat.

He knows at this moment, if he is to live, he has no recourse but to relinquish his sword. And in the now hushed chamber, it descends with a final, echoing clang of metal upon the stony floor of the cavern.

I release my adversary. I am now acutely aware of the sweat upon my brow, the fervent heat of my body, and the pulsing beat of my heart, my living blood surging through my veins. I am fully present. I am alive.

I see no further visions or spectres in the chamber. That is, except for the figure of Le Chevalier, who, in silence, gives me the most curious look. There is an unspoken reverence in his stance. A profound and all-encompassing stillness pervades the entire chamber. Casting my own sword to the ground, with a final clatter, I turn and depart from that forsaken abyss of torment. I shall never return.

CHAPTER 20 – NOSTALGIA

The inn was nestled midway down a narrow and quiet London street. Snug and inviting; a haven from the frenzy of the crowd. So slender was the lane that neither horse nor carriage could pass, and so the welcome guests of that little-known establishment were obliged to approach on foot. Thus, on a biting February afternoon, with the bitter wind whipping the delicate wisps of snow through the frigid air, Augustus, having left his faithful steed ensconced in a stable of soft straw and enfolded in thick blankets, turned a corner into that familiar street.

A jarring flare burst forth in his thoughts. A vivid heavy clang, harsh screeching metal against jagged rock. Augustus halted abruptly, blinded from the violence of the image and the emotions it wrought. The freezing wind whirled about him, chafing his cheeks until they hurt.

Yet he felt a strange gratitude, for it brought his mind sharply back to the present moment. The memory lingered, along with the sense that his soul had been snatched away the night before, taken. It was only through an immense effort – a prodigious surge of anger from deep within him, which had spilt over, that he had ultimately reclaimed himself, his life.

He had consciously, resolutely and definitively left that darkness and others like it. Yet still he struggled with its relentless claws, which would suddenly seize his psyche in an attempt to draw him back with its devouring grasp, into its turgid mouth.

He exhaled a gasping breath, which, as it met the cold air, expanded its ethereal, subtle white, as if his very soul had expelled a potent essence in defiance. After a moment, he felt he could continue on; his mind more level.

The inn, built some centuries past, had a half-timbered façade, with blackened wood framing the casements, and its rough-hewn exterior gave it a quintessential charm of a bygone era. As Augustus neared the modest inn door, he glimpsed the glow from the fire within, an inviting ambiance emanating through the small, leaded window of the entrance.

He opened the door and stepped within, to be greeted by the homeliest of surroundings, which instantly warmed and gladdened his heart. This setting offered a soothing embrace; a welcome relief from the contrasting cold outside and the inner terrors that had plagued him. At least for now, they seemed to have abated, and the refuge of this place was well-suited to keep them at bay.

He shook his greatcoat and stamped his feet upon the coarse matting, to free himself of the snow that had clung. A similar matting had always lain across the old stone floor, rounded and smoothed over centuries of welcomed guests who had sought warmth, a satisfaction of their thirst, and to take their fill of a friendly atmosphere of convivial companionship.

He wandered through the toasty oak-panelled rooms, where creaking wooden boards, low, comforting beams and a smoky haze from ancient stone fireplaces contributed to the rustic charm. The aroma of burning wood mingled with the earthy scent of the aged timbers.

He passed coteries speaking in hushed tones, until he finally beheld a glowing sight, both picturesque and heartwarming, surpassing any he had seen in a long time. It was his venerable friend, Dr James Ashford, snug in the embrace of the crackling hearth. The fire's popping denoted the moisture and irregular grain within the burning elm, whilst the pleasant glow cast a gentle golden light upon his familiar face.

Upon glimpsing Augustus, his friend rose with an air of vitality, joyously lively and exclaimed in his warm inviting tone, 'Gussi, my dear lad. Come here and allow me to embrace you.' As he enfolded Augustus in his arms, layered in the thick wool fabric of his rough earthy coat, he uttered in his ear, with a mellow voice laden with sentiment, 'I hoped, but never knew if we would ever be granted such a heavenly moment.'

These were the most heartening sounds Augustus had heard in many years, for it was not merely the words, but the affectionate tone, and the cosy setting that made this moment with his friend so deeply comforting.

'Come, my lad, have a seat, draw up a chair. I shall order some ale for you. Will you have the usual?' his friend cried out with warmth.

Augustus, beaming and still heady from the embrace and his emotions, which were so high on the surface, cared not what was served, but indeed the usual from years ago, sounded like perfection to him.

Soon his friend returned, bearing two glasses brimming with a thick and dark honeyed liquid, crowned with a frothy head, near-spilling over. 'The innkeeper professed he does not have your usual brown ale,' he said, placing the glasses upon the worn, slightly sticky wood of the small round table before them. 'However, he recommended the Porter, so I thought that we might sample it together.'

It was an oak table that had witnessed countless merry gatherings, which seemed to have seeped into its grain, along with years of brown liquids. Ashford's rounded frame bumped the table gently, as he turned to find his chair, swirling the liquid with no mishap.

He eased into the creaking timber seat, with a characteristic and expressive 'eh', and a deep outtake of breath, adjusting his position with a gentle shift from side to side. His stomach slightly protruded, he assumed his familiar pose, with hands loosely entwined, resting upon it.

Gratefully, Augustus raised his glass, and they exchanged a hearty toast, the thick glasses making a low, satisfying thud as the vessels met. They sipped the rich, dark and slightly bitter ale, and the older man emitted a contented sigh as he set his glass down. A faint froth of ale clung to his white beard, and it momentarily prickled and popped, before he brushed it away. His fluffy white hair, light and airy, almost obscured his face, leaving only his twinkling blue eyes visible beneath his brows. His cheeks, a blend of rose and creamy smoothness, and the rounded shape of his nose completed his comforting visage.

After a few moments of contented silence, Dr Ashford spoke. 'You know, Gussi, this is what I cherish most in the world: a conversation with loyal friends, and communion over a drink free of any hidden motives.'

He drew his cherrywood pipe from his pocket. Augustus had always thought it an unusual choice, as it was not of the common clay or even the more refined briar. Dr Ashford gazed at it with a touch of melancholy, and shook his head, despondently. 'Since returning from war, I find I no longer have the heart to smoke it,' he sighed, before slipping it back into his pocket.

Augustus understood his friend well, for it was a familiar sentiment that he had come to recognise since his own return. So many things now seemed banal and lacklustre, and were a pale contrast to the trauma and haunting visions that he so often now endured. Yet, only the night before, a flicker of his former energy had ignited within him, flaring up like a fire, valiantly fighting against the encroaching darkness that had threatened to consume him.

'James, my friend,' Augustus replied quietly. 'I know only too well what you are feeling.'

He took up his ale once more, savouring a sip of the rich, malty sweetness. As he set the glass down, he continued, looking at his white-haired companion, 'I know the pipe holds great meaning to you. If you forgo those simple pleasures in life, then we have lost. They would have taken these simple liberties from us.'

Augustus paused, observing the impact of his words, as James's light blue eyes began to glisten. 'What were we fighting for? Not the self-interests of those at the pinnacle. No, you and I fought for our liberty, the freedom to do exactly as we are doing now. To engage in free conversation, to sit in a public inn, drinking our sweet ale and smoking a pipe.'

He allowed the sentiment to settle as the fire beside them continued to crackle and glow, weaving its heavy woody smoke towards the companions.

'You are, of course, quite right, Gussi,' Dr Ashford said, using his friend's endearment, out of comfort.

'If you will not smoke it, I shall take it up myself, as someone must continue these traditions,' affirmed Augustus.

His friend chuckled, and the mood lightened. 'Very well, very well,' he replied, as his fingers fumbled in his snug coat pocket for his pipe. He cupped the pipe in his palm, and felt the weight and balance of the glossy cherry, as his hand moved in an undulating motion. 'You are aware that her name is Rosamund,' he said, searching for his tin of tobacco.

'Who is?'

'My pipe, of course. Did you not know? Perhaps I have not shared her origins,' said the doctor. His voice had a rugged quality, with a deep, raspy texture, but it also possessed an undercurrent of melody. He leaned forward, opening the tin of Virginia tobacco with a delicate metallic click. Placing it on the table, he gently unfolded the wax paper, which unfurled resembled a white sleeve ruffle, revealing the delicate curls of dark rich chestnut tobacco medallions nestled within. He lightly grasped some tufts and carefully packed them into the bowl of his pipe.

'A dear friend of mine was admitted into my care, suffering from a wound that would not heal.' He said this slowly, taking his time, as though preparing his sermon. 'I spent many hours by his side, listening to his tales. We often shared a pipe as comfort during those precious moments of companionship. Irrespective of the weather outside our tent, it achieved its purpose.' He paused as he gently pushed the tobacco into his pipe to allow room for more, before resuming. 'He would speak often of his love, whom he clung to as a source of strength.' He added more shreds of the nutty, brown tobacco to the cherrywood bowl, bushing it down with his thumb with meticulous attention, to level it. 'In the end, when he succumbed, I found a note in which he bequeathed me his cherished pipe.'

Having finished preparing the tobacco, he turned once more to his pocket, seeking his matchbox. Placing the pipe between his lips, he struck the match, which flared up with a familiar, searing sound. He then lit the tobacco, cupping the bowl within his thick hand, savouring the heat and taking several deliberate puffs. His extended draws, as he maintained the flame to the tobacco, indicated its freshness. The rhythmic, slow 'pop, pop, pop' of his mouth was accompanied by deep breaths audible through his rounded nose.

As the pipe came to life, he leaned back in his chair, holding Rosamund aloft, as he continued. 'I was profoundly touched, and now, as I smoke her, I think of him.' Parched from the draws, he raised his ale to moisten his lips, his beard cushioning the glass, as he tasted the union of flavours, the bitter tang taste with the smoky notes.

He placed the tip of the arched stem at the corner of his mouth and sounded a 'puck, puck,' the white smoke merging with the haze that wisped around him. 'I pondered long and hard upon what to name this pipe,' he continued, as he performed two more pops.

'Eventually, I settled upon Rosamund, in honour of my friend and the love that brought him solace.' He paused in quiet contemplation, then with the tip still at the edge of his lips, he said in his gruff voice, 'I hoped, too, that this name might offer me some measure of strength for my own trials, left as I was amidst the remnants of war.'

The tobacco burning softly wafted its smoke in a mixture of toast and a rich, roasted aroma, which combined with the subtle woody, nutty scent released by the cherrywood pipe.

Emboldened by his companion's tale, Augustus ventured to recount his own. 'I comprehend the need for solace, an anchor to which you may cling,' he began, pausing as if weighing the wisdom of revealing his inner thoughts. The smoke curled languidly through the air, drifting in clouds. He resumed, 'I often thought of home, yet more particularly, there was a singular vision to which I returned again and again.'

He gazed at his friend, who calmly held his pipe at the corner of his mouth with open acceptance. Reassured, he continued, relating his vision. 'It is always summer, and I am in a field of wildflowers, at the zenith of the season when the vivid blue of the cornflowers, nigella and scarlet poppies, with their grand and bold petals, are in their fullest splendour. A young lady that I once knew is bending as she plucks these flowers, her glossy chestnut tresses shine beneath the brilliance and scorching heat of the sun. I approach her, and she straightens, looking towards me with her laughing eyes, which are the hue of forget-me-nots. Tall yellowing grasses brush against her waist and she has a light blue lutestring gown, which clings to the grass as she moves to approach me. She extends her hands, presenting the wild flora, and that is all.'

He halted, overcome by the vividness of the images before him. His friend considered Augustus, and made a 'puck, puck'.

Augustus continued, 'I knew most likely she would not be mine, but at least, each night, envisioning her was a guarantee of solace. Wherever I might find myself, and regardless if I were mired in mud, or blood, in a quiet moment, I could always recall the same vivid colours of those flowers and her countenance. Indeed, at least upon closing my eyes, I might immerse myself in this vision, if but for a fleeting moment of human feeling, a respite from the harshness of the day, and the descent back to hell. Perhaps I was mad?'

The doctor slowly withdrew his pipe, gestured towards Augustus and replied, 'It is the mark of a true leader, to retain that bit of humanity each day and yet still face your enemy in the morning alongside your men, rather than losing your mind and dignity to this war.' He paused, reflecting upon his friend's words.

'And how do you fare now?' the old man enquired. It was a simple question, though almost elusive, unanswerable, but he would try to coax his young friend, if only to begin the process of healing for them both.

Augustus took a sip from his own honey-coloured ale, allowing the complexity of the malty notes to run over his palate. 'I am alive, when yesterday I was not. That is something. Though I cannot speak of what we endured.'

'Ah,' replied the sage physician. 'But it is important to reflect, for therein lies the path where you can heal, grieve and liberate your mind. On the ground, our focus was upon survival, with little time to reflect, no time to grieve. Now, we are granted the rare luxury which many others have been denied.' He gazed into the crackling fire, which was dying, and continued. 'We must, as you say, preserve those pursuits which grant us true freedom and that includes the liberation of our minds.'

He took a measured sip from his own ale. 'Yet,' he resumed, 'the cider tax has crept up in the aftermath. The war must be funded somehow, it seems. But why must they intrude so deeply into people's very homes – taxed for making cider from ones' own apples? Another infringement of freedom, even amidst peace. No wonder people are rioting.'

By this time, the doctor's pipe had smouldered its last ember, as if he had filled it with their shared troubles and puffed them into the air, affording Augustus a brief respite with his friend.

'Let us, then, take to this place each week, and here we shall grant each memory its due reverence. To converse, drink, and to share in laughter – these are among the finest remedies. And perhaps, one day, when you too have grown a beard, you too may find joy in sharing a pipe with me, and we may rest here as two old men in our dotage,' the aged doctor chuckled merrily.

CHAPTER 21 – REVELATION

The Thornbury Residence, London, Isabella Thornbury

My mother, Lady Ingram, Mr Thornbury and I were engaged in our morning repast some days after the ball, when a footman, clad in purple and gold livery arrived to deliver an invitation.

The February sun once more graced the tranquil scene with its gentle rays. Lady Ingram was in the midst of pouring rich, warm cream chocolate into a Famille Rose cup, and as she did so, I was greeted by its sweet aroma rising to my senses. Since her recent triumphs, I perceived that she had afforded herself many indulgences, and thus her hands were slightly less slender than in the summer, and the furrows of care seemed to have softened from her once-lined visage, so that she appeared more youthful than her five-and-sixty years.

As my mother received the embossed invitation, adorned with the red wax seal bearing the Earl of Cheltenham's crest, she appeared somewhat confounded by its unexpected arrival. In the two decades that we have been neighbours, not once have we received correspondence from the earl or countess, nor a greeting during Sunday service.

'It is an invitation to take tea with Lady Cheltenham this afternoon, should we be at leisure,' said my mother with mild astonishment, as she turned over the card to discern if there might be further elucidation as to why this request had arrived so unexpectedly.

Lady Cheltenham was a rather pale and elusive figure in all our imaginations, seemingly under the earl's sway, his commanding character taking precedence.

However, Lady Ingram appeared to discern the matter and remarked, astutely, 'The earl evidently observed Isabella's success at the ball, and now seeks to form a connection. It is scarcely surprising given the numerous hopeful suitors calling ever since.'

She sipped her chocolate, and as she set the cup back upon its saucer with a soft tinkle, her countenance grew even gentler. 'It is indeed a great distinction. Yet, I would not allow your head to be turned to Gussi, for it should not be taken as a sign that the earl will permit his eldest son to cast his gaze in your direction.' She wagged a playful finger towards me, giving a significant look, accompanied by a subtle smile. 'In any event, you must focus on Winterbourne.'

I gave a soft smile in return. I required no advice on that front and I sighed, as I had done countless times before, reflecting on my dances with Winterbourne. If I closed my eyes, I could feel my hand in his warm grasp, as he guided me to the floor, moving with a fluid grace and strength. As we turned briefly, we would then meet once more, face to face, our eyes lighting on each other in a tender and unspoken exchange.

'Isabella, do you concur?' asked my mother, dispelling any indulgent thoughts from my mind.

'Indeed,' I replied, surmising that my mother must be referring to the visit to the Cheltenham's. Yet, I would much rather indulge in sweet thoughts and await another call from Winterbourne. What if I were to miss him? I weighed up whether it was customary for dukes to make their visits weekly, or more frequently. He had called only once, on the day following the ball, and not since then. However, it had only been a few days and Lady Ingram appeared unfazed. The dowager would be the first to discern and inform us were anything amiss.

Amiss... Why had Cheltenham suddenly taken such an interest? I mused, as we continued with our breakfast repast. Mother and Lady Ingram continued to chatter, yet I allowed their voices to recede into the background.

Was Cheltenham searching for the book, too? I could only presume that someone must be searching for it. The notion seemed all too plausible, and the unease which had been lingering began gnawing and weighing once more heavily upon my conscience.

The thought of having kept the book was becoming increasingly unsettling. Perhaps I should find a way of disposing of it after all – burn it. Yes, I should have burnt it that day. Why had I not insisted!? How mortifying it would be if Winterbourne were ever to discover that I had it in my possession.

I bit the side of my thumb in anxiety, tearing the skin at the corner, causing a tiny cut where blood appeared. The metallic, iron taste touched my tongue and I let it go. I wrapped my thumb in my napkin under the table, twisting the white cloth around my digit until it became tight.

Breathing deeply, I feigned interest in the ladies' conversation, all the while preoccupied with my reflections and comprehending none of their words. The cold tendrils of anxiety crept through my limbs, chilling me. The clink of Lady Ingram's cup startled me, so frayed were my nerves, so agitated had I become.

Perhaps I had better contrive an excuse to avoid the visit to Lady Cheltenham. I left my chocolate untouched, so tight was the grip within my stomach and my throat felt somewhat dry and constricted.

I swallowed, then burst out, unable to restrain myself, 'May I be excused from visiting Lady Cheltenham this afternoon, Mother?'

Both ladies abruptly paused from their chatter and regarded me with inquisitive looks. Following a brief silence, my mother, her cup halted midway to her lips, responded, 'Why, yes, of course... though I fail to see –'

She was cut off abruptly by Lady Ingram. 'Indeed, what reason could you have to decline?'

Caught off guard by the suddenness of my own outburst, I faltered, not having prepared a convincing response. 'I... I...' I began.

'Nonsense,' Lady Ingram resumed in her brisk manner. 'Do not suppose that marrying Winterbourne will absolve you from the necessity of forging social connections.' Her emphasis was on the word 'absolve'. She shook her head, 'Quite the contrary. Your associations with the Cheltenhams and others of similar consequence will likely extend. His Grace will no doubt expect it.'

She affirmed this as she reached for the toasted brioche and took a bite, chewing rapidly, as she fixed her eyes upon me with great intensity. After a dry swallow, she continued, 'No, no, you shall not sit this one out. It is far too important.' She shook her head again, until her white pomaded hair, piled high, bobbed, before leaning over to take another bite of the brioche.

As strange as it may appear, I had not considered the social obligations that would follow marriage. My heady thoughts had wholly been consumed with Winterbourne.

I drew a deep breath, slightly shuddering as I exhaled slowly, and gazed down at the napkin, which bound my thumb, resting upon my lap. I had not foreseen this. The noose would only get tighter with the damning, incriminating book in my possession. Heloise and I surely must take action, and fast. But how?

I paced my chamber rapidly, with great agitation, my gown swishing with each turn as I awaited Heloise's return from her morning errand. I had left a message with the housekeeper, Mrs Mills, instructing that Heloise should come directly to me upon her return. The fire had died in the hearth and had not been rekindled, for I rarely return to my bedchamber after breakfast. However, a private space was necessary for our discussion.

The barren winter trees outside the window etched harsh, jagged silhouettes against the pale grey sky. Thin dark lines, as though scored by hundreds of claws, scraping against the window. The chamber itself was cold as bone, with the chill seeping through the cracks and crevices of the window casements. As I waited impatiently for Heloise, I had time to expand upon my thoughts.

I took up the book as I paced, feeling the soft leather texture of the cover, grasping it, kneading it with my fingers. I clenched it hard, almost as if doing so would break it, but it simply caused stress on my tendons and fingers. On my hand the whiteness of my skin was evident, except for the corners of my thumbs, which were raw. To my shame, I had now bitten upon the other thumb, having pressed it with force against the flatness of my teeth as I pondered. I had been unconscious of the small bites and before long, almost without my notice, I had torn the skin.

Heloise and I had resolved that we should at least bring Thomas Fairfax to Mrs Stoughton's attention at the next literary circle. However, this decision alone brought me considerable anxiety.

Although Fairfax's visit to Cheltenham was not necessarily definitively linked to the book, Cheltenham's sudden invitation did indeed appear to be highly suspicious, especially in its timing. I had seen Cheltenham at the ball. That was the crux – the timing – the long-awaited indication that perhaps pursuers were closing in. My only protection, truly, was to stay quiet, or destroy the book. The question was, could I let it lie?

I perused some of the pages, looking for Cheltenham's name with increasing urgency. It appeared several times in lists, presumably of council meeting attendees, and then I came upon this entry:

Cheltenham will bring his maid, one Martha Wood, to join the revelries as a regular. She will be as the other nuns, including associates of Fairfax.

Hastily, I flicked through the pages and saw more references to Cheltenham, this time in connection with the East India Company. It was evident he harboured some obsession with the matter, manipulating the government to the Company's advantage – and to his own. Mary's acerbic retort, 'You know not what you may provoke,' resonated with unsettling clarity.

The door creaked, and as I saw it move, I started; so agitated were my nerves. Heloise appeared in the doorway, gently closing it with a click before walking slowly and silently towards me.

The carriage clattered in the slush of the melted snow beneath the steely grey sky, as it conveyed us to Cheltenham's residence. I had shown Heloise the passage concerning Martha, and upon reflection, we were of one mind that it was too perilous to leave the book unattended. From hence forth, I would conceal it within my panniers or pockets. Heloise would glean what she could from the servants below, whilst I took tea with Lady Cheltenham upstairs. Despite its small size, the book felt heavy within my right pocket, and I was acutely aware of its presence.

As we alighted from the carriage, the cold air struck our faces, and I drew my cloak tightly around me. I dreaded, and yet knew, that Heloise in mere moments would be separated from us, and I felt as though I were venturing into a baptism of fire.

We were received by Lady Cheltenham in her drawing room shortly after Heloise had been whisked away. The room was grand and imposing, as one might conceive of a formal room with proportions resembling those of a palace, none of which conveyed any warmth of feeling. The countess was a pale wisp, a mere shadow, her voice soft and fragile, lacking any substance at all. Even her silk gown was a very faint pale ash-grey, and it seemed as though any ember of life had been stamped out of her long ago.

We were arranged formally around a circular table, whilst the countess reclined languidly upon a long cream sofa, drawn up beside it. There was little social chatter, until Lady Cheltenham turned to her maid, who stood awaiting instructions and almost in a whisper said, 'Martha, would you be so kind as to bring the tea?'

I became suddenly alert. My eyes struck Martha, and I looked at her intensely. This was she. Members are everywhere, moving amongst us, their identities concealed and only disclosed within the book. I studied her carefully. She was a young girl, with light hair and a plain face, plain and neat gown – unremarkable. She could pass as a maid within any establishment, and yet apparently, she was a member of Dashwood's Medmenham Abbey. My eyes narrowed and traced her until she left the room.

'My husband proposed to me that we should be acquainted, but unfortunately he is currently occupied with business, and so you see, he has left me to receive you,' said Lady Cheltenham, almost indolently. 'Miss Thornbury, my husband informs me that you made quite a mark during the Harringshire ball.' She was barely looking at me, but rather her eyes drifted around the room.

It was quite disconcerting and I was uncertain how to respond. However, the trusty dowager never failed. 'Indeed, this is Isabella's first season, but she has been most honoured to be amongst those noted,' she said, enlivened and with vigour. 'The gown Isabella wore is made of the finest silks sent from India by Sir Nicholas, and the design is most distinct.'

'Indeed,' came Lady Cheltenham's sigh, and she did not press the subject. Turning to Lady Thornbury she said, 'Lord Cheltenham tells me that your husband is much engaged with the East India Company and was but recently knighted on account of his associations.'

'Yes, he is indeed associated with the Company,' came my mother's reply, 'Though we hope that he will leave his vocation very soon, for the situation where he is located intensifies and he grows uncomfortable with the dealings.'

'Indeed,' sighed Lady Cheltenham once more, 'Lord Cheltenham never allows himself to be uncomfortable. He simply ensures things are bent to his will.' She gazed into the distance, almost as though she herself had experienced this, and was left resigned to the fact.

Shortly after some inconsequential chatter, for I really had started to wonder why we were here – evidently, our host did not appear enthused to receive us – Martha appeared with the tea. As she walked slowly across the room, I was acutely aware of her movements. I could sense her standing just inches away beside me, holding the china teapot, before carefully placing it before me. She did the same with the small white china milk jug. It seemed almost incredible that she could be inches from me, and yet also inches away from the book which revealed her membership.

I glanced up at her countenance, which revealed no expression, and then over to Lady Cheltenham, who was still reclined in a most languid position, ethereal, grey, silent. Was she aware of her husband's dealings and did she even hold any concern? Possibly she was simply a tool to facilitate them. I felt the book within my pannier. I placed my hand where it rested, visualising it in my mind, reassuring myself it was still there.

'Pray, pour the tea, Martha,' came Lady Cheltenham's ethereal voice. She was, it appeared, lacking the energy to do so herself.

Martha picked up the teapot. From my proximity, I could see the strain on her small cream hand as she grasped it and poured the amber liquid, steadily, slowly, trickling, into each of our cups. I tensed, and could not look at or acknowledge her, rather focused on her hands. She paused each time to lift the tea strainer from one cup and place it on the next. Finally, she set the pot back on the table and, with a silent curtsey, to my relief, she left us.

I realised that I had to release my breath, for I had seemingly held it the entire time. I focused on the teacup before me, the steam rising from the liquid. The once inviting delicacy, now marred, it lay tainted and unpalatable; I could not bring myself to consume it. The nondescript chatter continued as I allowed it to wash over me.

Then, the door to the drawing room opened once more. I wondered instantly who it could be. The maid? Lord Cheltenham? I held my breath again, anticipating either. Perhaps Lord Cheltenham would have been the worst to encounter and yet, it was most likely.

Instead, there stood Augustus. He was most dashing, dressed in a smart but not overly snug coat of deep blue, with embossed gold trim. He strode over with self-assurance towards us and bowed with a pleasant, relaxed smile. 'Ladies, it is such a pleasure to see you all.' He seated himself next to Lady Cheltenham, who adjusted her posture, sitting more upright to allow him space.

'How are you all? Lady Ingram, Lady Thornbury, Isabella? I truly am most delighted to see you,' came his warm voice. It was such a contrast to the atmosphere moments earlier, that the entire company could not help but be enlivened.

'We are well, thank you, Gussi,' came my mother's tinkling, laughing voice. 'And we are most pleased to see you in good health. We have missed you at the recent events.'

'Well, I have otherwise been engaged,' said Augustus, running his fingers unconsciously across his nostrils. 'But I hope to attend many more events during the season.' He paused, and then to affirm it, added, 'I hope very much indeed,' and he gazed over at me with a most curious expression, his eyes bright.

I was grateful for the warmth and cheer he had brought to our little gathering. It almost made me forget the book. And yet, it could not entirely leave my thoughts. It puzzled me greatly that Augustus should be mentioned, his character seeming so incongruous to it at this moment. Yet, if one were to judge the maid, one would not suspect her either. Clearly, not all are as they appear to be.

Suddenly, the door opened once more, and Heloise entered the room. 'Heloise,' said my mother, quite surprised, for it was very unlike her to disturb a party whilst visiting. 'Is everything alright?'

'Yes, my lady, however, might I have a word with Miss Thornbury?' she asked. I could not discern the expression on her countenance.

I was naturally most curious. However, was this not something that could wait until our nightly collations? I wondered, whether it was truly urgent. Nevertheless, I rose and excused myself, following Heloise into the entrance hallway, closing the door behind us.

I then trailed her silently down a darkened passage. There was no one else about, but she looked around cautiously, leading me to the far end to ensure our privacy away from any who might use the stairs.

'What is it, Heloise?' I asked, now in quite some suspense.

'I have discovered a great deal,' she replied in a serious tone. She glanced about again, before lowering her voice further. 'Martha told me all she knows.'

I gasped, 'How did you? We do not know whether we can trust her – will she not inform –'

'Shhh...' Heloise reminded me to lower my voice and continued, 'No, no, we can trust her, I assure you.' She glanced around once more. 'Martha is not at the club by choice. If she does not attend, she will lose her position, without a reference. You are aware this could mean destitution if she cannot find another position.'

I could not form a response as the matter began to fall into order.

'She informed me that it is a private society established by Sir Francis Dashwood, very exclusive and designed to allow members to revel in ways they would not openly in public view.' Heloise paused, allowing me to absorb the information. 'For Dashwood, it is chiefly theatrics and a measure of drinking – they have a banqueting hall and such – but others take things further.'

I nodded again. 'And what of Cheltenham?'

'Cheltenham,' continued Heloise, initially forgetting to lower her voice, then adjusting it back to a whisper, 'Cheltenham, is there for political and business connections, primarily to maintain influence in Parliament. He nearly has Bute in his pocket, but not quite. His motivation is to ensure his interests in the East India Company are fully supported by Parliament. That is evidently where his interest in you lies, not to mention your success at the ball.'

I felt somewhat deflated at this, yet also relieved. 'So that is why we are here?'

'Not entirely.'

'Why then?'

'Augustus,' Heloise replied.

'Augustus?' I exclaimed.

'Lower your voice,' Heloise urged. 'Yes, Augustus.' She continued, 'Martha witnessed the most shocking duel only last night between Augustus and Winterbourne.'

I gasped again, scarcely believing what I heard. 'Winterbourne was there?'

'Yes, Winterbourne. Martha provided the full account as to what sparked the duel.'

I was stunned by this revelation. Winterbourne had not even been mentioned in the book. Was there truly no one exempt?

'Augustus was also compelled by his father to attend,' Heloise added. 'But Martha believes that after his escapade, it is likely he will not attend again. He had a fire in his eyes such that she had never seen before. He was dangerous and emboldened.'

This was in complete contrast to what I had expected; it was as if my eyes had been opened to a new reality.

I repeated, 'Augustus? Winterbourne? Augustus?' as though trying to grasp the reality.

'Martha tells me that Winterbourne – prepare yourself for this,' Heloise whispered, casting a glance at me. I nodded, indicating that I was braced for any revelation. Heloise then recounted the wager between Winterbourne and the Duke of Harringshire, detailing Winterbourne's boast of pursuing me for my fortune and his intention to persist in his libertine ways even after our marriage.

This was indeed a great deal to absorb. All I thought I knew of Winterbourne had come crashing down. We had all been deceived. None of it had been genuine.

After the initial shock, I felt my eyes prickle slightly and there was a sharp sensation in my nose. There in the darkened passage, Heloise allowed the silence to fill the space. After a brief period she said, 'We have been quite some time, and the party will be wondering where you are. Here,' she handed me her light kerchief. 'I thought you should know now, since you are sitting with Augustus. He is a valiant gentleman. He defended your honour. I do not think Winterbourne will continue to pursue you,' she said this quietly, allowing the words to linger.

I nodded, though I could not speak. I dabbed my eyes, for tears had started from them. My chest heaved, and I shuddered as I fought to control a sob, which threatened to escape. I took in a breath and then exhaled slowly.

'You are right. I shall have to return to them,' I said. I felt a remaining tear cling to the lashes of my right eye as I closed both of them to prepare myself.

Heloise held me firmly by my shoulders as if to give me strength and we faced each other, sharing a moment of understanding. Then she took the kerchief from my grasp, and applied one last gentle dab at my eyes, as I whispered, 'Thank you,' before I turned back down the long, dark passageway.

I took another deep breath before I grasped the brass door handle to the drawing room. Cold as the metal was, I allowed my hand to rest there for a moment, as I composed myself further. Then I turned the handle and swiftly entered, brightly as though nothing had happened, placing myself back in my seat, as I joined the party.

Despite my absence, the conversation appeared not to have moved much further, and no one commented on my disappearance.

Martha entered again, with a fresh pot of tea. She walked over to me, standing again inches away. This time, as she poured the amber liquid into my cup, I gazed up at her and into her countenance, studying her delicate features. I felt a true compassion now for this maid, ensnared as she was. What alternative fate did she have? I glanced out of the window and into the grey, wet, cold streets of London. It was barely a choice. My head swirled, and as I regarded Lady Cheltenham, languid on her sofa, I wondered if she knew.

What would become of this family if the truth were to be revealed? What about Augustus? If he defended me, I am sure, now knowing his character, that he could do something similar for her, though I doubted his power to persuade his father. Was there anything that I could do for this poor soul, clearly living in a nightmare? Indeed, I reflected for the second time that day, those around us are not as they appear to be.

As Martha set the teapot down upon the table once more, I took up the cup and, bringing it to my lips, I said cordially, 'Thank you, Martha.' She curtsied and was gone.

I now found myself irresistibly drawn to glance at Augustus. It was as though after the stretch of seven long years, I now beheld him in his truest light for the first time. However, Augustus also looked over at me, sensing something was different as my eyes met his. I felt a slight flutter. In that fleeting exchange, something unspoken yet deeply felt passed between us, illuminating a tender bond that had always been there, hidden beneath the surface. What was more, he had defended me against Winterbourne, though he had not, and likely would not, reveal his actions to me. At least now I knew.

As we made our way home in the carriage, jostling along the uneven cobbles, I gazed out at the grey, sombre sky, my face turned from my companions, in case they discerned the tumult of my emotions. It was evident now that Winterbourne was not the man he had presented himself to be. That was clear. I had been foolish, swept up by his allure. He had not truly felt for me. It had all been an illusion, contrived for his own purposes.

I closed my eyes and again felt the fleeting warmth of his hand as it clasped mine. It was not real; it was but a mere fabrication. It was what he wanted me to feel, for his own ends.

Biting my lip, my thoughts wandered to our moments in the chocolate house. A part of me had been flattered, yielding to temptation. I recalled his words, spoken in his rich, velvet voice. The memory now filled me with excruciating humiliation, which then led to a surge of anger as I clenched my fists tightly, though conscious not to draw the others' attention. I forced myself to breathe deeply, striving to set aside the painful and mortifying feelings that overwhelmed me in that moment.

Turning my thoughts to Augustus, the book had been at odds with all that had been known of him – those carefree days spent playing amidst the wildflower fields, and in the orchard. Then he had gone away and had not returned.

That was, until now, and in a very different setting. Evidently, he had changed into a distinguished and dashing young lieutenant colonel. Yet, I could still discern traces of his former self. How could I have imagined he might be involved in such a society? It was the very antithesis of his true character.

The carriage jostled on, splashing through the slushy, grey London streets, when I felt a tentative hand gently rest over mine. It was Heloise's. I did not turn but kept my gaze fixed on the street outside the window, yet the warmth of her presence was a comfort. I could feel her there and I was grateful.

CHAPTER 22 – ALL IS FAIR IN LOVE AND WAR

'Ladies, do lend me your ears, for I have the most thrilling news to impart!' exclaimed Mrs Stoughton, exuding her effervescent spirit, as she stood in her drawing room, where the literary club was seated in their customary circle. Her eyes had a spark of excitement as she brandished a modestly bound, off-white periodical, its plain cover belying the marvels she professed lay within. Mrs Stoughton's energy contributed to the rising warmth provided by the fire which blazed high on the hearth.

'Miss Thornbury, your presence at the Harringshire ball caused quite a sensation. *The Gentleman's Magazine* has included a most remarkable account of you and the exquisite silk gowns, spanning two full pages.' As she said this, Mrs Stoughton waved the magazine dramatically before presenting the pertinent pages to the seated Isabella. 'There is even an illustration of you exhibiting your gown.' This caused Lady Ingram to lean in eagerly, peering over Isabella's shoulder.

Mrs Stoughton was almost singing with excitement, 'Indeed, what will surely set all hearts aflutter, is the mention of a certain duke. Do read for yourself!' She jabbed at the relevant text on the page. 'Imagine! With such splendid publicity, the entirety of London will undoubtedly anticipate your imminent engagement. Oh, my dear, I could wish nothing more for you. Indeed, were I still in my bloom, I dare say I might have found myself taken with him as well.'

So intense was her passion that she opened a drawer in a dresser and retrieved a fan. It was evident that the news had thoroughly warmed her, as her rosy cheeks glowed. She fanned herself vigorously, although to Isabella it was as though she were fanning the flames.

In contrast. Isabella turned cold as her heart sank. As she read the article, her eyes came to rest on the following:

There is considerable speculation and many whispers circulating within the circles of London society, suggesting that a proposal from the esteemed Duke of Winterbourne to the lady featured in this article is anticipated imminently.

There it was, in writing, for the consumption of not only London, but all of Britain, so extensive was the periodical's readership.

The journalist had long since left her mind, with all the possibilities and allure of the capital utterly dispelled, yet society's expectations of her remained unchanged, as though nothing had altered. She had mourned the loss of the very concept of Winterbourne or any other charming gentleman. However, the article served as kindling to the flames, the publicity searing when combined with her humiliation, to make it all the more painful. She could only hope that with time, this would all abate.

With quiet resolve, she remained composed, determined not to betray her feelings to the group. In the recesses of her mind, she also remembered her duty concerning Fairfax.

Lady Ingram had swiftly taken the fallen periodical from Isabella's lax hands and was hungrily devouring its contents. Meanwhile, the other ladies were engaged in an animated discussion about the article. To Isabella's relief, the conversation soon shifted to the Wilkes.

'My husband and I were not in attendance at the ball,' Mrs Wilkes explained, 'for there were some amongst the number, who are highly influential, and who Mr Wilkes has displeased most severely.'

'Indeed, I have heard that he is at odds with Lord Bute,' replied my mother.

'Indeed,' confirmed Mrs Wilkes, 'my husband has been attempting to expose the Prime Minister in his periodical, *The North Briton*. The charges are grave. You must have heard: bribery, nepotism, placing favourites in all areas of government, and undue influence over the King, all for personal gain. It is corruption at the highest level, but essentially our institutions enable it.'

'This is troubling,' replied my mother, her tone growing serious. 'What can be done about it?'

'I have heard enough,' Lady Margaret interjected, to everyone's surprise. Though generally conservative, she was now resolute. 'I have been endlessly discussing this for nearly a year now. We should not remain passive; the matter is too grave. We are close to and at times even witness the malfeasance, yet we could assist in exposing it.'

'Well, we would certainly require more evidence than speculation,' replied Mrs Wilkes.

Lady Margaret leaned in slightly, lowering her tone. 'I have observed it firsthand at the palace. As I intimated earlier, not to put too fine a point on it, Lord Bute engages in frequent and clandestine assignations with the Dowager Princess of Wales. I am not mistaken, and Fairfax is undoubtably complicit. I witnessed it myself just last evening.'

'Might I comprehend,' said Lady Thornbury gravely, 'that you are implying another example of Bute's undue influence upon the young monarch? I must agree, no single individual should possess such an undue concentration of power. Was this not resolved in the aftermath of our civil war?'

'Yes, but when one is in comfort, such dangers are all too easily disregarded. This insidiousness arises when one believes the past cannot repeat itself – that the nation has progressed. Yet, it is precisely this complacency that allows such behaviour to slip through unnoticed,' said Mrs Wilkes. 'Quite so, and even if we are aware, we convince ourselves that it is of no consequence to our everyday existence,' Lady Margaret rejoined with vehemence.

'Oh, but it does affect the people,' retorted Mrs Stoughton, who had joined the conversation after fanning herself to gain composure. 'Have you not heard? There are riots over that cursed cider tax. There has been word from my maid's relatives that unrest is spreading like wildfire in Exeter.

Mrs Wilkes asserted, her tone sharpening, 'My husband and I are steadfast in our belief that the only remedy is to enlighten the public through the press. If the populace remains uninformed, how could they ever hope to defend their liberties?'

'Indeed, we must deliberate on what action we might take,' said Lady Margaret.

'I doubt we will accomplish anything at all,' were Mrs Wilkes' private thoughts.

Carter, the footman, whom Isabella now recognised as Mr Thomas Fairfax, entered bearing the wine and refreshments.

Isabella tensed, realising she would need to broach the matter of Fairfax with Mrs Stoughton. It would be unjust to leave her in ignorance, especially given that this man, whatever his motives, resided in her house with access to, well, frankly everything of hers. But what if she had been mistaken?

She studied Carter as he poured the wine into several crystal glasses, his movements deliberate and almost too precise, as though anticipating Isabella's betrayal. Mrs Stoughton had picked up *Paradise Lost* once more and laid it upon her lap. The book remained there, untouched, its words unread, a silent testament to the pretence of propriety to which they clung, a veil over the indulgence in gossip and wine.

The fire crackled in the hearth, but its warmth did little to dispel the chill that had crept into Isabella's bones. Was it truly guilt, or was it something darker – an unspoken fear that she was teetering on the edge of danger, something which could not be undone once spoken aloud? The question lingered in the air, unvoiced yet laden with weight, and Isabella's gaze returned to Carter as he turned and left the room.

She felt a need to relieve the tension from within her, and whilst the rest of the company continued their discussion, now was as good a time as any to talk with Mrs Stoughton. Lady Ingram was still absorbed in *The Gentleman's Magazine*, and no doubt nurturing dreams for her young charge; dreams that would now never come to pass.

'Mrs Stoughton,' Isabella began, 'I find myself compelled to confide a matter pertaining to your footman, of which I believe you should be aware.'

'Oh, and what might that be, my dear? Are you in search of a footman yourself? Perhaps you have designs upon Carter for when you establish your own household with a certain gentleman?' she replied melodiously, with a wink to Lady Thornbury.

Isabella then endeavoured to recount clearly the peculiar conversation she had held with Fairfax by the piano-forte during the previous literary circle. Additionally, she revealed his clandestine visit to the Earl of Cheltenham.

'Am I to understand correctly? My footman?' said the astonished Mrs Stoughton, 'You are not in earnest.'

'I assure you, I am entirely serious,' Isabella replied.

After some effort persuading Mrs Stoughton, the vivacious matron concluded, 'Well, if you are absolutely convinced, then I shall ask Carter directly when he returns, but it could be most embarrassing for the party if I accuse him and this comes to nothing.'

The moments preceding Carter's return appeared to elongate and stretch interminably. Isabella felt as though she were a criminal, divulging the transgressions of one who might yet be entirely innocent. To soothe herself, she took a lock of her chestnut hair, and wound it gently around her finger like a snake, the motion a poor solace amid her growing unease. Lady Ingram glanced up at her with a disapproving tut, prompting Isabella to release the coil and straighten her posture.

The door opened smoothly, as Carter brought in the cheese tray.

'Ah, Carter,' said Mrs Stoughton, 'might I have a word?'

'Indeed, yes ma'am,' he replied.

'Pray tell me, are you indeed a footman, or do you merely only profess to be one?' Mrs Stoughton said this with a hint of playful irony, anticipating his answer.

'Ma'am?' he replied, his uncertainty evident, before glancing towards Isabella.

'There has been a rumour that, and I can scarcely believe I am uttering such an accusation,' she directed a significant look towards Isabella, pausing before narrowing her eyes. Then, adjusting her countenance to reengaged Carter, she said, 'Are you the younger brother of Mr Fairfax? Forgive me, Carter, you were seen entering Lord Cheltenham's residence on your own business.'

Before Carter could answer, Lady Ingram burst out a, 'What?!'

Isabella's countenance flushed deep crimson as she shifted uneasily in her seat. Mrs Stoughton's words for the second time that day stung, causing her to wince. This was exceedingly uncomfortable, and she was filled with a sense of treachery. She could not bring herself to look up at Carter.

As she adjusted her position, the rounded edges of the book pressed against her skin through the pocket where she had secured it. She had her own secrets, which she had to resolve and which had lingered far too long. Yet, she could not help but wonder if this were the very same Fairfax entangled in the book, or if this were in fact his brother. However, she hoped the answer lay in the identity of the man who stood before them now.

A profound silence seemed to settle over the room, as the party's attention became wholly fixed in anticipation of what might unfold.

Carter delicately set the tray upon the table before them and cleared his throat.

'Ma'am,' he began, his voice slightly wavering, 'I am Mr Thomas Fairfax, the most unfortunate younger brother of Mr Fairfax and Miss Thornbury's account is, regrettably, true. I did meet with the Earl of Cheltenham recently. However, I assure you, it was not with any nefarious intent. I was compelled to sell my horse. I cannot afford to retain him, and the earl is the sole acquaintance remaining who will deign to converse with me, if only in pursuit of a favourable arrangement.' He seemed to falter and swallowed. 'I was compelled to part with him, for I possess naught else. He was my sole asset, the only means by which I could afford a lawyer to investigate my case.'

The ladies exchanged bewildered glances. Isabella, however, squirmed. This was most dreadful. Fairfax's voice faltered once more, and he stopped to collect himself, his figure now less upright, his countenance despondent, as he lowered his gaze.

'As I informed Isabella, I had held a life estate whilst my father lived, and on his recent passing, it was expected that my brother would provide for me by granting me an estate in Surrey, thus ensuring an income. Unfortunately, without explanation, I found myself barred from admittance. I was left to satisfy my creditors with what remained in my bank account.

Consequently, I was forced to find another way of life. I had hoped that serving as a footman might afford me access to society, enabling me to further investigate my circumstances. In my former life, I had not frequented society to any great extent, preferring to stay ensconced in the country. To my mortification, I resorted to writing my own reference, using my own seal to attest to my service within the Fairfax household. That is all, and I have regrettably made no further progress in uncovering the truth.'

With that, unprompted, he found a nearby vacant chair and sank into it, his hands covering his face. He was utterly spent; the weight of his narrative having drained him completely.

Isabella struggled to restrain herself from fleeing the room. How mortifying it was. However, as she finally forced herself to look upon the broken man, she felt such a deep compassion that she set aside her own feelings.

'But Carter,' Mrs Stoughton began at last, breaking the silence, her voice so uncharacteristically tempered, 'You must be unaware.' She spoke with deliberate slowness, herself reeling with the shock, preparing to deliver yet another blow to the man before her. 'Your brother staked the Surrey estate in a game of Faro against Cheltenham.'

Mr Thomas Fairfax uncovered his face and regarded Mrs Stoughton, as if this were the first he had heard of this, as though a revelation was unfolding before him, which he never thought would come.

'And he lost. Cheltenham now possesses the estate,' Lady Margaret concluded, understanding that her friend could not.

Fairfax straightened slightly and blinked in disbelief. 'Cheltenham? Cheltenham had my estate in his possession when I visited him to sell my horse? I distinctly conveyed to him the reason for parting with my horse. And yet… he knew.'

The weight of these words fell heavily on every person in the room.

After some moments, Lady Margaret rose from her chair and said, 'If Fairfax has done such a thing to his own brother, then we can assume his character is such that he would act ruthlessly for his own gain. I have always maintained that he is an advocate for Bute. In fact, I had always believed his placement in the palace was due to Bute's influence. Bute has his loyal spies infiltrating and influencing everywhere in the palace and Parliament, including Fairfax.'

'I have even encountered difficulty in securing a reputable barrister to take up my case,' said Thomas

Fairfax, despairingly. 'They are quite aware of my brother's position of power, his connections with Bute.'

'Indeed, all of this, all of this... corruption,' Lady Margaret almost spat the last word of that refrain, and it was as though it were smeared across every surface of the drawing room. 'It is insidious. It has been seeping through society and it is present in our own drawing rooms.'

'Yes, but what are we to do?' said Lady Thornbury.

'We have to find some way of taking action,' said Mrs Wilkes. 'People's lives are being destroyed.' She glanced over sympathetically at Thomas Fairfax.

'That is why I am here,' said Fairfax. 'I have nothing left but to pursue this and take action. My life as I knew it is gone. There is nothing left.' He straightened, as though resolved now. 'Might any of you assist me in securing a position as a footman in Bute's household? I am confident that together we may acquire the evidence we seek.'

It was a most audacious proposal, an almost impossible fight. Though none of them articulated it, each possessed, to varying degrees, an awareness of this. Only those with the strongest of stomachs should meddle with Bute. In such a world, perhaps one needed to fight fire with fire.

'Well, if we were to acquire evidence of the corruption in Parliament, we could give it to my husband to publish,' said Mrs Wilkes.

'He would be a very brave man to do so', said Thomas.

'And so are you,' said Mrs Wilkes.

For the first time, Thomas Fairfax's eyes brightened again, as though he had some semblance of hope in this world, not that his estate would be restored to him, but that there was a possibility of some form of justice.

'How shall we manage to gain Mr Fairfax entry into Bute's residence?' asked Lady Thornbury.

'I shall take care of it,' said Mrs Stoughton with resolve. The fire was within her once more this evening.

CHAPTER 23 – IMPRESSIONS

'Kindly hold it there, Your Ladyship,' said Joshua Reynolds. 'I am most nearly complete.'

The eminent artist was concluding his initial skim of the Prime Minister's wife in her drawing room. Neither had been content with the preliminary arrangement, and numerous alterations to the furniture and poses had been made before they finally settled on this composition.

At that moment, Mrs Stoughton was announced and entered, but not without some difficulties with the door, for the furniture having been hauled towards the corners of the room, had somewhat obstructed its opening.

Once clear, and notwithstanding her rather ungraceful entrance, Mrs Stoughton comported herself and strode in with her usual lively yet commanding presence.

Lady Bute, relieved to be liberated from the tiresome pose, sprang from her seat and exclaimed, 'Mrs Stoughton, what a delightful surprise! To what do I owe this honour?'

Recognising the inevitability of his defeat, Reynolds threw down his pencil in frustration.

'I thought I would call upon you, having been so remiss since your most splendid salon in January,' replied Mrs Stoughton.

'That is no matter,' Lady Bute replied. 'In truth, I have been quite occupied, as you can imagine. Smythe, please would you bring in the tea,' she requested of her maid, who had announced the visitor moments before. Lady Bute then ushered Mrs Stoughton to a seat, which she drew towards a table, before acquiring one for herself. Thus, in a rather disordered manner, their tête-à-tête began.

'You must recount all that you have been engaged in of late,' said Mrs Stoughton.

'Ah, so many engagements and obligations,' Lady Bute responded, with a hint of weariness. 'The wife of a prime minister is ever hosting, so I have discovered.' She had a slight tinge of tiredness about her eyes, no doubt from all the late evenings.

'I can scarcely conceive,' said Mrs Stoughton in a sympathetic tone, 'And of course, you must have increased your household considerably since your husband's appointment, to manage the additional events and such. Indeed, this is your first full London season in your new role.'

'It is indeed wearisome, and yes, we have engaged a few new hands in our service,' said Lady Bute.

'Indeed, one cannot have too much help. I understand the pressure you must be under. I could fully appreciate it during your salon.'

'Oh? How so?' said Lady Bute. 'Was it perceptible? I thought it proceeded quite smoothly.'

'It did indeed, though there were one or two remarks regarding the insufficiency of staff, but I suppose it cannot be helped during the season, when there is such great demand,' Mrs Stoughton said, shaking her head wistfully and allowing these remarks to settle.

Not wishing her comments to appear too critical, as she knew even a nudge would suffice, for her ladyship took great pride in her role as hostess, she quickly added, 'I must say, the performances of Handel were exquisite. You truly surpassed all expectations. You are well aware how greatly I esteem his work.'

Mrs Stoughton glanced around the room, noting Reynolds as he packed away his instruments, then turned her attention to the scene where Lady Bute had been seated for her portrait. She observed with some puzzlement that Lady Bute had been placed beside a harp – an instrument in which she was acutely aware her ladyship was wholly untrained.

Lady Bute, noticing Mrs Stoughton's eyes resting on the harp, said, 'We tried so many accoutrements and none would suffice. At last, we settled upon the harp, of which I am so fond. I suggested it, as it conveys virtue and harmony, and who would not wish to convey such an impression?'

The irony was not lost on Mrs Stoughton, particularly in light of her assignment, yet she chose to let it rest as much as she could manage.

'Indeed,' she replied, almost in a whisper, as if in a bisbigliando, slightly put out by the misuse of her favourite instrument.

The earlier remarks of Mrs Stoughton had evidently unsettled Lady Bute, who returned to them. 'Pray, forgive me, but you mentioned there were remarks made at my salon concerning the insufficiency of staff?'

'Nothing to concern yourself with, I am certain, and I trust you have resolved everything by now in preparation for your ball, in the coming week,' replied Mrs Stoughton, as she smiled to herself.

'Resolved?' Lady Bute echoed, alarmed.

'Yes, I trust you have done everything possible to resolve your staffing issue, as you always do,' said Mrs Stoughton, as Mrs Smythe entered and set down the tea before them.

Lady Bute, beginning to feel somewhat uncomfortable, raised her lace kerchief to her brow, which did very little to ease her mind.

Mrs Stoughton, glancing at her over the rim of her teacup, perceived that she was making progress and seized the moment, exclaiming, 'You look somewhat out of sorts, Lady Bute. Are you quite alright?'

'Yes, yes...' Lady Bute replied, 'quite well...' though her thoughts lingered.

'I know it is almost impossible to find staff in the midst of the season.'

'It is... I wonder how I shall manage?'

'If required, I can certainly assist you, at least initially,' offered Mrs Stoughton. 'I have a most reliable footman, whom I would be happy to lend you, as a favour. I am sure Carter would be delighted to oblige.'

'Yes... yes, I suppose I shall have to engage some additional servants...' Lady Bute's voice trailed off.

'At least for the ball, I suspect,' enforced Mrs Stoughton, taking another sip of her tea. 'Do not look so concerned; it is all taken care of. There is nothing to worry about.'

Lady Bute seemed to snap out of her drifting thoughts. 'Thank you, Mrs Stoughton. I would be most grateful.'

'To be sure, I shall speak to Carter directly upon my return home. I am certain he can join you in the coming days,' said Mrs Stoughton, her objective accomplished. Now it would be up to Mr Thomas Fairfax to see what he could uncover.

CHAPTER 24 – ON TRIAL

'Are you quite well?' enquired Lord Bute. The Prime Minister was in his home study, writing at his bureau with numerous papers scattered across the surface. The room was as one would expect of a Prime Ministerial Earl; heavy furniture of walnut and dark, high-backed Queen Anne-style upholstered chairs. The opulent hue of the leather was rich and glossy brown, with undertones of smouldering crimson, where the light caught the surface, revealing a warm, wine-red depth beneath the polished exterior.

It was all quite as it should be, except that the painting above the hearth depicted a majestic figure draped in ermine and velvet, a figure so regal that one might easily mistake it for a king – which was perhaps the intention. A similar portrait, but of even grander proportions, was displayed in the entrance hall of the residence, capturing a different, but equally regal pose.

'Indeed, Your Lordship, I thank you. I am merely seeking to ensure that your every need is fulfilled,' replied Fairfax.

In fact, the new footman to Lord Bute did not look entirely well. A light sheen had glossed his brow and he could feel the dampness across much of the rest of his form under his thick, well-fitted livery.

Whilst he was required to attend Lord Bute in his study at that moment, Thomas Fairfax felt as though he were an imposter. He sensed the eyes of Lord Bute's portrait bearing down upon him, seeming to break the domain between appearance and reality, but he was unable to escape their witness.

As he moved to place the teacup upon the writing table, he was conscious to make it a smooth transition, and endeavoured to evade the papers strewn. Yet there was a minute shake as the teacup landed upon the green leather writing surface.

Thomas Fairfax's eyes darted across the table. Papers, papers, papers, all likely official and even above board. He would need time to study. Perhaps there were letters which would be significant to their plight. He was so near to the figure of the man who controlled so much and so many, even the King. Then Lord Bute manoeuvred, swiftly pulling the top righthand drawer of his writing table open, removing a leather-bound book and sliding the drawer shut with a jarring snap.

'That will be all, Carter,' ordered Lord Bute. 'I shall ring should I require you,' he said, without glancing up as he perused the scribblings in the book.

'Very well, Your Lordship,' said Fairfax, as he crept with some relief out of the study. It may have been his conscience, however; as he stepped out of the room, the weight of the portrait's watchful eyes remained with him. Their presence, celestial and terrestrial, were everywhere. As Fairfax made his way down the corridor from the study to the entrance hall, he was indeed once more faced with those eyes, the intensity of which ensnared his own and they remained locked, as he self-consciously traversed across the room.

After a week of discreet enterprise within the service of Lord and Lady Bute, Thomas Fairfax had yet to gain a private moment in his target's study. Only the first footman and the butler, being long-standing servants, were permitted there alone.

However, he had become well-acquainted with the layout and routines of the household. He had observed the comings and goings of the staff, noting the timings and patterns that might afford him an opportunity.

One evening, after noting that Lord and Lady Bute had departed for yet another event and that the servants below stairs were resting in the servants' hall after dinner, Fairfax determined that the odds tonight were in his favour.

Therefore, under the pretence of retiring early for the night, he seized his moment. With a cautious glance down the servant's corridor to ensure it was deserted, he ascended the narrow stairs to the ground floor and slipped unnoticed into the corridor leading to Lord Bute's study.

He had no justifiable cause for being there, and he was well aware that even the slightest detection could result in his immediate dismissal. However, he was also a man who had nothing to lose, and it was not only his cause.

He padded slowly down the corridor, as quiet as a badger. He saw the mark's door open a chink. A sliver of light shone from the early March Worm Moon, which in its eminence illuminated the anteroom. He would wait to hear if anyone were within.

He moved carefully up to the door, listening intensely to the growing silence. There was nothing at that moment except for his pulse and breath. To him the mechanics of his heart were audible and he waited for it to lower. Then he listened between breaths, laden with anxiety. As he peered through the crack, the moon glistened off his eyes, which were focused on the threshold to Bute's study. At last, deeming there to be no one, he silently slunk into the anteroom.

Though it was dark, his eyes soon adapted to the moonlight, which cast a fortunate beam. He continued to move silently across the small chamber and up to the study door. He grasped the round brass doorknob and attempted to twist it slowly, to prevent any sound from escaping. It moved a fraction and then halted. He attempted once more, enforcing slightly more pressure, but to no avail; the door was secure. He slowly released the tension on the brass spring, back to its quiescent state.

It was in the ensuing days, as Fairfax continued to adjust to the quiet routine of the household, carefully observing Lord Bute's daily schedule, that the solution came to him. After a week of meticulous strategising, and having despatched a note to Mrs Wilkes to confirm the necessary arrangements, his plan crystallised, and he was ready to fulfil his audacious task.

One afternoon, after placing Lord Bute's teacup in its customary position amongst the scattered papers, and having observed His Lordship now engrossed in writing in his book, Fairfax calculated that the conditions were optimal. He withdrew from the room, allowing Lord Bute a few moments of undisturbed focus.

Then he steeled himself. There was no one else in the darkened corridor outside the anteroom. All was quiet. It was the quiet before the crime. The hush before the execution. He stood upon the threshold, withdrawing an envelope from his livery pocket. The address appeared to have been hastily scrawled with urgent intensity.

Entering the anteroom, he approached the study door. He raised his hand to knock, letting it linger over the oak for a moment too long, as though an invisible force – perhaps his conscience – were balancing a heavy weight, before tipping over irrevocably. He let the pendulum fall. Three firm knocks.

'Enter!' commanded Lord Bute.

Thomas Fairfax forced himself to grasp the doorknob and twist it, the sweat of his palm causing it to slip slightly. The action exerted greater strain than usual on the tendons of his wrist and stress between his knuckles. The door unsealed with a groan, and Fairfax stepped towards Lord Bute. With a bow he presented the missive asserting, 'My Lord, an urgent message has been delivered by express courier.'

Lord Bute was deep in thought, temple in hand, his elbow propped on the bureau. He looked up wearily, as though so accustomed to urgency, that the news raised barely a flicker on his face. Accepting the letter, Bute broke the deep red seal of the House of Fairfax. That was perhaps the first indication of the deception within, incongruous to the urgency. However, this remained undetected by the unsuspecting gentleman as his eyes surveyed the missive.

All at once, Bute sprang up, as if driven by the report of a pistol, exclaiming, 'I must leave at once – instruct Hayward to secure these papers safely!' As he strode out of the room, he muttered, 'Foolish Henry! He will ruin us all,' before cursing under his breath.

A few leaves of parchment fluttered as Bute swept out, leaving Thomas Fairfax alone in the study. Silence descended, but before making any move, Fairfax waited to ensure Bute would not suddenly re-enter the room.

CONSEQUENCE OF POWER

As the sound of footsteps gradually faded down the corridor, he knew he must act swiftly. He began to sift rapidly through the papers with his own urgency, gathering disordered stacks, scanning and scanning. What he sought, he knew not. He read:

The meeting minutes from the previous departmental briefing have been compiled and are now available for review...

No significant deviations from the expected outcomes were noted during the recent audits...

His eyes tore through page after page of innocuous comments, both confusing and seemingly insignificant. Then his orbs were arrested and drawn to Lord Bute's small leather-bound book, open upon the writing table. He scattered the jumbled letters and papers across the emerald leather of the board and picked up the book tentatively. It appeared to be a more personal ledger of reflections.

Fairfax skimmed through it, and though he could not wholly decipher its meaning in those few precious minutes, his instinct conveyed to him that he had stumbled upon something of considerable significance. He could not delay through contemplating further. In the distance, footsteps of hard polished shoes striking stone reached his ears.

In an instant, he flew to the sash window, his fingers fumbling as he unscrewed the catch and prying it open. He quickly dropped the book into the bush below, then slammed the sash shut with a loud roll and shudder. Fairfax then strode out of the study as though with purpose, but in truth nearly blinded by panic. As he rounded the door from the anteroom into the corridor, he almost collided with Mr Hayward, the butler.

'Carter, good heavens! What is the meaning of this?' asked Hayward before he regained his customary calm composure. 'Lord Bute dashed out, exclaiming something about Henry – whom I can only presume to be Mr Fitzwilliam – challenging Sir Francis Dashwood to a duel.'

Fairfax feigned mild surprise.

'I might believe it of Mr Fitzwilliam,' said the puzzled butler, 'but not of Dashwood – surely these are theatrics?' He shook his head in contemplation, then proceeded into the study to place everything in order and secure the papers.

Thomas Fairfax, with some relief, had to restrain himself to ensure he did not appear to depart too hastily from the site of the affair. He would yet have to endure the repercussions of the commotion – the revelation that the letter was a fabrication, and the subsequent, perhaps more horrifying discovery, which might require another day or so: that the book was missing.

He would regrettably be required to remain at his post, until Lord and Lady Bute had found a suitable substitute of their own, before he could return to Mrs Stoughton. He would need to brace himself for suspicion, which would inevitably be cast upon him, even if the evidence were merely circumstantial.

The following morning, sooner than Fairfax had anticipated, the household staff were summoned to the kitchen, where they were informed that Mr Hayward would be conducting a thorough search of each of their sleeping quarters.

However, Thomas Fairfax was ordered directly to Lord Bute's study. This time, there were no papers scattered about; rather, Lord Bute sat in a posture of silent contemplation at his bureau. As Fairfax approached the bench, he felt the eyes of Lord Bute's portrait bearing down upon him once more. He deliberately avoided both pairs of eyes; those of the likeness and those of the earl in the flesh.

Bute launched directly into the interrogation. 'Yesterday, you delivered a missive purportedly from Mr Fairfax. However, it was a sham, a fraud!' Bute emphasised the last few words, before articulating the case. 'It was evidently sent with the intent of calling me away and facilitating the pilfering of papers from my study.'

He paused, observing Fairfax for any sign of reaction. Lacking evidence, Bute continued his line of questioning. 'Who delivered the letter?' His enquiry was served as a latent threat.

'Your Lordship, it was delivered by express courier, or so I believe,' testified Fairfax, with feigned composure and emotion, as he perjured himself in the judgement of the sceptical eyes of the sitter's gaze.

'Hayward asserts that he did not attend the servant's door.'

'I observed the express courier from the window and attended him myself,' came Fairfax's well-rehearsed statement.

'Hmm…' Bute appeared to deliberate. 'Needless to say, I have instructed Mr Hayward to search the sleeping quarters of all the household staff.'

Fairfax brightened within, as it dawned upon him that a special investigator had not been summoned. The Prime Minister was evidently conducting the questioning himself. Fairfax further deduced that he must surely have stumbled upon a most fortunate discovery with regard to the book.

'I am certain you understand, Mr Carter, that suspicion falls upon you. Have you anything to confess?'

'None at all, Your Lordship,' replied Mr Fairfax steadily.

'None, hmm...' The Prime Minister appeared to deliberate further. 'You are aware that the pilfering of confidential information from me constitutes not only common theft, but potentially treason.'

Fairfax remained silent.

'What is the punishment for treason, Carter?' asked the earl, his tone silky.

Once more, Fairfax was unable to find his voice and his throat was dry. Time seemed to stretch interminably. Finally, he croaked, 'Most severe.'

He dared not utter the fatal implications aloud, for fear of manifesting them into reality; yet in his mind, the Sword of Damocles hung suspended directly above his head. The tip pointed down inches from his crown, swinging from a thin, tenuous thread, like a pendulum, which could snap at any moment.

'Most severe,' Lord Bute repeated.

Once again, the silence stretched. Fairfax pondered, with the knowledge that there was no tangible proof. Yet, did the Prime Minister truly require proof to execute punishment?

'You are dismissed from my service. You must understand that I cannot afford to take such a risk,' Lord Bute declared.

Fairfax closed his eyes in relief, hoping it would be interpreted as despair at the loss of his position. He knew he would likely remain under scrutiny, but for the moment, his task was complete. He would return to Mrs Stoughton, where he might stay, at least for the present.

CHAPTER 25 – PANDORA'S BOX

Beneath Medmenham Abbey, Mr Henry Fitzwilliam

'Henry Fitzwilliam, you old rogue,' comes a charismatic voice.

I glance up from my exertions, rolling an oaken wine barrel out of the Buttery, to see the squinting face of John Wilkes. His jaw protruding and animated features, to me at this moment feel jarring and uncanny. I question myself: is it he or is he a figment of my mind?

'I should not be surprised at your antics,' Wilkes continues. 'I keep away for a few months, and upon my return, I hear whispers that you challenged Dashwood to a duel, and Bute of all people had to be summoned to prevent it.'

I have committed sufficient real delinquencies to contend with, without the additional burden of fending off false accusations. Yet, I find myself questioning whether I did in fact commit such an act? Was it during some drunken stupor of which I have no recollection? It frightens me, leaves me on edge. What might I do, unaware?

But most grievous of all is the guilt. Guilt has taken root within me, growing stronger with each passing day. I find no pleasure in anything now. The spirit has been drained from me, like wine from a glass. Every last drop. Now what is left is only guilt, a pulpy sediment, which stains everything. It has become entirely unmanageable and I am at a loss to comprehend how it has come to this.

And yet, there is more that has been let loose to the world. Stories may emerge should that infernal book fall into the wrong hands. It must be contained and if found, confound it – burnt! Perchance to purge, perchance to save me from burning. Le Chevalier – I shall seek out Le Chevalier tonight and discover what progress has been made.

Wilkes' peculiar countenance, with its remarkable elasticity, makes me nauseous. How could Dashwood allow him into our club, to rifle through our caverns, risking all our secrets? A journalist too, even if he is a purported member. Traitor! I know Bute will have him out, if he notes Wilkes' return.

'I have my own little scheme planned for this evening,' says the leering Wilkes to me, his eyes twinkling, one larger than the other. He makes my skin crawl.

'Get thee gone!' is my vicious, acerbic retort to the figment. 'Get thee gone, poisonous spirit.' My retort is not vicious enough, for he laughs to torment me. My head throbs, whilst a knife cuts piercing into my right temple, above the eye.

I endeavour to redirect my attention to the task of rolling my wine barrel. A draught is all I require to steady my nerves, and once I am more settled, I must speak with Le Chevalier.

The barrel rumbles, deep and resonant from its weighted contents, as I continue to roll it over the jagged rocks and rough surface of the abbey's cave.

I leave that spectre, whomever he is, behind in the Buttery and keep rolling the barrel until I can find a nook of my own, a place of solace to gorge. I pass through the darkened tunnels lined with torches on the wall, which blaze to give an intermittent glow as I roll by.

The barrel scrapes along the floor, the iron hoops get caught on the serrated rock, which claws and grates, to a sharp screeching sound, which I cannot bear. I exert myself to push the barrel over a particularly harsh protrusion, when it gives away all of a sudden. There must be a slope, for it gathers momentum and has come away from me, rolling uncontrollably and out of reach.

It disappears into the darkness beyond. Then I hear an almighty eruption, which reverberates up, up, up through the tunnel and into my already on-edge being, the blade piercing deeper into my psyche.

By the time I emerge from the tunnel and arrive at the scene, the aroma of the leathery tannins has already assailed my senses. Yet, the rivers of wine, like blood, flow thick, dark and sinuous over the cavern floor, their stain unrestrained, even clinging to the rough walls of the cave.

The oak has splintered into sharpened stakes, like needles drenched in blood, glinting ominously in the dim torchlight. I slip upon the slick surface and fall onto the wet liquid, the crimson staining my white robes, and I scramble pathetically, desperately, catching the fabric on the rugged ridges, cutting my flailing hands on the sharp teeth of the rocks, my robe now coarsely shredded in places. At last, I succumb and lie still, exhausted not from physical exertion, but from the strain upon my mind. The seepage smears my cheek as I lie there, the points of the rocks pressing into the flesh.

At some moment that evening, I know not when, I manage to raise myself. With a throbbing head, for I have had no sustenance despite the drenching of my robes, I follow some such echoing murmuring which sounds like a gathering.

I reach one of the larger caverns, a hive of activity, and pass through the crowds of my compatriots. Some draw back on impulse and disgust, when they obtain but a fleeting glance of me. I must present a horrifying vision seeped in crimson; a manifestation born of my darkest nightmares. The drenched, now sticky, clinging fabric adheres to me in parts as I move, much as the memories of my past deeds cling to my being, my mind. Perceiving this, others instinctively recoil, fearful of being tainted themselves.

Through my blurred sight I make out the shape of Le Chevalier, leaning casually, as is custom, against the wall in a corner, also observing the scene. As I move towards the dashing figure, wide-brimmed hat cocked with luscious plumage of feathers, there is no flinching from the practitioner. That is, despite the horror I must present and, I suspect, Le Chevalier's reluctance to permit the transfer of stains from my own appalling garments onto immaculate attire.

'Bon soir,' Le Chevalier is the first to speak. 'It has perhaps not gone so well for you, cette soir.'

'Have you any news of the book?' I cut straight to the heart of the matter, given the severity of my requirement, my desperation to save my soul.

'Malheureusement, nothing yet, but I persist,' Le Chevalier replies.

As my eyes widen in intensity, shaking with tension, I impulsively step towards Le Chevalier, as if to grab a crisp white collar of intricate lace. At once, a refined finger is wielded in the air, arresting me. 'Ah, ah, ah, mon ami, I would not advise it in your state,' Le Chevalier reacts delicately.

The power of the gesture from that single raised index finger lies in the psyche; the apprehension and awareness of its master's capabilities. It is this very understanding that has led me to enlist Le Chevalier's aid.

I relent, stepping back to allow a respectful distance. Yet, within me, my emotions writhe like a poisonous snake. They are full and brimming just beneath the surface. It would take but a slight push to tip me over the edge, back to the cavern floor. More troubling still, a mere nudge could return my mind to the darkened place it has inhabited these past few nights. Though my vision is blurred and dimmed, I struggle to gather my focus, letting my sore reddened eyes rest on the delicate tip of Le Chevalier's finger, hovering in the air, so composed, immaculate, untrembling and self-assured. My very antithesis.

I compose myself sufficiently to pose my question in desperation: 'When?'

'Tout en son temps,' replies Le Chevalier with unwavering confidence, still leaning against the stone. 'As I recounted to you, I am methodical.'

'But can I have your definitive assurance that you will find it?' I ask, tense and shaking uncontrollably once more. I press the fingers of one hand against my tightly shut eyes in a futile attempt to wipe away the blur, the fatigue, the violence of my mind. 'I am in dire need of it.' I expel these words in a quiet gasp, breath laced with the vapours, the intoxicating stench of grape.

CONSEQUENCE OF POWER

Le Chevalier does not stir, save for a scarcely perceptible flare of a single nostril, as the fumes reach it. 'I have never faltered,' comes the smooth reply.

The serpent writhes once more in the depths of my stomach, compelling me to stagger away from Le Chevalier, throwing myself against the cave wall a few feet distant, lest I taint him with any expulsion.

Le Chevalier, with quiet composure, straightens and moves away with grace, merging into the crowd, presumably in search of a more peaceful alcove.

My emotions are just too raw. I slump against the rugged wall, hands splayed now as I continue to gasp, moisture streaming down my cheeks and a clammy dampness enveloping my form as I close my eyes once more. The still-wet fabric of my robe sucks at my legs with every movement, sending a chill through me. Whatever it is within me, I feel it drawing me in deeper and deeper into the netherworld.

I sense a figure beside me. I fervently hope it is not another leering, uncanny visage.

'Henry, Henry,' a gentle voice speaks, trying to gain my attention. As I open my bleary eyes, I am greatly relieved to find Dashwood's friendly countenance.

'Come, my friend, allow me to tend to you. You appear as though you have traversed through the very depths of hell,' he remarks with a chuckle at his own jest, though in truth, I am scarcely far from such a fate.

Dashwood, with a delicate yet firm touch, takes hold of my elbow, carefully ensuring not to make contact with any other part of my form, and guides me out of the vast cavern chamber, as the sea of figures part to permit our passage.

He pulls me through the tunnel and into the robing chamber, where at last he relinquishes his grip. There appears not to be an attendant present, and Dashwood himself commences sorting through various garments suspended on pegs and folded in stacks, until he makes a selection which he deems suitable for me.

'Refresh yourself, my friend; it is not as grievous as it seems,' he says, offering me a tunic.

Shivering, I remove my sticky, clinging, soiled material and cast it upon the floor.

As he continues his search, I stammer, 'B-b-but it is!' Mustering what little strength I possess, I grapple with the tunic, wrestling it over my head. 'I have committed so many offences.' I emphasise the word 'committed,' before spitting out, 'And that accursed book…'

'Peace… peace… there is no cause for concern. Do I appear troubled? If anything, this shall immortalise us as legends,' he soothes, ever the optimist.

'Dash it – Dashwood! You are not so… implicated.'

'Henry, Henry,' he continues in calming tones. 'You are so tormented. Now, I suggest,' he pauses momentarily distracted, before finding what he is seeking – some linen with which to cleanse my face and such, which he tosses to me. 'I suggest you take a respite,' he continues. 'Remove yourself from society for some time. Find a place of rest so that you can restore and heal your troubled mind. I shall even assist you and can advise of a suitable sanctuary abroad.'

'But, confound it – the book!' I exclaim, using the linen to dry my visage, the cream fabric turning a tinge of purplish-red in places. 'And Wilkes is sniffing about this evening with that gurning face, unsettling everyone. From what wretched woodwork did he emerge, the conniving worm?'

'Ah, but Wilkes is as much a member as any of us. This is why we have the rules. They are there to smooth over any such friction, at least while the club is in session.

Would you have us all torn apart?' replies Dashwood, characteristically unperturbed.

I have nothing to say to this, except to return to the book, as my mind ever does. 'The book, Dashwood,' I hear my own pathetic, feeble voice utter those words.

'Pray, Henry, take heart; all of this shall surely pass,' he says, tilting his head and offering a sidelong smile. 'People forget. It is human nature, especially in politics. Such matters occur in cycles. Go away, and in a year, two years at the very utmost, the public, periodicals and peers will have forgotten. They will be on to the next damn thing that outrages them.'

I try to consider this, but deep within me, I am uncertain whether I shall be able to forget.

'If aught, the pressure is upon Bute and myself,' he chuckles. 'Nevertheless, should all collapse, Bute will assuredly secure me a position more suited to my interests, perchance within the palace. Master of the Great Wardrobe, eh? That sounds far more diverting, and indeed, more suited to my disposition.'

He glances over at me. I feel more composed, relieved of the sticky garments and comforted by Dashwood's reassuring tone.

'I digress, but the point remains, there is no cause for concern,' continues Dashwood. 'We occupy the highest of society; and it follows therefore that it is our privilege, nay, our duty to enjoy ourselves. Therefore, I entreat you, take my advice and retire for some time to recuperate.'

Placing a reassuring palm upon my shoulder, he says with twinkling eyes, 'Come, St Wily Wilkes tells me he has a treat in store for us all; a jest, I fancy. That will put you at ease.'

'Will it?!' I exclaim with alarm.

'We must maintain a level of order between the brotherhood, setting aside differences,' he says as he leads me out of the robing chamber, back down the darkened winding tunnels.

As we return to the main cavernous chamber, we find ourselves amidst a considerable congregation, evidently in a flutter of excitement. That is to say, except Cheltenham who remains naturally unmoved, with his customary stony façade intact, and Le Chevalier, who has found a new nook, and has resumed an elegant pose, leaning nonchalantly against the cavern wall.

The remainder of the evening's attendees are circled around a mahogany chest of prodigious proportions, which reaches Wilke's waist as he strains to manoeuvre it into the centre of the cave.

'This had better be good,' coos Sandwich.

'At least someone is endeavouring to enliven the evening,' chatters Fairfax, who stands beside him.

I find myself much less bleary eyed than before and can discern some of the figures amongst the assembly. Winterbourne, Bute... not Augustus, though one could scarcely blame him for that. I too should stay away and heed Dashwood's advice.

The torches blaze on the walls of the cavern, casting an ominous glow, emphasising the shadows where the light cannot reach. Heat emanates from these and the closely gathered assembly. Yet, this does not warm me, rather I feel a chill creeping from my spine and throughout my limbs as a hush descends.

Wilkes stands next to the well-positioned chest, evidently ready. He swivels his eyes around to various individuals. I cannot help but notice them linger on Bute, with a particular squint. The chamber is now thick with anticipation.

In one swift move, Wilkes throws open the chest and scrambles away in an instant. A demon leaps out, its russet fur stark on end, with thrashing arms, perched on hind legs. Its sharp horns are red as fire, with thick sabre fangs poised. Enraged and now released from captivity, it screams at members of the assembly with a ferocity of purest evil that would summon the devil himself. Its piercing shrieks cut like knives into my head and through to my soul. Claws running fast across the stony floor echo through the chamber and the tunnels, as though a hundred other demons were scrambling to join the pit.

The assembly, wild in panic, screeching, push, and fall over one another in a desperate attempt to flee the scene. Chaos ensues, as the demon strikes out at the nearest being, and then leaps to the other end of the chamber, where in great haste the crowd parts. I too, witless, having sprawled, now scrabble across the floor in an attempt to flee.

Then, I see Sandwich caught in the grip of the demon, flailing his arms and pleading for it to spare his life. At last, he is able to fling the horned spirit off his person and across the chamber. Then he pushes his weight through the waves of bodies, seeking to save himself, with little regard for those around him.

Finally, my deepest fears are manifest, as the devil has come screaming in consequence of my sins to shatter my mind.

CHAPTER 26 – ENFEEBLED

As Isabella ran her eyes across the features of her friend's face, she traced the thin, delicate ridges of her brow; the remnants of years of effort and well-meaning care devoted to her loved-ones.

Isabella's gaze moved over Lady Ingram's eyes, which were gently closed as she rested, and to the crow's feet at each corner, like the parched beds of rivers, bearing silent testimony to a prior vitality and once-vigorous spirit. Her dusty white hair, usually pinned in a modestly fashionable style, had, even in the presence of friends, been permitted to relax, and now lay softly loosened upon the pillow.

Isabella had entered the bedchamber of the usually formal lady, to ascertain how her once-indomitable friend now fared, and saw a vision of fallibility, which she had never before witnessed. Her mother had assured her, on the good authority of the doctor, that there was truly no cause for alarm. Lady Ingram had merely overextended herself in recent months, and given her five-and-sixty years, such exertions had taken their toll.

Yet Isabella, was first struck with a pang of guilt, like a glass shattering; a sensation which progressed to a blunt unsettling in her stomach, the contents stagnating, the shards still pricking. In truth, she harboured a private conviction that she had, in some measure, been the cause of Lady Ingram's decline.

Lady Ingram's growing realisation that Winterbourne no longer sought Isabella's hand, his absence conspicuous since his single call a few days after the ball, had undoubtedly contributed to her present malaise. The venerable lady's hopes, once so triumphant, had faded, and she saw her efforts had been for naught.

Even other suitors, many of them most eligible and at first eager to call upon Isabella, had gradually trickled into nothing, as the young girl's interest in them became markedly lacking. However, she had been unable to mask her despondence with feigned enthusiasm for these new suitors.

Mr Thornbury had taken to lying at the foot of Lady Ingram's bed, as though keeping a vigil. He appeared to have fallen into a depression, perhaps sensing the absence of the energy and warmth from one of his favourites, which had previously influenced the ambiance of the household.

As he lay, he would of course, raise his head from his paws the moment a tray was brought into the bedchamber, his rounded black nose quivering gently as he sniffed the air to discern which delicacies had been prepared for them. Yet, as the offerings were notably plainer than he was accustomed, one could hardly attribute this to a secondary motive behind his watch.

Indeed, he felt deeply for those dear to him, particularly for this most vivacious of ladies, and he regarded his duty to provide comfort as one of his most important.

'Come, Isabella dear, shall we take a turn about Hyde Park?' said Lady Thornbury, as she quietly entered the peaceful scene. She observed Isabella's countenance deep in thought as, seated beside the bed, her daughter's eyes lingered intensely over the sleeping lady's visage.

Lady Thornbury approached her daughter and whispered gently, 'She will be well in time. The strain of the past few months has merely exhausted her.'

She paused, as though to settle in her mind how to broach a subject that had long occupied her thoughts. In a whisper, she continued, 'I am of the opinion that it would be most prudent to return Lady Ingram to the country, away from the excitements of town. Spring will soon be upon us, and our garden may offer the tranquillity she requires for her recovery.'

Isabella's face softened a little, as she turned towards her mother, comforted by the welcome news.

'We may be able to arrange for you to stay in town,' continued Lady Thornbury. 'I could enquire of Mrs Stoughton if she would be your chaperone for the remainder of the season. I dare say, she –'

'Oh no, please!' Isabella's desperate voice interrupted her mother, 'I cannot stay here, not after... Oh, please take me with you, I beg of you. I have had enough of the city.'

'Why of course, if you wish, my dear,' replied Lady Thornbury. She was not entirely surprised, for she had long felt her daughter's growing misery, even before Lady Ingram's decline. She then affirmed the mutual feeling with, 'I agree. London does not entirely suit either of us.'

Lowering herself, she embraced her daughter tightly. Unbeknown to her, over her shoulder, Isabella allowed a tear, which had been buried and fiercely restrained for weeks, to at last escape.

CHAPTER 27 – THE GARDENER'S COTTAGE

Reverend Fernsby bore a certain lively spirit in his stride, as he made his way from the vicarage to the Thornbury's comfortable family home in Henley. Spring's breath was floating on the late March air, and the tight, hard buds of the oaks, ash tree and sycamores seemed poised and on the brink of yielding, ready to unfurl and reveal to the world their long-awaited verdant hues. The daffodils had begun to flower, as had the wood anemone, heralding the arrival of spring, the tentative bees and the Thornburys.

After three long months of winter without the family, life now appeared to have improved for the vicar. Whilst he stepped with a sprightly gait, he thought to himself that Lady Ingram would soon benefit from the restorative freshness of the spring air and nature, which could not fail to be a balm to the soul.

Mr Thornbury had sensed that Lady Ingram had improved sufficiently and that he could in good conscience leave her bedside. Therefore, he was stationed at the drawing room tea table with Lady Thornbury and

Isabella, and was able to greet his much-missed favourite as the vicar entered.

After Lady Thornbury had poured the tea, reassuring the reverend that the dowager would indeed likely be well soon and had recounted some of the highlights of London, Reverend Fernsby felt it incumbent upon him to impart some of the latest news from the village and its neighbours.

'Reverend Littleton, of our neighbouring parish, is advancing rather swiftly in years. It is a great pity, for since Sir Nicholas' departure, he remains the only one who engages me in a stimulating philosophical debate. Regrettably, he was obliged to miss our regular dinner last Thursday.' The Reverend Fernsby said this as he lifted the Famille Rose cup, allowing the sweet Hyson tea to waft under his fine-tuned Augustan nose.

'That is a pity, however we are hopeful that Sir Nicholas will leave his position in India soon, though we remain uncertain as to the precise time of his return,' replied Lady Thornbury brightly.

'Ah, that is marvellous news!' replied the reverend with enthusiasm.

'Indeed, I received word from Sir Nicholas before we departed from London,' affirmed Lady Thornbury, removing the latest edition of *The North Briton* from the table and making room for the scones which Mary was, at that very moment, presenting to the merry company.

'The prospects for Lord Bute are not favourable,' mused Reverend Fernsby indicating to the paper. 'You will, I am certain, have encountered him whilst in London,' he said, as he leaned to accept a plate of dense buttery pound cake, with a golden crust, from Lady Thornbury.

'Indeed! Cream, Reverend Fernsby?' came Lady Thornbury, as she passed the jug of the rich temptation before resuming. 'Yes, indeed, it is most shocking. One scarcely knows where to begin. The Peace Treaty appears to have been a poor settlement, at least as reported by the newspapers.'

'Yet it has at least conferred one benefit, from a personal perspective. Cheltenham's son has returned from the war. I had heard that he had been in London for a time, but he has now returned to the village.' The reverend said this whilst pouring the viscous cream slowly over the pound cake, allowing it to soak into the crumb. 'I had the pleasure of seeing Gussie only yesterday, enduring his new curricle on our woefully stony path and took the liberty of stopping for a conversation. Do you not recall that he was my former pupil?'

'Indeed, we had the opportunity to see Gussie a number of times in London, but we were unaware that he had returned here,' replied Lady Thornbury.

Isabella felt a warmth when she reflected upon the service Augustus had performed for her, yet she had not spoken of it.

However, what had been discussed before leaving London, was the surprising success of Thomas Fairfax's assignment. Mrs Wilkes was of the opinion that the book retrieved from Lord Bute's study contained material sufficient to yield further revelations in the forthcoming issue of *The North Briton*. However, since this triumph, Bute's general unpopularity had from the press, public and Parliament only increased. Their additional input might be perilous, but would douse the fire with further fuel.

Later that day and for the first time in many months, Isabella and Heloise ventured through the verdant meadow bordering the Thornbury family home, accessed through the orchard. They passed the location where the exotic nigella would bloom in some months to come and the irony struck Isabella, as she reflected upon its evocative names; Love-in-a-Mist, which had proven to be more a Devil-in-the-Bush.

The memories no longer stung, rather, she would make a concerted effort not to be blinded again in the future. Late March was too early for wildflowers, yet Isabella could still picture the cornflower blue heads bobbing and the petals of scarlet poppies moving gently on the breeze.

They continued across the meadow and ascended a hill until they came into view of the Cheltenham's imposing residence. Constructed of light Ketton stone, in the Palladian style, it boasted twelve Corinthian columns across its façade. The central four pillars were crowned with a masterful pediment, while the ornate frieze and elaborate foliage of the cornices enhanced its overall grandeur and presence. One might call the house beautiful, but Isabella could not disassociate the hardened mind of its custodian from the appearance of its stone aspect, despite the fact that it was built of soft limestone.

Whilst she sought to avoid Lord Cheltenham's company, whom she presumed still resided in London, she was equally desirous of paying her respects to Augustus. This was particularly in consideration of the services he had rendered to her. Were it not for Augustus, she might now be engaged to Winterbourne, a thought which now caused her to tremble.

As they approached the daunting stone steps of the front façade, a footman in purple and gold livery greeted them. Lord Augustus was not presently at home; however, it was highly probable that, should they cross the formal gardens to the eastern side of the estate and proceed beyond the copse, they would discover the master in the Head Gardener's cottage.

It was a pleasant surprise to both ladies that they could avoid the austere and likely colossal marble halls, exchanging them for something more pastoral. They were not disappointed. As they approached the modest dusty red bricked gardener's cottage, clad in deep green ivy and the promise of wisteria's frills of purple cascades soon to adorn the porch, there lingered a distinct scent of a sweet honey, suffusing the air.

They gently tapped on the wooden front door, and moments later, Augustus appeared, in a relaxed attire. His snugly fitted frock coat, embellished with gold, had been exchanged for a simpler, more loosely fitting garment made of fine wool. This one, was devoid of ornamentation, and the muted blue off-set the natural colour of his teal eyes.

At first, he greeted them with a relaxed smile, evoking memories for Isabella of a distant dream. It was as though a gossamer veil had been lifted, and a breathless silence descended between the pair. Then, as though unable to conceive that she was truly before him, his eyes widened, catching the light as they met her forget-me-nots. For a moment, he forced his eyes tightly closed, drawing an almost imperceptible breath, though Isabella felt it within her own chest. The anticipation of this moment had spanned many years, and now, in its realisation, it was even more vivid than he could have imagined.

Years of memories flooded his mind: image after haunting image. Yet each was overshadowed with that single, enduring vision of hope, which remained. During the course of those seven years, he had seen Isabella as through a dim mirror, but now they stood face-to-face. Having endured two of the three virtues, he now welcomed the third and greatest of them all. As he opened his eyes to the light streaming through the open threshold, he regarded her standing before him in physical form. He gazed upon – dare he hope, even in a dream – his future.

Heloise broke the silence with a customary greeting, but as if fearing that even a glance away might dispel the illusion, Augustus held an unwavering sight on Isabella, as he wordlessly gestured them into the parlour.

The cottage had rough stone-flags, equally-matched oak benches and a large well-scrubbed table, bedecked with an assortment of bowls, tree rind, leather tomes and greenery. Long-dried lavender and various herbs hung from some of the beams, providing the inevitable mixed infusion, which mingled with the rich-honeyed scent.

Through a passageway appeared a tall, venerable gardener, with a tree-bark visage, his loose white shirt sleeves rolled to the elbow, leafed in simple earth-stained breeches. However, as a fragile silence of unspoken sentiment pervaded the room, and Augustus and Isabella continued to regard each other, it became immediately evident to the gardener that his friend's love, of whom he had so often spoken, had at last arrived. Though unacquainted, Heloise and the seasoned man, with his weathered countenance, exchanged a glance of mutual and astute prescience, as though both perceived the depths of what was unsaid in the moment.

Although fully aware of the identity of his visitor, the gardener, intent on coaxing the young shoots out of the earth, made an effort to encourage conversation, asking, 'Will you introduce me to your acquaintances, Your Lordship?'

Augustus, as though roused from deep contemplation, shifted his gaze slowly towards the gardener, as if the mists of a dream were lifting. 'I beg your pardon?' He said this with confusion compounded by the man's unfamiliar formality.

'The ladies, Your Lordship?' urged his weathered companion.

'Ah, yes, indeed,' Augustus stammered, regaining his composure. 'Isa – Miss Thornbury, Miss Mayfield, allow me to introduce my dear friend, Mr John Lightfoot. He is the most esteemed Head Gardener for this estate.'

'I hope I have not intruded,' said Isabella.

'Not in the least. You have arrived at a most fortuitous time,' John interjected, with enthusiasm. 'His Lordship had the splendid notion of redirecting a portion of our estate's production from cider to mead, providing an equally delicious alternative, free from the burden of taxation.'

'Indeed, but do tell Isabella what you have discovered, I believe she shall find it most intriguing,' urged Augustus, forgetting himself.

'Oh, what could it be?' asked Isabella.

Visibly more at ease, Augustus turned to the ladies and remarked, 'John has unearthed a method from Abyssinia. In truth, this is for our own interest. John?' He nodded to his friend to continue.

Chuckling and clearly very proud, the gardener began explaining. 'I have been showing His Lordship my findings, made possible after he so generously lent me this book.' John picked up an open volume from the table and began turning its pages, saying, 'It is a translation of Dioscorides' *De Materia Medica*, dating from the first century, which includes ancient recipes for mead. We have been experimenting with its production, using the homemade T'ej process and a leaf from an Abyssinian shrub.'

Then, winking at Augustus, he continued. 'Sourcing this was quite an endeavour, but His Lordship, ever fond of, let us say, unique challenges, thought it would be intriguing to replicate the most ancient known mead-making process. Perchance you noticed the honeyed aroma as you approached the cottage?' He glanced up from the book, beaming and in his element. Then placing the tome back upon the table and regaining his presence of mind, he offered his guests refreshments, saying, 'May I offer each of you a glass? The Abyssinian mead is still maturing, but we have a modest quantity of our local from a previous batch.'

Then gesturing to the bench, he said warmly, hoping to ameliorate the path for his friend further, 'Please make yourselves comfortable,' before returning down the passageway.

'I am so glad to see you well, Gussie,' said Isabella, as she sat beside Heloise on one of the benches.

'Indeed, I feel as though I am more truly myself in this place,' Augustus said, his voice tinged with relief. 'My time abroad brought many challenges. Though my father ordered me to London upon my return, I did not enjoy it, save for those rare moments in your company.'

He hesitated; however, he was reassured as Isabella gazed at him more intensely, and a subtle smile briefly lightened her features.

He nevertheless shifted his tone. 'I was most fortunate to re-establish my connection with an old friend of mine. He is a physician whose company brought me some solace. Yet, after some weeks of our meetings, he advised me to seek the tranquillity of the countryside, believing the serenity of nature would offer me healing.'

'Healing?' Isabella asked.

At that instant, Augustus's notice was taken by an early mayfly which floated across his sight. It danced until coming to rest on some of the herbs hanging from the beams above them.

Augustus took a moment. 'A mayfly,' he mused, as they all glanced up at the insect. The mayfly took to the air again, hovered and then flew swiftly out of an open window towards the lakes beyond.

'Some mayflies live only a few hours,' he said, as his gaze drifted out of the window. 'How fragile life is, and so fleeting.'

As he turned back to Isabella, his expression softened. 'Towards the close of the war, there occurred a defining moment for me.'

Isabella became acutely alert at the word war. Augustus had never directly spoken of it, and until then, it was a vague notion to her mind. He gathered his thoughts as the sunlight filtered through the window, casting a warm glow over the room.

'Pray, continue,' Isabella nodded empathetically, affording him the opportunity to recount.

He began, 'There was an occasion when I found myself trapped, defenceless, upon my knees in a clearing of a wood, at the mercy of a French soldier. His rifle was levelled at my chest from no more than ten paces.'

Augustus paused, as if reliving the memory, and Isabella and Heloise's breath too caught, as they attempted to imagine the scene. He continued, 'Unarmed, I accepted my fate, braced for the shot. I closed my eyes and felt the deep regret for the futility of it all.'

He blinked, as though still in disbelief. 'I was convinced I had died, as time seemed suspended. Yet, I had felt nothing. When at last I was compelled to relieve the tension in my eyes, upon opening them I found, not heaven, but the empty clearing, with no one in sight.'

The lieutenant colonel's countenance revealed the remembrance of his relief. 'I collapsed in the dust, clutching at the soil in sheer thankfulness. I could not comprehend why the soldier would spare me, or indeed if it had been a divine intervention, despite my flaws. I had to question the man's very existence, but in any case, I felt an indescribable appreciation for the simplicity of life. Much like the mayfly, every moment now holds great significance. Each moment counts.' Augustus's words hung in the air like the mayfly itself. 'Would you not agree?' he appealed to Isabella.

'I would,' she replied, impulsively reaching out and placing a hand gently upon his coat sleeve. 'And yet,' she continued, 'having endured all this, you would still fight for what you believe in, would you not?'

Recognising her knowledge of his encounter with Winterbourne, he nodded slowly. 'Yes, despite everything.'

Gently interrupting the moment, the gardener emerged from the passageway, bearing glasses filled with translucent amber. At his arrival, Isabella released Augustus's arm to accept a glass. Yet the pair continued tandem in their thoughts which, as in nuptial flight, danced in their shared sense of philopatry.

As they took a sip of the rich, fermented honey, it unfurled its aroma further, evoking a sense of soothing nostalgia.

'I am truly glad you have returned. Will you remain here?' asked Isabella, conscious that her words were inadequate after Augustus's reflections.

'Indeed, I intend to,' answered Augustus. 'And yourself? Will you stay?'

'Indeed,' Isabella replied with conviction, 'I will remain here.'

The words lingered in the air, blending with the now heady aromas of nature which filled the rustic room.

CHAPTER 28 – THE PRECIPICE

'At last, we may have discovered the precipice,' mused Lord Bute, sitting in his rich crimson leather chair behind his study table. A thin finger had unconsciously moved to his delicately pursed lips as he rocked gently in thought.

Sir Francis Dashwood reclined at ease on a chair opposite Lord Bute, an attitude which irked the latter during this critical moment, as they teetered on the brink. Bute did not convey his disdain for the gentleman across from him. Had the impending crisis not concerned Dashwood at all? Perhaps not; he seemed to regard everything so lightly. Most likely, he was more desirous of spending further time at his clubs and in the company of his cronies. Dashwood had neither sacrificed nor striven with such fervour as he had. It was maddening to be in this position.

Calmly, Lord Bute let his finger drop to his writing table as he glanced up to consult his portrait. Maddening, truly maddening, it responded in confirmation.

'I concur,' replied Dashwood. 'The situation has become untenable. We may be compelled to admit defeat and move on.'

There was a discernible trace of regret in his voice, but even Dashwood had to acknowledge that his talents lay not in economics, but in other pursuits. It had been an exceedingly disagreeable experience for him. He infinitely preferred to be liked. Rome, Florence, another Grand Tour beckoned him, now that the war was concluded and these new thoughts brightened his mood.

'You take it so lightly, Dashwood,' observed Lord Bute quietly, drawing himself up in his chair. Then, with a dangerous, silky edge, his voice turned, 'Regardless, I shall navigate this. The palace may possess a drawbridge that can be lowered in our favour.' Bute added silently to himself, 'or at least in mine.'

Dashwood, well aware of his political colleague's sentiments, remained silent, for in truth, he was indifferent to the matter.

A chill pervaded the room, for the cool damp of early April required a morning fire to abate it. However, since the incident of his stolen book, Bute did not permit a single soul – be it butler, footman or colleague – to be left unattended in his study, much less to add yet more fuel to the fire. Thus, he was compelled to conduct this unscheduled, extraordinary meeting with Dashwood in the cold.

Naples before Rome, thought Dashwood, reflecting on the warmer southern climes and the proper order of progress if one were to begin a tour at this time of year.

A rap at the door roused both politicians from their private strategic thoughts.

'Le Chevalier,' announced the footman, as the dashing figure of fashion strode in, flourishing a bow while removing a wide-brimmed hat adorned with a full, sweeping, white, feathery plume.

'Bonjour, Messieurs.'

'Bonjour,' Dashwood greeted, standing and returning the bow with nearly equal flourish.

'Good day,' murmured Lord Bute, without rising. Before any business could commence, he bit sharply, 'Chevalier, is this critical?'

Le Chevalier, maintaining a smooth and sophisticated demeanour, replied, 'Pour vous? Peut-être.'

Suppressing his irritation, Lord Bute leaned back in his chair, his lips still pursed, and with a smooth gesture of his hand, dropped a single-word command: 'Proceed.'

'Are you aware of the whereabouts of Mr Fitzwilliam?' enquired Le Chevalier.

'No one has seen him since the last meet at Medmenham Abbey,' replied Dashwood. 'To say Wilkes gave him a fright with that devil-baboon jest is an understatement – gave us all a good scare – abominable! Even I would scarcely dare to conceive of releasing a masked wild beast from a chest.' He chuckled. 'Henry is likely abroad, recuperating. I advised him as much before. My supposition is that he has elected to pursue a period of reflection and one can only hope that he will reform himself.'

Bute placed the tips of his thin fingers together in a triangular formation and remained silent.

'Quelle dommage, for I believe I have retrieved the book which he so desperately desired,' said Le Chevalier.

'Ah, good!' exclaimed Dashwood, delighted.

'Oui, however, finding him absent, I shall pass it into your – er – trustworthy hands.'

In an elegant gesture, a book was produced from an imperceptible location on Le Chevalier's person, and presented to Lord Bute. 'I took the liberty of perusing it.

Mr Fitzwilliam suggested it belonged to Dashwood, but I find that it is, in fact, yours,' said Le Chevalier lightly.

At the sight of the book, Lord Bute became more attentive, raising an eyebrow. Maintaining his composure, he slid the volume from Le Chevalier's palm into his table drawer, locking it with deliberate care.

'Indeed, I would be more careful, Lord Bute; a book with such contents reveals much. Perhaps you should keep such matters locked in your mind.' Le Chevalier, tapped a finger on the forehead, implying far more than this.

Dashwood appeared somewhat deflated, saying, 'Ah, you are certain that is not my pocketbook, which has been missing for months now? Oh well, I suppose we shall never recover it.'

Le Chevalier replied in a consolatory tone, 'Je suis désolé. It is most disappointing, but at least I could be of service. I shall continue the search for yours.' Turning back to the Prime Minister, Le Chevalier added, 'And are you not curious from whom I retrieved your – shall we say – your plans?'

'Most definitely,' replied Lord Bute smoothly.

'May I venture a guess?' Dashwood perked up, 'Was it Fairfax? No, no, let me try again – Lord Bute is in such a quandary at the moment, one hardly knows where to start –'

'Non! It is not Mr Fairfax. It is someone far more dangerous.'

'Wilkes,' pronounced Lord Bute, his fingers repositioned with each tip meticulously, once more pressed against its counterpart.

'Très bien,' replied Le Chevalier.

'I have much on my mind at present, but rest assured, Wilkes and his associates will be dealt with,' mused Lord Bute, his eyes flickering in Le Chevalier's direction.

'Non, non et non. It is not for me,' declared Le Chevalier. The contents of the book seemed most distasteful to Le Chevalier, and it would be best to be removed from any association with its poisonous taint. Sweeping a bow, and a 'Bonjour,' Le Chevalier evanesced from sight, much to Lord Bute's chagrin.

CHAPTER 29 – SPRING'S BREATH

April released its warming breath upon the first of the buds, which finally stirred to present a bold and vibrant display. The sycamore and horse chestnut trees led the way, with their moist, tightly bound coils, unfurling to reveal the fullness of their vivid, expansive leaves.

So too had Isabella and Augustus gradually permitted their mutual understanding to unfurl. There was an unspoken arrangement that Isabella would daily encounter her neighbour in the meadow.

When the golden orb deigned to throw its warm embrace upon their world, coaxing the foliage into vibrant life, the couple would wander across the meadow and lie below the horse chestnuts, which spotted the hillside. There, amidst the marvel of the spring, they cherished the precious moments together, where so recently there was winter and grey uncertainty.

However, when the crystalline drops of spring fell, this was no less an exhilaration to the pair. Though Isabella's chestnut hair grew a deeper hue, her waves heavy, and Augustus's light hair, darkened in the rain, they would find their natural canopy, and drank in the verdant scents.

Isabella's mother never questioned what may have appeared improper to Lady Ingram, had the venerable lady known; for she only wished to see her daughter content, and observed that the anxieties of the past months had dissipated. Moreover, she and her beloved Sir Nicholas had always harboured a fondness for Augustus and having secretly hoped for such a union, their betrothal was simply the crowning joy of that spring.

'Well, I cannot profess to be surprised,' said the Reverend Fernsby, placing his napkin over his left shoulder, as preferred, ready to receive the first service – the creamy lobster bisque. 'I believe you alluded to the peril facing our Prime Minister and Chancellor, Lady Thornbury, upon your return from London.'

The dinner had been well-planned, as usual, by Lady Thornbury. Lady Ingram, unfortunately, still preferred to take her repast in her bedchamber, not yet equal to joining the company. However, since the engagement, additional attentions had been made, for the guests attending the frequent Thornbury dinners had expanded from simply the vicar, to include Augustus and his younger sister.

Lady Catherine was but a year away from her debut in society. She was strictly governed until a suitable strategic alliance could be forged by her father, the earl. Until this time, she remained in Oxfordshire with her governess, whilst Lord and Lady Cheltenham – particularly his Lordship – were meticulously conducting their London season.

'Indeed, who could have foreseen that Lord Bute would resign, followed closely by Sir Francis Dashwood with his own resignation just the following week?' cried Lady Thornbury, as she lowered her spoon into the smooth liquid, garnished with bright red-orange gems of coral roe, illuminated by the contrasting lightness of a cream swirl.

Bute and Dashwood had fallen from grace in the face of public anger over the Treaty terms and, unsurprisingly perhaps, the loathed cider tax. The general sentiment of the table was that the less said on those latter most lamentable topics, the better.

However, Mrs Stoughton's most recent letter to the Thornburys conveyed that the revelations from Lord Bute's book had yet to be published in *The North Briton,* and they awaited each day on tenterhooks.

Despite the political upheaval, the literary circle ladies and Thomas Fairfax were still unanimous in the opinion that exposing the malfeasance was imperative. They regarded it as their contribution towards the abolition of these dishonourable practices, the very rot, as it were, that permeated the ranks of power.

Isabella, having oscillated in her deeper, secret concerns regarding Dashwood's book, had found some solace in the Thornbury household's removal from London, which provided the illusion of safety, as they were ostensibly out of reach of those who might seek the volume.

Conversation soon turned from politics to more agreeable matters, specifically the forthcoming nuptials of Augustus and Isabella, over which the Reverend Fernsby would, of course, proudly officiate in the summer.

'I am most delighted not only to have my brother returned for good, but also to have gained a sister,' expressed Lady Catherine. 'It will transform the house into a far less desolate place.'

'Indeed,' responded Lady Thornbury, 'but you are welcome to dine here regularly, even daily. I could not be more blessed to have my daughter so close by when she is married; in truth, I am simply gaining a son rather than parting with a daughter,' she added, raising the warm soup to her lips.

The convivial company continued their usual lively conversation, after which Isabella and Lady Catherine delighted them all with a performance of *Sonata in A Major*, from Händel-Werke-Verzeichnis, 361. The harmonious blend of Lady Catherine's violin and Isabella's piano-forte produced a most charming ambiance. The company's attention was drawn to the bond shared by the future sisters-in-law, which brought smiles and joy to all. The quality of their performance was of little consequence; instead, it was the heartwarming moment that resonated with everyone.

These performances had become a cherished feature of their comfortable evenings, adding to the atmosphere of familial warmth that was greatly beloved by all, and particularly for its novelty, by Lady Catherine.

CHAPTER 30 – IF WALLS COULD TALK

The Tower of London, Mr John Wilkes, MP

I press my face against the right side of the thin vertical slit, then to the left, my bulging eyes straining gruesomely. My vulnerable neck extends so that I can glean as much as the narrow cell window will permit.

The Tower of London's formidable ragstone fortification, dense and deep, further impedes my vision, confining the view to walls and yet more walls, and the partial lawn below. It is much like the game that I have long played: what can I gather, glean and thus reveal?

I glimpse a raven landing heavily on the green, in a stark contrast with its ebony funereal garb. Shadows drift and another falls beside it, and then another: a full conspiracy. Yet, I have been seized from the clamour of Parliament and thrust screaming into what I now fear will result in my murder. The birds caw and strut, perhaps to pick at the forthcoming carrion, though the rot and stench came much before.

The black-feathered omens fall out of my sight. They have not strayed far, for even the ravens are, in their own manner, prisoners and bound within these walls. It is a long-held tradition to keep them here, to thus prevent the Tower's fall and with it, perhaps even the kingdom. And so, deemed a threat, I find myself within these prison walls.

Perhaps all fall eventually. For now, I too succumb to my own descent, sliding down the ragged rock to the dark, cold floor, the walls drawing closer around me. It is indeed a descent, though one that I have precipitated myself. As a Member of Parliament, I, John Wilkes, anticipated some measure of immunity, and yet, I ought to have known that all that my status will grant is a more comfortable cell. It is much as it was for the many occupants who preceded me, Milton, Raleigh, even princes.

Evidently, my adversaries will stop at nothing to reach their ends. Yet, that question hangs over me, like an axe or more noble-option – sword. I have much time to contemplate, nay dissect. Shall the final, ultimate blow be struck within these Tower walls, or shall it occur at the more public spectacle of Tower Hill?

I weigh up the scales of judgement, the crime. Officially it is sedition. Though I was so cautious not to implicate the King or government, rather to expose the rot within the system. For how can one allow it to fester and decompose, "this scepter'd isle, [...] This other Eden, demi-paradise."

I press my living body against the rough, biting stone, thankful just to feel anything, even the blood coursing through my veins, however chill. Then a realisation of horror causes me to fling back away from the stone – the wall reveals its secrets. I feel them, their innocent, untrialed fingers reaching out through the wall to me in appeal. I shudder, only inches from the bodies disencased from these walls. The bodies of the murdered princes in this tower.

Thus, the truth cries out so boldly and resonates throughout my flesh – the body of a cursed man within this cell. The matter is not in one's standing, but one's understanding: There are consequences to wielding power, yet to what lengths should one dare to tread? Indeed, what are the consequences of inaction to oneself and others? In either case one may be condemned.

Then I hear them. Their delicate child-like voices prevail, plaguing my thoughts and compelling my imagination to linger. Who but the public can save me now? Yet, unlike the princes uncovered in these walls, I may be buried within and never discovered.

CHAPTER 31 – POST-HASTE

The Thornbury Family Garden, Henley-Upon-Thames, Lord Augustus

'Oh, my dear, pray come quickly!' Lady Thornbury called out as she hurried from the house and across the lawn, brandishing a letter. She rushed frantically towards my betrothed and I, as we strolled leisurely together through the apple orchard within the Thornbury family gardens, pausing beside the Bramleys.

'It is most dreadful!' Lady Thornbury cried upon reaching us, breathless from her uncharacteristic haste. 'Most dreadful,' she reiterated with tender urgency, regaining her breath.

I could perceive Heloise and the Reverend Fernsby emerging from the house in the distance, making their way to join the company, their curiosity no doubt matching that of my own.

'Pray, what might be the matter?' Isabella enquired, disconcerted.

Having steadied herself only somewhat, as the party assembled, Lady Thornbury unfolded the letter. I observed her hands trembling in haste as she related, 'I have just received a most troubling message from Mrs Stoughton.' Delicately smoothing the parchment with care, she continued, 'John Wilkes has been detained… he is imprisoned in the Tower of London on charges of sedition and I know not what else.'

I gasped, 'What? This surely cannot be. He is a Member of Parliament.'

However, the colour drained entirely from Isabella's face, as I felt her grasp upon my arm tighten, unsettling my stance and drawing me towards her instinctively. Reverend Fernsby and I, whilst confused by this commotion, were both concerned with the Thornburys' evident distress.

Lady Thornbury glanced down at the letter she held; her voice trembled as she related, 'Mrs Stoughton reports that the book Thomas Fairfax had rescued from Bute and delivered to Wilkes is nowhere to be found. It may have been taken from John Wilkes's home when he was seized and our friend reports that – that,' here she wavered, as though holding back some emotional turmoil, before stammering, 'we – we – may all be implicated!'

'How? How could this be?' asked Isabella, seeming to find her voice as I grappled to understand.

'Lady Thornbury, it is grievous for the gentleman,' interjected the Reverend Fernsby, 'but you must strive to remain calm. This cannot be good for your health.'

'You do not fully understand, Reverend,' Isabella responded.

Lady Thornbury appeared to be anxiously crumpling the letter in her grasp. Releasing my arm, Isabella prised it out of her mother's hands and passed it to the reverend and me, as we rapidly surveyed it.

Lady Thornbury began to sink, but regained her footing, with the aid of Heloise, though her visage was ashen.

'It is our fault and yet, it is no more than we deserve,' Isabella said, her voice was unsteady, as she gazed in contemplation at a spot on the lawn. Then, after a brief moment, as the breeze picked up a large lock of her hair, she grasped it. I witnessed her with great concern.

The reverend had no words, and having finished reading the letter, he crumpled it. As I digested its contents, my stomach felt as though a large stone had plunged to the murky depths of a pool. I began pacing up and down the lawn before facing Isabella.

'Have you entirely lost your senses?' regrettably my words blazed forth, whipping through Isabella, though I could not suppress them. Finally, we were so close to bliss. To have it snatched away would be unbearable. 'What could have driven you all to do such a thing?' Again, my voice rose in desperation. Grabbing her arm and arresting her, I exclaimed looking at her full in the face, 'The Prime Minister – Bute? What – What – do you truly grasp the nature of the individuals with whom you are dealing? I fear you do not.'

'I do,' she replied, her eyes conveyed the weight of the siege. It was evident from her reaction that she understood to some extent, and perhaps knew more than she had disclosed to me.

I confess, I felt somewhat betrayed that she had not entrusted me with any of this. I may have been able to provide some protection, perhaps prevented this and preserved our future. Speculating on the resources that these individuals may have at their disposal, I realised they may be en route to us at any moment. In my mind I grappled how to convey the urgency, without causing more distress to the party.

'We had no notion that our actions would lead to such a consequence,' exclaimed Isabella.

The April breeze had risen in intensity, and the garden seemed colder than before. Lady Thornbury had fallen mute and stood still, staring into the distance, one hand firmly clamped across her mouth, where it remained.

Isabella, it appeared, could scarcely look at anyone, much less myself, though in truth, all I felt was a deep concern as I studied her. 'You are not safe here; we must find a way to ensure your safety,' I said, breaking the silence. 'They will know it is you, God's truth. You have letters circulating everywhere.'

'What?' Isabella's voice trembled as she looked up in shock at me.

'You cannot stay.'

'What?' she said, lowering her tone.

'Immediately. We must all leave.'

'But where to?'

'What of the wedding, and Lady Ingram?' Lady Thornbury interjected, slowly withdrawing her hand from her mouth.

'This is a matter of survival. There will be no wedding,' I responded with firm resolve, and yet it felt as though the voice were not my own. This instant felt not of this world, as our future slipped through our grasp.

'Wait, wait,' the reverend said, raising his hands to calm us. We all turned to him. 'There may yet be a solution.'

He appeared to take a moment to consider and somehow, a faint glimmer of hope arose within me, against all reason. We all clung to his words, as though our very lives depended upon them, and in some way, I felt that they did.

Then, almost unable to bear the suspense, Isabella offered innocently, 'Perhaps we might go to Gretna

Green. Many are married there, and it would be a considerable distance from here.' However, full panic had set in, and she could not hide it from her voice.

'It is not possible,' I interrupted. 'Lord Bute is from Scotland; it is there he wields his greatest influence.'

'Indeed, it is true,' mused the reverend, a finger touching his pursed lips, though I could see in his eyes as they moved rapidly from side to side, that his thoughts raced through a multitude of possibilities. 'Not Scotland... but France. Indeed,' he rubbed his chin now with his thumb and two fingers. 'France... more specifically Normandy.' Looking up and breaking his contemplation, his brow lightened a fraction. 'France lies nearer to us than Scotland, and crucially, out of our government's jurisdiction. Lord Bute may no longer be Prime Minister, but as he has demonstrated, his power still has reach.'

'France?' uttered Lady Thornbury softly.

'Indeed, there may be no alternative,' I replied with understanding.

Isabella glanced at me, and I believe something unspoken passed between us. She understood the truth; the depths of my fervour and concern must have been etched upon my face. It was not for my own sake, but entirely for hers and in a desperation, that I had spoken so rashly earlier.

The vicar continued with his proposal. 'There exists a small community of Catholic monks at Mont-Saint-Michel. I had the fortune of visiting the abbey on a pilgrimage many years ago. There is nothing but myself connecting you and I am confident, for my sake, the brethren will extend their protection.'

I could perceive the words taking hold to differing extents among the company.

'But, Lady Ingram, she cannot be moved... I shall not leave her,' cried Lady Thornbury desperately.

'It is true,' said the vicar. 'We may have to seek alternative arrangements for Lady Ingram, but for now, you must join us. Indeed, I can escort you there myself. I shall make the necessary arrangements with Reverend Littleton. He may be able to help find a supply reverend to absorb my duties.'

'This is too dreadful,' said Lady Thornbury, as she shook her head. 'I shall not leave her. I cannot.' Then, turning to her daughter, she embraced Isabella. 'But you must go.'

Isabella began shaking her head, which her mother must have sensed as she clutched her. 'But she has Mary, and Heloise will stay and help,' Isabella cried.

'No, no, do not argue with me. You will go. I am firm on that. Besides you, I am all Lady Ingram has in the world. I shall not abandon her,' Lady Thornbury insisted. Then, turning to Reverend Fernsby, she took his hand and grasped it. 'I know you will take care of my daughter.'

'As if she were my own,' he replied, and we were all certain of his conviction.

'I shall join, of course,' I said resolutely. 'I have been parted from Isabella once. I shall not be parted from her again.'

As the gathering dispersed momentarily, for a brief interlude to prepare, I departed for my home to make ready for the journey ahead and say farewell to my sister. As I left the Thornbury family home, I observed Isabella and Heloise proceeding up the staircase.

Only a few moments later, Isabella and Heloise found themselves in Isabella's bedchamber, making preparations for the journey. Augustus had departed to make his own arrangements and bid farewell to his sister, whom he trusted implicitly to keep their flight a secret. He packed a portmanteau with some modest clothing, which he had acquired from the gardener. Aware of the gravity of the situation, he reluctantly slipped a dirk, his hunting dagger from the war, within the folds of his coat, should it be required. Yet, he resolved to keep this precaution hidden from his companions, lest it provoke undue alarm.

Reverend Fernsby was already en route to Reverend Littleton's vicarage in the Thornbury carriage, with the intention of consulting his friend on the matter of finding a curate or another to fulfil his commitments, as the elder reverend was unlikely to be able to manage them himself. Once the reverend had made his own preparations, they would exchange the Thornbury carriage for the afternoon post, to avoid being conspicuous at the various toll-posts and inns along the way.

'I can scarcely believe this is happening,' said Isabella, opening a drawer in search of a shawl.

'Nor can I,' replied Heloise, withdrawing a carpet bag, which she began to fill, 'and so suddenly.'

'Indeed, I am uncertain what is best. I have never undertaken such a journey, and what if we are pursued?'

'It is, I hope, unlikely that you will be followed,' her companion replied, though in truth she could only speculate. 'However, you must remain calm and composed, maintain a low station and follow Augustus's example.'

'I do feel safe with Augustus,' admitted Isabella, warming to this thought.

'Yes, he is more than capable of caring for you, and you will also have Reverend Fernsby,' replied Heloise reassuringly.

'But not my mother, nor Lady Ingram, nor you... How shall we all bear it? I am so afraid of leaving you all.'

'Fear not, I shall take care of them both.' Then, with a smile and a slight hint of a sparkle in her eye, she said, 'I am very resourceful and servants often remain unnoticed by society. I shall remain discrete, as it were.'

Isabella crossed the chamber and embraced Heloise. 'Please be safe.'

Heloise, meanwhile, was quietly devising her own, rather more local contingency plans for the remaining family, should there be any cause for their removal. She resolved to maintain a vigilant watch and to keep one or two holdalls conveniently packed with supplies.

Once Isabella released her from her embrace, Heloise made her way to her own sleeping quarters to fetch some items, returning with a plain fawn-coloured gown of coarse cotton. It was evident that it had not been one of Isabella's older gowns, which Heloise would customarily wear, yet it would serve the occasion well, allowing Isabella to be less conspicuous among the other passengers during the journey.

As Isabella gazed at her reflection in the mirror, she also observed Heloise combing her chestnut locks, for what might be the last time, as she could not say when she would see her again. Reflecting on her life, she felt profoundly blessed to have such a circle of family and friends.

'I am certain that, in due course, matters will settle,' said Heloise, perhaps with a touch too much optimism, 'and Lady Thornbury will signal that it is safe for you to return.' She continued to focus on combing Isabella's hair with great assiduity. When she had finished, she observed warmly, 'There, you are perfection itself. You may even return as a married lady. Lady Kant, I believe, and then in time, Lady Cheltenham. How fine that sounds!'

Isabella smiled politely at the comment, for she had scarcely considered the change in title, and indeed it mattered even less to her now, given the gravity of the present circumstances.

Instead, this past month her thoughts had simply been absorbed in what seemed to her the miraculous prospect of uniting with Augustus, whose sentiments were so like her own. His spirit bore a familiarity and yet he continued to reveal the depths of his character with each passing day, and most strikingly in the face of adversity.

With each challenge and the more she discovered of him, she had found her admiration and respect growing deeper. Her heart melted with the tender realisation, like a delicate primrose, unfurling in the morning light, its petals blending hues of burnished gold and gentle pinkish-purple.

CHAPTER 32 – THE DIVINE OFFICE

As the carriage jostled over the cobbles, the golden sun dipped towards the horizon, casting its burnished oranges, coral pinks and purples, across the shimmering sea, with smooth smudges of soft copper-peach across the sky. Isabella had, until that journey, never beheld the sea, and this resplendent display took her breath away, as though she were entering heaven.

'Each sunset that I have witnessed,' Augustus mused beside her, 'seems so unique, even from the same vantage. It is extraordinary how nature is ever-changing, devising new beauties to keep us in awe.'

'Perhaps it is your perception that alters too,' she responded. 'I wish I could capture this moment, so that I might retain it in my mind eternally,' said Isabella wistfully.

Augustus reflected on the moments he had himself captured and long held in his own thoughts, replaying them over and over. Those images of Isabella had in their own way saved him, or at least his mind. Now he realised that he could finally release them and there would be new and vivid memories to take their place, as their future unfolded before them.

As they approached the sweeping view of the bay, Reverend Fernsby assured them, 'It is not long now. We shall soon approach the island and must abandon our hired fiacre, to traverse the mudflats by foot. They act as a natural defence of the island, but it appears that the tide is beginning to ebb, so we shall have a fleeting opportunity to cross. Then we shall enter through the medieval entrance gate into the village.'

As they continued on, Isabella drew down the shutter and leaned out of the open window. She observed the medieval abbey rising up in the distance as they approached. Its spire towered above the mount; a beacon of purity bathed in a pristine, even divine light. The closely clustered buildings of the community encircled it, which in turn was embraced by a holy rampart for the fortified island.

'I believe we must disembark here,' the reverend observed, as the carriage came to a stop. 'I must advise you that this is a treacherous crossing, but I am somewhat familiar and believe we have timed it well, the tide now having receded. The sea around the island possesses its own will. It may deign to grant safe passage or it may resolutely deny our entry. It has been known to advance rapidly and unbeknown may swirl around the unfamiliar traveller, encircling them. Follow me closely,' he emphasised.

'Is there no other way? Perhaps there is a boat?' suggested Isabella.

'Not before nightfall and you will be quite alright if you take hold of Gussie's hand and keep close to me.'

As the sun continued to set, the scarlet light crept across the sea, which continued to draw out, enabling them passage. The strong east wind began to rise and as they commenced traversing the mudflats, they did so in silence, their feet slightly sinking into the wet sand with each step, their eyes fixed upon the island approximately a mile ahead.

Reverend Fernsby took the lead by a few steps, and at times Isabella could see his heavy trudge slowing his pace with an immersive suck, mud clinging to his boots each time he was able to free them. The wind gently whipped up his cloak, stirring the scent of the salt-sea air, which combined with the musty mudflats. Isabella felt the same sensations, and yet, the reverend appeared unafraid, rather determined to deliver them to sanctuary. This sense, and with Augustus by her side, brought to her a similar determination and comfort.

At last, they entered the village at the foot of the abbey and they meandered through the streets. Their sandy soles initially slipped gently on the stone paths, drying as the grains dusted off naturally, whilst they ascended through the now darkening narrow streets up the mount towards the medieval sanctuary. When they arrived at the abbey's entrance, Reverend Fernsby marvelled, 'I did not believe I would ever set eyes upon her again. There she is in her beauty, our Celestial City.'

He advised that he would first consult with the brethren, should Isabella and Augustus be willing to wait outside until he signalled. They agreed and watched the amicable clergyman ascend the grand medieval steps of the abbey.

The couple waited some time following Reverend Fernsby's admittance. Twilight was setting in and as the light cooled and dimmed, the temperature began to lower. They maintained the silence which befitted the setting, almost as though it were ordained, and gazed across the miles of expansive bay and glistening mudflats from their west-ledge vantage atop the mount.

Evidently, the reverend was engaged in a long discussion with one of the Order. However, it granted Augustus and Isabella a tender moment together in which to marvel at their location. So far removed from their lives prior, it could be easy to forget why they were here.

Augustus allowed the silence to engulf them before uttering a pledge into the stillness. 'Regardless of whether they grant us admittance, I shall ensure that we are safe.' The tide was already pulling in, almost as though in divine answer that they were in his embrace. 'Soon, when all of this is resolved, I promise you, we shall have a home of our own, which shall offer us sanctuary, removed from all the troubles of the world. Although,' he continued with a smile and glancing at his future bride, 'One might imagine this prospect as a glimpse of heaven itself, and I would be most content residing here beside you for eternity.'

'I am content just to be with you. In our brief time together of late, my most valued moments by your side have been in simplicity. I do not desire the complexity of this world,' replied Isabella.

She gazed into the distance, in further contemplation and Augustus said, as though he heard her deepest thoughts, 'Do not fear for them Isabella, I am quite certain they are well.'

The abbey entrance, being at the highest point of the mount, the vast expanse of the bay lay before them and they witnessed the dramatic change of the tide as it began to rise and close up the mudflats they had just crossed. The sea was now a darkened liquid silk, rippling across the vista. Calm had descended in the deepening twilight. Through the windows of the village houses, they observed candles being lit and, in turn, they cast their own low glow out onto the world. This welcoming peace would set the tone for the coming experience, and at a point, before the stars had begun to speckle the dark sky, the Reverend Fernsby appeared at the grand illuminated doorway of the abbey and beckoned them in.

Over the course of the following days, the three began to adjust to a very different existence; that of the Benedictine Order. It was one of peace and simplicity, untainted by the outside world and most crucially under the protection of the abbey's jurisdiction.

Given the indefinite length of stay, the Abbot had suggested that they might benefit from adopting some of the monks' practises and schedule. However, given the strict vows of celibacy, the monks did not admit ladies in certain areas of the monastery, particularly during specific rituals and times of prayer and reflection. Nevertheless, Isabella was permitted to join practical activities such as gardening, cooking and mealtimes, the latter of which were always partaken in silence. They were assigned a mentor by the name of Frère Ambrose, a brother of the Order.

'Notres devise est, "Ora et Labora". Cela reflète un équilibre entre la prière et le travail,' advised Frère Ambrose.

He had supplied a parchment outlining the schedule of prayer and work: the Divine Office, so that they may follow it, should they wish.

Augustus and Reverend Fernsby experienced the first of the schedule, not at dawn, but at one o'clock that first morning. They were awoken at a single toll of the bell for the Matins Nocturns. As they entered the darkened corridors, they were able to discern in the moonlight, which came streaming through the hall windows, numerous monks walking in silence towards the church, where they would congregate.

Each wore a simple, dark habit of coarse material, which fell almost to the floor. Some had their cowls pulled over their heads to provide further privacy, enabling them greater focus for their prayers. Augustus and Reverend Fernsby, having been supplied with the same attire, felt a sense of safety and cohesive community, as they blended seamlessly. This was the quiet service symbolising the darkness before the dawn, both physically and spiritually.

Once in the church, over the next hour of solemn reflection, they recited psalms and hymns, accompanied by readings from scripture. Isabella awoke gently to the sweetest sounds of the monks' voices chanting in Latin. A profound and hauntingly beautiful rise and fall of song drifted on the night air, appearing to mingle with her dreams.

Unbeknown to Isabella, it was the *Missa Cum Jubilo*, and with her thoughts in harmony with the hymn, she joined the communion in her mind. There was a deep sense of calm and reflection throughout the abbey.

Once more, at five o'clock they were awoken from their brief rest for Lauds, which was shorter and lighter in tone, as they gave thanks for the coming day, interspersed with joyful hymns. This had greater energy than the previous Matins, as they welcomed the dawn. Surrounded by the monks, who had accepted them and generously offered sanctuary, they had a sense of community.

Immediately afterwards, at the six o'clock Prime, the gentlemen and the monks received their assignments for the day, followed by a short prayer service before they began work. The activities included agriculture, gardening, scriptorium work such as illumination and other manuscript tasks, cooking, cleaning and general management of the abbey. One of the key aspects was guesthouse management, where monks tended to pilgrims and guests who sought sanctuary.

It was during this period of the day, on the first week of their sojourn, that Reverend Fernsby accompanied Frère Ambrose on a visit to Isabella, who was residing in one of the guesthouses. It was a separate stone building, with thick walls and vaulted ceilings, but was sympathetic to the gothic architecture.

'My dear Isabella, Frère Ambrose, is accompanying me and attending to the needs of the guests. He desires to know whether you would grant us a moment for a brief discussion. Would this be convenient?' asked Reverend Fernsby.

'Why yes, of course, I would be most glad,' replied Isabella, ushering them warmly into the sparse living quarters, which she now inhabited. It had only the essential furnishings, chairs, a table, a bed and Isabella's few necessities that she had brought with her. It was a room of intentional simplicity, as though each artifact was laden with a symbolic sense of purpose and significance. Her own simple fawn-coloured coarse gown, now accompanied by a brown wool cloak provided by the abbey, was most befitting.

'Welcoming guests and offering sanctuary is a practice deeply embedded in the abbey's spiritual environment. Indeed, they treat and care for guests as though they are receiving Christ himself,' mused Reverend Fernsby, when the three had settled on the wooden chairs around the table.

'Oui, comme le Christ,' said Frère Ambrose, nodding solemnly to confirm the gravity of this truth. His face was that of a man deeply content, as one who is acutely aware of the troubles in the world, observing them pass frequently through the abbey entrance, accepting them and ultimately comprehending the role each would undertake in the service of God.

Reverend Fernsby commenced, 'Frère Ambrose already appreciates the situation in which we find ourselves, but should you not object, he would like to personally console with you and offer his council.'

Frère Ambrose reached his hand out to Isabella and said, 'Je peux vous assurer que vous êtes en sécurité ici. Er, here you are safe.' Then Frère Ambrose gave a modest inclination of his head, and a gentle gesture with his hand, reminding the reverend of the brother's concerns.

'Ah yes,' exclaimed Reverend Fernsby, 'Frère Ambrose has confided in me that he perceives there may be something more, beyond our plight, that weighs upon your mind. Possibly your mother?'

'Yes, I have concerns for those dear to me whom I left behind,' replied Isabella, but did not elaborate.

However, the experienced brother gestured further and turned to Reverend Fernsby, saying, 'Ah, but there is something more – Je le ressens profondément – I feel it, non?'

'Are you certain there is nothing else?' enquired Reverend Fernsby.

'I am certain,' said Isabella hesitantly.

After some contemplation, Frère Ambrose murmured to Reverend Fernsby, who nodded and turned to her asking with empathy, 'My dear Isabella, if there is anything weighing on your mind, ask yourself if you can justify bearing the burden. What good can come of it? I can see that Frère Ambrose is quite adamant that he discerns your unease, and he is desirous of offering assistance.'

The experienced brother nodded sagely.

'It is not our place to prescribe your course of action, but the Benedictine way is that of simplicity, and seeks peace beyond the concerns of society,' continued Reverend Fernsby. 'It was this attraction to the philosophy and my own longing to explore it, that brought me to the abbey many years ago. Frère Ambrose advises through inward examination and reflection, in time, God will guide you from the darkness of your troubles.'

Not wishing to press Isabella further, Frère Ambrose rose to depart, however, not before placing a Bible upon the table, and tracing a cross over Isabella's forehead murmuring, 'Que Dieu te bénisse. I am here, should you need me.'

'He has blessed you, as do I,' said Reverend Fernsby, and parting from Isabella, they left her to her thoughts.

Once alone, Isabella drew out Dashwood's book from her carpet bag. Then, clasping it with both hands, her gaze remained fixed upon the Bible. Slowly she sank back into her seat, a soft sigh escaping her lips, in solemn contemplation of Frère Ambrose's sentiments.

CHAPTER 33 – SOWING THE SEEDS

Having spent a fortnight at the abbey, they were now comfortably familiar with the rhythm and doctrine of the monastery. Further, Augustus and Isabella had been assigned gardening duties together, much to their delight. They adhered to the Benedictine rule of self-sufficiency and care for creation. Therefore, guided by the monks, they approached their tasks with dedication and attention to detail.

Tending to the many varieties of vegetables which served the community, together they not only witnessed the tender vegetation sprouting in the late spring, but also gained a deep understanding as to the purpose of each for the monastery.

Frère Ambrose taught them that the peas and beans, whilst staples and good sustenance, also provided nourishment to the soil, enriching it. Therefore, the beans were rotated amongst the other vegetables to ensure the health of the earth. During the early stages of spring, the brethren had already prepared the fertile soil, ensuring it was well-drained, as these were most preferable conditions for the beans.

By May, the soil had warmed, and now Augustus and Isabella began sowing the seeds. Together with care, they planted runner beans, setting each a distance of two palms apart, and interspersing them with sunflowers as companions and a natural trellis for the climbing vines.

As Augustus delicately pressed each bean with his fingers into the fertile earth, he lingered in that sacred moment, relishing the feel of the rich, loamy soil. On first reflection, with a quiet voice, he appealed to Isabella to do likewise. Together, they would scoop a portion of the rich, dark, almost ebony soil, which bore a tonal reddish hue and allow the soft moist, grainy matter to cascade, clinging gently to their fingers, as if reluctant to part.

In their care of the plants, they were cautious to ensure the right balance of moisture, to avoid root rot and yet, also to retain wetness. To suppress weeds, they sprinkled grass clippings, which also safeguarded the beans from the vicissitudes of heat and cold. Moreover, they planted marigolds nearby, and imbued the soil with a splash of ash and lime to discourage slugs and snails.

When it came to herbs, thyme, sage, rosemary, mint, lemon balm, fennel and lovage, not only provided a beauteous scent as the couple progressed through their tasks, but were grown for teas, as well as culinary and medicinal purposes.

Sage, with its muted silver-green hue, was held to be a powerful herb for healing, used for easing digestion, as a balm for sore throats, with the ability to strengthen both the memory and the body. This connection to the process and the earth was, in itself, a form of meditation that brought much-needed healing, slowly washing away the concerns which had previously consumed their minds.

It was towards the close of this second week that Isabella received a letter from her mother. It came almost as a stimulative, breaking the usual calm pace of abbey life, so cocooned were they from the outside world. However, it was, of course, most welcome.

Before Isabella opened it, she was conscious to feel the parchment between her fingers, savouring the precious missive and understanding that this was a rare gift. In doing so, it also allowed her to reflect, bringing a strong reminder of those whom she had left behind, and with it a pang of sadness. Upon reading the letter though, she was most encouraged:

Henley-Upon-Thames, 7th May 1763

Dearest Isabella,

We trust that you have all arrived safely and are now comfortably settled in your life at the abbey. I am certain the brothers are most kind and generous; Reverend Fernsby assured me as such before he left.

Now I have the pleasure of imparting not one, but two encouraging pieces of news. First, Lady Ingram appears to have revived somewhat. At least, in recent days, she has been able to leave her bedchamber and take her meals with us. She seems more like herself, engaging in vibrant discourse in a manner with which we are all so familiar. I am so relieved to see her thus, and Mr Thornbury has likewise increased in spirits.

However, it is not the only glimmer of hope that we can glean in the darkness, for I have been informed by Mrs Stoughton that Mr John Wilkes has been released from the Tower. It is truly the most miraculous news and perhaps signals that it may soon be safe for you to return.

In other developments, Reverend Littleton introduced us to our temporary supply, a Reverend Laurent. He appears to be French, which I find most unusual, given their usual Catholic persuasion. I could not discern how the Reverend Laurent came to reside in England, but we were most grateful, of course, that he could assist at such short notice. In order to make him feel at home, we served him dinner in a style that we believe he is accustomed: service à la française.

He appeared pleasant and interested in the community, having visited all the neighbours and has an observant manner. His sermons are not so very different from Reverend Fernsby, that is to say, they are brief, though less lively, than our dear friend's. Reverend Laurent has, dare I say – I know not how else to describe it – a somewhat feminine and graceful touch to his manner. It is almost as though he possesses a duality of nature, as though two spirits reside within them, each vying for expression.

He had dined with Heloise and me, though Lady Ingram was not well enough to descend the stairs, at that time. However, in recent days, Reverend Laurant seems to have vanished. After I enquired with Reverend Littleton, he could also by no means account for this.

I surmise that perhaps, having been called to us so suddenly, our new pastor may have left his own affairs in disarray, thereby necessitating his attention to them.

I have taken up Heloise as my companion, though Mary seems somewhat put out. However, in my sometimes otherwise solitary state, Heloise has been a true balm. In truth, I could not do without her whilst you are away.

I have not received any letters from your father. However, I am certain he sends his love, as do I, Lady Ingram, Heloise, and Mr Thornbury.

Your ever-loving mother,

Isabella was much relieved upon reading her mother's letter, and at first hurried to inform Reverend Fernsby and Augustus of the news. However, she was obliged to discipline herself to wait until None, the brief mid-afternoon prayer service, had concluded. Being well aware that their prayers would soon be answered, she discovered them both in the garden, amongst the garlic beds, during the designated work period, where she was also due to join them.

'I have received the most wondrous news from mother,' she whispered close to the reverend and Augustus, in keeping with the peace of the surroundings. This drew the reverend's attention from his deep meditation on the marigolds and he lowered his tin watering can with care to the granite, ensuring not to make a sound and he mopped his brow from the afternoon heat.

Scarcely pausing for breath, Isabella resumed in an audible whisper, 'Lady Ingram, it appears, is almost recovered, or at least she is much better and you will scarcely believe it, but Mr Wilkes has been released.' She uttered the last word with relish.

Reverend Fernsby and Augustus took some moments to comprehend the enormity of this news, after which Augustus embraced Isabella with abandon. The reverend threw up his hands in joy, exclaiming, 'Ah, wondrous Isabella,' and temporarily forgot himself in the natural stillness.

This caused some brethren in one corner of the garden to glance up in astonishment from their vegetable beds, given the brief breach of observance. However, with gentle smiles, they soon settled back to their tasks, understanding all was well.

'Surely, we can return home soon, now that all is safe,' Isabella said eagerly, still encircling Augustus's neck, her bare arms resting on his worn scapular and gazing into his visage which was so alive, his teal blue eyes sparkling in the sunlight.

'It appears we can, although there is no hurry. Indeed, it may be wise to wait a short while,' said Reverend Fernsby. Then after a pause he continued with a lightness, scarcely succeeding in restraining his voice, 'Indeed, I shall tell you now of some news of my own. I have conferred with the Abbot about your forthcoming nuptials. He has agreed that I may preside over them myself on these consecrated grounds, provided,' and he raised his hand here to imply the significance, 'we respect the customary process, which is most reasonable, of course. In fact, I would be required to insist upon this in my own parish. Namely, the banns shall be read out as per usual over the course of a month, and so by the beginning of June, I believe you may have a summer ceremony.'

'Ah, in such beautiful surroundings, a true midsummer's dream,' mused Isabella playfully and romantically. 'Or a little before,' she said, and they all laughed, for this was indeed unfolding as if in a dream.

'That is, of course, if you are at ease with the notion that your mother, Lady Ingram, and Heloise will not join us,' said Reverend Fernsby.

'Indeed, I am certain they will understand, and in truth, I do not think I can wait much longer. Will we not also have a celebration upon our return?' replied Isabella joyously. 'Think of your dear sister, Gussi. She will no doubt be so excited to join our celebrations.'

'Our time here together has been most enjoyable, and the prospect of remaining a while longer appears quite pleasant. The thought of marrying you here, Isabella, is a dream to me,' exclaimed Augustus. He reflected to himself that in this curious and isolated place, they had been able to nurture their affection, away from the noise of society. Just as they tended to the plants, it had rooted even more deeply.

'I cannot explain it. Though we have a schedule, I feel more alive than ever, away from constraints. Is this not pure?' mused Augustus further, quite overcome. He embraced Isabella again, releasing her only in respect of the brethren in the corner of the garden, who, in fact, could never begrudge such joy.

The sun became ever more fervent over the course of the following week, as the island progressed towards summer. Augustus and Isabella basked in its rays during the day, and towards its close became increasingly aware of the privilege of beholding nature's many varied and spectacular sunsets. Such scenes appeared to grow in depth, moving towards the spectrum of burnt oranges, vibrant fiery vermillion, and even crimson reds, reflecting the intensity of the world's life-giving orb in its final moments before it dipped beneath the horizon.

It was upon one of these serene days, when the sun stood at its zenith, casting its midday heat, that Augustus chanced upon Isabella in the garden. Her burnished chestnut mane glistened beneath the sun's golden rays as she stooped to water the Damask roses. Their highly fragrant blooms, in purest white, softened into pink with an ethereal glow, as if the roses themselves were blushing in the warm embrace of the sun.

Earlier in the week, during a communion, some of the brethren had imparted to Augustus a poem, in knowledge of his impending nuptials, which he had preserved for the appropriate moment. Finding his betrothed amongst the roses, he touched her upon her shoulder, and entreated her to listen to his piece on the transcendent nature of true affection, confident that it would move her heart. From a sheaf, he read the verses of Pierre de Ronsard:

En la beauté des fleurs, en la verdeur des herbes,
En l'ombre des rameaux, en l'émail des jardins,
En les tendres arrêts des amoureux destins,
Et en mille doux nœuds des amoureuses gerbes;

Nous mourrons doucement sous la terre endormis,
Et quand des Cieux amis les lampes se baisseront,
Les Amours éternels ensemble nous berceront
En des parfums heureux, de roses endoloris.

'How beautiful,' Isabella mused, enraptured by Augustus's mellifluous gallic tones. 'I would so love to hear its translation.'

To this, Augustus responded that he had shared the very same desire and had devoted time to rendering it into English, before continuing his reading from the sheaf:

In the beauty of blossoms, in the lushness of grass,
In the shade of the boughs, in the garden's bright hues,
In the tender pauses of lovers' fates,
And in a thousand sweet ties of amorous sheaves;

At this moment, Augustus broke off and quietly offered Isabella a Damask rose, which he had thoughtfully pressed for her, before resuming the verse:

We shall gently rest beneath the sleeping earth,
And when the friendly stars of Heaven dim their light,
Eternal Loves shall cradle us together
In joyful scents of wounded roses.

They meditated on the words in silence until Augustus finally spoke, whispering, 'I pressed this rose for you,' as he gestured to the dried flower Isabella held lightly between her fingers. 'Perhaps it is fanciful of me, but I thought we might bear it home as a cherished memento of our time here together.'

With that, he revealed his own; the counterpart of Isabella's, carefully hidden within the folds of his habit.

CHAPTER 34 – CASTING THE FIRST STONE

Meals were taken in silent communion, fostering spiritual reflection. The entire monastic community gathered within the expansive refectory, a room with grand, lofty vaulted ceilings, yet otherwise simple, reflecting the Benedictine way of life.

It was during such a meal, seated at one of the extended wooden tables, arrayed in rows, that Isabella turned her meditative thoughts to the sustenance before her. It had been a day of particularly intense labour and the heat had caused her greater thirst than usual.

Therefore, she had an overwhelming sense of appreciation for the cool, refreshing water as it touched her lips. She was at once aware of the careful harvesting of rainwater, which now allowed her this sensation from yet another life-giving element.

The sun, the water and the soil had, in the passing weeks, become intensely significant, for the three had so intimately connected with the very elements which nourished and sustained them.

She reflected upon past moments and whether, in her former existence, she had savoured food with such profound appreciation. True, she had relished the aromatic allure of the chocolate from the chocolate house; its rich, sweet and velvety essence, subtly perfumed with a touch of vanilla. Yet, she had not truly grasped the origin of this most divine of beverages.

Thus, in the quietude of the refectory, she permitted herself to meditate on the complex origin and significance of an ostensibly innocent dish of chocolate.

She was well aware that cocoa beans were not among the commodities her father had dealings with in the East, but were more frequently imported from South America. The cocoa beans, having been cultivated by farmers in a climate so vastly different from that of the monastery, were likely grown in tropical conditions, and perhaps, this struck her profoundly, by those subjected to enslavement. That was a life so vastly different from any she had known in her past or present that she could not comprehend.

She consciously resolved to delve deeper into the study of cocoa beans and the lives of those who tended them upon her return home. She was certain however, that they would have made a long and treacherous journey, and she wondered whether understanding their origins, much as she now understood the origins of the beans she grew, might bestow a new layer of meaning upon her experience of the chocolate.

As her thoughts wandered, she revisited a previously pleasant, but now excruciating, memory of the past; her temptation at the chocolate house and her discourse with Winterbourne. With the physical distance and that of time between them, she had gained a more objective perspective, and with greater wisdom, trust in her own feelings. She now recognised her senses and emotions had been intoxicated entirely. Winterbourne's words echoed in her mind: 'It is important to manage temptations. I strive to govern mine.'

She understood the words for what they were now, and the chilling contradiction in the creature who uttered them.

Now Isabella would be more vigilant and felt a renewed inner strength. She looked forward with self-assurance to her future with Augustus, who, though not without flaws, though neither was she, possessed a pure spirit. Together, in their own Edenic refuge, they might guard one another against the world's temptations.

Indeed, neither of them had any inclination towards societal ostentation, for the gardens of the monastery had taught them that true happiness resided in the simplicity and communion within.

Augustus, likewise was in deep contemplation of his repast, as he sat beside his betrothed. However, towards the end of the meal, as one of the Order read aloud from the bible, whilst the gathering listened in silence, Augustus glanced up to survey the community.

Alighting his eyes upon each soul in turn, he contemplated those he recognised. Frère Ambrose, in quiet reflection, his brow smooth, conveyed his inner peace, yet he understood the sorrows of many, offering solace in his experienced manner.

Another seated beside Frère Ambrose was equally silent and meditating on the simple stew of vegetables from the monastery earth, grown not many steps away.

Augustus continued regarding various visages, contemplating their paths to sanctuary, when he alighted upon the face of a pale, young gentleman. He was more withdrawn in posture than the others and had chosen to draw his cowl over his head. However, as Augustus pondered and observed more closely, he felt that the man's countenance had a somewhat familiar aspect, which he could not quite place.

He continued to study the figure as he took his repast. Then, towards the end of the peaceful meal, the man slowly drew his eyes up to meet Augustus's, as though aware of being observed, though they were vacant in their expression, before withdrawing them once more and reflecting on his repast.

At that moment, Augustus was struck by the intense familiarity and was certain he knew the countenance, though from where, he still could not understand. Perhaps his regiment in the war? An enemy soldier? Might it be someone from Oxfordshire or London, perchance? He resolved to discover.

It was not long afterwards, whilst he was tending the vegetable beds, that this particular monk entered the garden. However, he kept to the walls surrounding the potager, as though he were a shadow, pulling his cowl over his head once more, to darken his visage. Then, keeping his head bowed, he continued to one of the farther reaches of the kitchen garden.

Augustus was in quiet discourse with Frère Ambrose and Reverend Fernsby over the condition of the garlic bulbs, but observed the young monk's actions in their entirety.

Awaiting an appropriate break in the discourse, he ventured to enquire of Frère Ambrose the identity of the withdrawn figure.

'He is... how you do you say – Il ne souhaite pas être derange,' muttered Frère Ambrose, somewhat reluctantly.

'But I sense a familiarity with him. I have wondered for some time, and at first could not place him, but now, I am sure. Are you aware that is Mr Henry Fitzwilliam?' enquired Augustus boldly.

Frère Ambrose's expression was one of mild surprise, but he retained his usual composure. However, he nodded slowly, before reluctantly relinquishing his knowledge, 'C'est vrai. He was once Henry, but now he is Frère Jean, an apprentice of the monastery.'

Firmly Augustus countered, 'Henry is by no means a character one would desire to admit to this community. He is reckless, a drunk, if you only knew his past, the stories –'

He was uncharacteristically cut off by Frère Ambrose's raised hand, signalling a request for peace.

'Avez-vous oublié? It is not for you or I to judge who is worthy.' Paraphrasing the bible he said, 'Let those without sin cast the first stone.'

Then, as though having exhausted his linguistic abilities, the brother murmured in rapid French to Reverend Fernsby, whose countenance in turn change to unguarded surprise. He glanced at Frère Ambrose, then at Augustus as though to speak, then back at the brother as if to verify that he had indeed understood. Frère Ambrose, in his calm way, gestured to the reverend to communicate his message.

Hesitantly, the clergyman related, 'Mr Fitzwilliam came here by his own accord, vulnerable and in truth a broken man. The brethren understand that he is tormented by his past, but the very purpose of this sanctuary is for God to accept those who seek forgiveness. You must dismiss this from your thoughts. He is no longer Mr Fitzwilliam. He has cast off his old self, and must be allowed to heal in peace.'

Frère Ambrose interposed at this juncture. Augustus felt the brother earnestly grasp both of his hands, and though gentle, his grip trembled with the intensity of his entreaty, as he attempted in English, 'Forgive your brother of his wrongs, yes, as… as he would forgive you.'

Augustus, still held by Frère Ambrose, felt the words 'As he would forgive you,' resonate within him. He too was no stranger to sin. His mind drifted to that turning point during the war, when kneeling in the clearing, his fate had rested in the hands of a French soldier. He may have continued his descent, were it not for that moment of divine intervention, where he had been granted a reprieve.

Then, glancing over at the figure of Henry Fitzwilliam, now Frère Jean, he observed him, truly observed him in his entirety. Where there had been coldness towards Henry, there now stirred within Augustus an unexpected understanding.

CHAPTER 35 – BONE OF MY BONES, FLESH OF MY FLESH

Returning to the guesthouse after her morning walk through the grounds, Isabella prepared for the late morning duties. Whilst awaiting Reverend Fernsby and Augustus, who were due to pass by on their way to the garden, she busied herself, tying a fresh white apron around her waist, and tidying some of her garments and books which were scattered about her living quarters. She had quickly learned what she had long taken for granted, which included keeping her bedchamber in order without Heloise's assistance.

As she contentedly tidied, she reflected upon the Merveille, a particularly striking gothic cloister on the north side of the abbey and one of the most serene and spiritual areas within its confines. She had spent considerable time that morning circulating through the double rows of intricately carved columns. These outlined the parameters of the courtyard, and as she absorbed the fragrance of the herbs in the central garden, these in turn stirred up her thoughts.

So immersed was she in her reflections that, on hearing a light rap on the door, she opened it immediately, poised to rush out to join her companions, when she was suddenly halted. There on the threshold stood a figure dressed in a dark cloak, not of the Order, but as she surmised, one of the other guests, perhaps a pilgrim.

'Bonjour, my child,' said the figure, their countenance calm, almost serene, 'I am pleased that I have encountered you here. I have been interested to meet you.'

Isabella was quite surprised, not only to see the figure, but that they seemed to know of her. 'It is likewise a pleasure to make your acquaintance, I am sure. Might I be of service?' she asked.

'Perhaps you may. Might I be permitted to enter?' came the smooth, delicate French accent.

One of the brethren had mentioned her to them, she thought. The calm demeanour put her at ease and she welcomed the guest, saying, 'I am expecting my companions at any moment, as we are due to tend to the garden this morning. However, I am certain I can spare a few moments until they arrive. Do come in and rest a while.'

She ushered the guest into her living quarters, ensuring the door remained unclosed, to permit her companions admittance when they arrived and the sun to stream in, lighting the otherwise cool, dark room and bringing some warmth. Her guest did not appear inclined to take a seat, perhaps sensing that Isabella was about to leave and would not linger long.

'May I ask with whom I have the pleasure of speaking? Are you on a pilgrimage?' enquired Isabella.

'Oui, oui, of sorts. I have an objective which has led me here,' replied the pilgrim. 'Et vous? What had brought you here?'

Isabella, though at ease, was not willing to disclose the entire narrative of their plight. Therefore, to keep her response cryptic she replied, 'Indeed, my companions and I were seeking a place of sanctuary, and I believe we have finally found peace.'

The pilgrim waited patiently, as though expecting Isabella to continue. Silence in conversation is so often uncomfortable for many, that they tend to fill the space, thereby risking the disclosure of more than one ought.

'My betrothed and I are due to be married here in only a few weeks, before returning home,' Isabella said, predictably filling the silence. She reflected on these sentiments as she uttered them, in turn also enveloping her with a comforting warmth.

'As I said, I have been curious to meet you. Indeed, now that I have the pleasure of seeing you, I find you most intriguing,' mused the pilgrim.

As the sun approached its highest point, so near to midday, it cast a brilliant light that streamed into the room.

The visitor continued, 'I had long wondered what manner of person would dare to meddle. With such audacity, they must themselves be either most powerful or possess courage such as is rarely seen, or even be driven by a profound conviction.'

The pilgrim leaned against one of the stone walls, one leg slightly bent and subtly visible beneath the folds of the cloak. They continued, 'It was this curiosity, I must confess, that compelled me to seek you out. However, so inconspicuous as you are, it was surprisingly difficult to discern that it was you that I sought.' They paused before resuming in a measured tone, 'I believe you are well aware of what I speak. This brought me here – this, and a promise made to someone most desperate to recover what he had lost.'

These final words hung. A creeping sensation began to spread through Isabella's being. It was as though a fear buried deep within her had at last taken form and now stood before her. Yet, as is so often the case, it did not manifest as she had imagined and was far removed from the dramatic and dynamic terror.

Silence once again permeated the room. Both understood at that moment and an unspoken recognition passed.

Isabella was frozen, and an age moved. Eventually, Le Chevalier broke the silence with, 'I believe you have something in your possession that does not belong to you.'

The atmosphere was charged. Isabella remained motionless, though her eyes were locked on Le Chevalier, almost as though making any move would precipitate the conclusion; the very one she feared the most.

Countering and unyielding to her desperation, Le Chevalier remained equally still, like a stone carving, emotions impenetrable in the silence of the impasse.

Near unable to endure the strain further, Isabella felt herself beginning to yield, perhaps confess, questioning the worth of the burden. As they remained in a state of silence, they began to hear the sounds of footsteps pacing on the granite, moving towards the guesthouse. They grew louder, matching the beat of Isabella's heart, though she barely dared to breathe.

At that moment, Augustus and Reverend Fernsby appeared at the threshold. Augustus, absorbing Isabella's stricken expression, directed his eyes towards the visitor and instantly understood. With barely a moment of hesitation, on impulse, and with startling proficiency, he drew his dirk from the folds of his habit, directing it with well-practised resolve towards Le Chevalier's breastplate.

With unparallel mastery, Le Chevalier parlayed with a counter parry. The memory of muscle and sinew twisted the ivory handle of the dirk, away from their own form and towards the attacker, piercing the flesh between Augustus's ribs. He was held in statue, before Le Chevalier released him to the earth.

Silence penetrated the room.

Le Chevalier, grasping the now crimson coated dirk, shifted their gaze towards Isabella, as if for a moment comprehending the next motion. Releasing the inlaid dagger, it fell with a clatter to the stone floor. It met the deep red plumes of life, which expanded and flooded from Augustus, as a hyacinth, unfurling towards the statue of Apollo.

CHAPTER 36 – GATHER YE ROSEBUDS WHILE YE MAY

As the sun pierced the horizon, and slowly began its ordained journey towards its zenith, Isabella tidied her room with unwavering assiduity. She swept the stone floor meticulously, taking care to clear every crevice. Indeed, she did so repeatedly and in silence that morning, so devoted was she to the task, her mind wholly absorbed in the discipline.

The light streamed through the open door, warming the cool, dark room. Isabella continued with her tasks, arranging the bedclothes, and ensuring that the space beneath the bed too had been swept.

At midday, Reverend Fernsby appeared at the entrance to the room and paused at the threshold, observing Isabella's voluntary duties of the day.

'My child, are you ready to accompany us?' he enquired in his gentle manner.

Isabella did not reply, but continued tidying, arranging her few books once more on a shelf, ensuring the dust had been kept away.

'My dear?' Reverend Fernsby spoke, breaking the silence once more.

She hesitated a moment, before continuing. The clergyman moved into the room, ducking his head as he passed the low doorway, and placed a palm atop her hand, interrupting the process of her acute purgation.

'Come my child, it is time,' he murmured quietly, before guiding her towards the door and out into the abbey grounds.

As they made their way towards the monastic cemetery, where the brethren had begun to gather, the Death Knell tolled once, twice, thrice. Each single toll, signified one of the Holy Trinity, to invoke the solemn reflection.

After a beautiful monastic service, they gathered by the simple graveside. The loamy, dark earth, which gave such nourishment to their sustenance, was piled high in a mound besides Augustus's final resting place.

This was not the lavish gold ceremony befitting an Earl's son, nor would he be placed in the cold marble mausoleum on the Cheltenham family estate. Neither was he encased in military attire, befitting a lieutenant colonel of such distinction.

Instead, this simple hallowed place seemed to most closely embody his true soul, one that she had known and loved. There, he was placed in the earth of the abbey, amongst nature. Here, where their bonds had blossomed, and their minds had played in harmony within these gardens, in the peaceful simplicity of natural beauty.

Isabella had retrieved Augustus's pressed Damask rose, the counterpart to her own. Now she held it in her hand, pausing to reflect on the poem he had shared with her, and the love that they had held. Then she gently released it into his grave, where it fell to be with her betrothed.

She then reached to gather some of the loose, moist soil in her hand. So familiar, it clung between her fingertips, before she released this too into the grave and over Augustus.

In the grand scheme of life, and against the struggle to find one another, they had so few moments together, painfully fleeting, as the lives of mayflies.

A deep desperation rose within Isabella. In her eyes, he had one condition, only one imperative: to stay alive. Yet, in his endeavour to protect her life, he had lost his own. The injustice was more than could be encapsulated in a moment, for it would continue as her life endured, with no amends.

Isabella lingered one final moment at the grave of a man whose complexities were largely misunderstood by much of society. To her, he was not the son of an Earl, a rank, nor a mere piece on a board. He was Augustus, of which his true self he had revealed to her, in those simple moments.

CHAPTER 37 – DO NOT GO GENTLE INTO THAT GOOD NIGHT

The roses in the Thornbury family garden were in full bloom once more. A bumblebee was busying itself, collecting pollen, for yet another batch of Mr John Lightfoot's mead. It hovered over the flowers, alighting briefly on a Damask rose, before floating over the hedgerows, back to the gardener's cottage.

Lady Ingram was at her usual appointed place at the garden table under the arbour. Though her body had not regained its usual strength, her mind had somewhat recovered. The Reverend Fernsby was gladly receiving a dish of aromatic Young Hyson tea from Lady Thornbury, and Pudding had resumed his post beside his favourite.

Isabella picked up a fig and bit into the velvety skin, which had a slight resistance, and gave way to the sweet, soft interior, contrasting with the mild nutty seeds. She savoured each moment of the experience, whilst meditating on the fruit and its cultivation.

She had been largely silent since Augustus's passing, awaiting the fading of the initial shock, though she knew not what the future might hold without him. Though she had returned to her home, she could not enjoy it as she had done previously. She understood that Augustus was gone, but almost everything around her was a reminder of him.

The savouring of meals, the bees, the roses, her very garden and the meadow beyond, were imbued with a bereaved reverence. What she delighted in most, and had now learned to appreciate, evoked memories of him. Further, though it had been almost a month now since her return, a persistent sense of something unresolved remained.

Her mind had been so unsettled by events, that it could find no rest. She endlessly replayed what fragments her shattered mind could recall of those final moments with Augustus – so sudden, so swift. His life, their future, snatched in an instant, in a delicate motion, perhaps reflective of the fragile nature of existence, which hangs by a thread, ready to be snapped, severed at any moment. The figure had vanished moments after, leaving Reverend Fernsby and Isabella in the guest room in motionless shock.

Yet, now she felt for the first time a motion stir within her, a reminder of Augustus's nature. She leaned back in her chair that afternoon in late June, absorbing the natural surroundings. As she did so, Augustus spoke to her; each blade of grass, each insect, each watchful flower, expectant.

Her thoughts returned once more to Dashwood's book and her persistent inertia, her lack of action. Yet, she found herself incapable of destroying or parting from it – not while the possibility for some good still lingered.

CONSEQUENCE OF POWER

At that moment, in her garden, she silently resolved to confront the only person she knew who held influence over the core of that society that had pierced her world with such violence. That individual's land bordered her own. She need only pass through her garden and the meadow to confront him at his house. As she contemplated her strategy, she felt an anger, a rage, surge up within her.

That very evening, she strode through the meadows, advancing alone towards her objective. For only the second time in her life, she entered the courtyard as the grand Palladian house loomed over her. Its Corinthian columns seemed to rise to the occasion, as she paced closer and closer. With steely resolve, she ascended the steps to the towering door and seized the brass doorhandle, rapping with a firm strength, before the purple and gold liveried footman could anticipate her arrival.

'I am here to see Lord Cheltenham,' she said with an authority, which appeared to belie questioning.

After some moments, almost to her astonishment, the footman informed her that she would be granted admittance to the earl's presence and he would receive her in the long gallery.

She followed the servant through the seemingly endless marbled corridors, their feet striking the stone at a swift pace which appeared to echo throughout the many hollow chambers and further corridors. Otherwise, in the many minutes that it took to reach the east wing, they remained in silence. As she proceeded through a final corridor, the many portraits of Cheltenham's ancient lineage gazed down upon her with accusing eyes, as though she were the one at fault. Yet, undeterred, she pressed forward, decidedly. Nothing would stop her.

As they approached the intricately carved wooden doors, the footman opened one to allow her admittance, closing it behind her once she had entered. She was confronted with the long gallery. It was empty, save for the numerous white marble statues of frozen forms, many with Grecian visages of various emotions and in states of action. However, Cheltenham was not to be found.

She began pacing up and down the gallery, at a loss as to how else to expend her energy. She passed the many statues, again and again. She did this for so long that, in time, she could not help but notice some of them in greater detail. Pyramus and Thisbe were both depicted, symbolising, she thought, societal constraint, as well as the inability of those lovers to live without each other, or avenge their tragic fate.

Isabella halted at another of the stone figures and gazed into its carved face. Its eyes, alabaster-white in keeping with the rest of its form, absent of pupils, she knew was intended to represent stylistic and idealised constructs of beauty, divinity and heroism, creating a sense of abstraction. However, she recognised them for what they were.

In an instant, the door opened nearby and undeterred; she cast her eyes from one soulless pair to that of another pair without soul, as Cheltenham entered.

Moments passed as the polarities stood facing one another in silence.

Every ounce of her strength had been concentrated towards that moment, and now that it had arrived, she found herself wondering how she could possibly summon the words to begin.

Death had pierced with potent precision, rupturing the careful strategy, the future of that ancient family. Nothing, not even all of Cheltenham's influence, could alter that fate. As she gazed steadily towards the earl, she could see that he had been consumed entirely, swallowed up whole, and now appeared to be waning, being digested, inexorably worn down, his fight extinguished.

Finally, the earl broke the silence. 'I can understand your struggle to express yourself at this moment. I have been informed of everything which took place at Mont-Saint-Michel.'

Isabella offered nothing in return.

'We have both suffered a great loss,' the earl conceded.

'I am well aware,' returned Isabella.

More moments passed before she continued, 'I have the book in my possession. I also know everything where that is concerned.'

'I am aware,' his voice wavered in reply, his granite façade eroded. 'I trust you have come to return it.'

'Indeed, I have not,' she replied defiantly.

The marble statues continued to witness in silence, which was shattered only by Isabella's declaration, 'However, you may have it, so long as you disband the Order. I cannot bear living with the knowledge that this will continue to poison our society. Surely you, above almost all others, must understand this now.'

The earl's hollow eyes gazed upon her steadily, before confessing, 'If this is your concern, you have nothing to fear. The Order has dissipated entirely, shortly after Lord Bute and Dashwood's positions in our government, as I am sure you are aware. I can assure you that not a soul will discover the part that you played.' His voice had a tinge of remorse.

Augustus's pleas, whilst they engaged in chess in that very gallery, resonated deep within him. He understood now the ramifications of his own actions, though he could not bring himself to speak them, as he placed his palm across his visage, over and over, to console himself.

In measured tones, Isabella spoke, 'You do have the power to make some amends.'

The earl retained his palm against his cheek, motionless.

Isabella pursued her demand, 'Mr Thomas Fairfax lost his estate to you, through his brother's gamble. Would you return it to him?'

The earl gazed at her and replied, 'Would this bring you any consolation?'

'It would bring some justice at least, considering there has been so little,' she countered. Isabella continued to assert her demands unwaveringly, 'And, I believe it is in your best interest to release Martha, with good reference, perhaps to Thomas Fairfax's estate. Do this for me and for Augustus's sake, and I shall hand you the book.'

Cheltenham hesitated for a moment, reflecting on the remarkable nature of her requests and, indeed, her fortitude in defiance of him. After some contemplation, he acquiesced to these requests for redress.

CHAPTER 38 – MAKE A HEAVEN OF HELL

The Wildflower Meadows, Henley-Upon-Thames, Isabella Thornbury

I rested at last beneath the shade of one of the expansive horse chestnuts, dotting the hillside within the wildflower meadow. It remains one of my most cherished places, despite – or perhaps because of – the memories it holds. The crickets sizzled, singing their incessant chorus in the heat of June, unaware that Augustus would never grace this place again. I suppose nature and life continues its course.

Glancing down at the pressed Damask rose that I held, the very one which he had bestowed upon me but a few days before his demise, I was reminded of the place where its counterpart resides.

The meadow's vastness usually affords one ample time to observe an approaching visitor. However, I must have been lost in deep contemplation for some time, for

I had not noticed a gentleman on horseback before me until he spoke.

'Good day, madam. Pardon me, might I trouble you to enquire if I am headed in the right direction to town?' He said in a bright gentlemanly voice.

Startled, I glanced up. His visage had a kindly smile, radiating warmth, and his eyes conveyed a soul, which had true compassion. However, it changed to one of concern as he enquired, 'Are you quite well?'

I replied instinctively, 'Ah, yes sir, I am quite well. I thank you.' I had not been conscious that my countenance might have appeared so mournful during my unguarded moments of reflection. Yet, perhaps it was indeed – at least enough to elicit his kind enquiry.

'Truly, you look quite unwell,' he countered with concern, making as if to dismount his horse.

'I assure you, there is no cause for alarm,' I replied, forcing a smile as I began to rise. 'I am merely contemplating nature, and – and – the beauty of this rose,' I added haltingly, at a loss for words, not wishing to divulge the true nature of my thoughts.

'Ah, yes, nature can indeed offer great solace,' the gentleman mused, *"In the beauty of blossoms, in the lushness of grass, In the tender pauses of lovers' fates."*

His words lingered in the air. Then, composing my thoughts, I said, 'My apologies, sir. You wished to know the direction to town? Indeed, if you move passing by the hedgerows there, and out of the meadow, you will find the path leading to the Broadway.'

He fleetingly cast a glance to the direction I indicated, before turning to me once more. He gazed at me appraisingly, as though deliberating. Then, as if reassured, he said in a most sincere tone, as he looked down upon me from above, 'Well, if you are certain, I shall bid you good day and wish you well,' he added in his valediction.

'I thank you, I am. Good day, sir,' I replied.

He seemed satisfied, perhaps not with the words of my reply, as much as his general assessment. With that, he removed his hat and rubbed his brow from the heat, for it was midday. Then, conferring his hat upon his head, he inclined it, urged his fine stallion forward away from our crossing point, and trotted towards the hedgerows, finally joining the rough path that led in the direction of the Broadway.

I resumed my seat upon the grass beneath the horse chestnut and returned to my reverie. Then I gazed into the distance, shading my eyes with my free hand, while delicately clutching the pressed Damask rose with the other. The gentleman's choice of words at such a moment provided a measure of comfort.

As I come to terms with what happened over the last few months, I recognise that we have a choice in how we choose to think and direct our lives. Indeed, in my experience, I now feel the truth of the words:

"The mind is its own place, and in itself
Can make a Heav'n of Hell, a Hell of Heav'n."

CONSEQUENCE OF POWER

ABOUT THE AUTHOR

Sabrina Lund is an English-Danish author with a lifelong passion for literature. Specialising in historical works and fiction from the Renaissance to the nineteenth century, her family's enthusiasm for literature inspired her from a young age.

She is currently working on the next novel in the *Consequence of Power* series. In this eighteenth century series, she seeks to bring the rich historical period and its themes to life, reimagined for the modern reader. Sabrina launched a book club, which provided inspiration for Club de Vin.

Raised in London and Copenhagen, she now resides in Hampshire on the River Hamble, which influenced some of the descriptions of nature in her writing. She holds a BA (Hons) in English Literature and Language from the University of Exeter and an MA in Shakespeare in History from University College London. In addition to writing, she has a career in Finance and holds a MSc in Finance from the London School of Economics.

Contact the publisher to connect with Sabrina Lund:

Websites: www.goosehousepublishing.com

www.sabrinalundauthor.com

Email: contact@goosehousepublishing.com

www.ingramcontent.com/pod-product-compliance
Ingram Content Group UK Ltd.
Pitfield, Milton Keynes, MK11 3LW, UK
UKHW011407150625
459713UK00004B/103